THE
WAITING
LIST

THE
WAITING
LIST

MATILDA WILDING

RAVEN BOOKS
LONDON · OXFORD · NEW YORK · NEW DELHI · SYDNEY

RAVEN BOOKS
Bloomsbury Publishing Plc
50 Bedford Square, London, WC1B 3DP, UK
Bloomsbury Publishing Ireland Limited,
29 Earlsfort Terrace, Dublin 2, D02 AY28, Ireland

BLOOMSBURY, RAVEN BOOKS and the Raven Books logo
are trademarks of Bloomsbury Publishing Plc

First published in Great Britain 2026

Copyright © Matilda Wilding, 2026

Epigraph extract of *Homeland and Other Stories* by Barbara Kingsolver
reproduced with kind permission from Faber and Faber Ltd

Matilda Wilding is identified as the author of this work in accordance with the
Copyright, Designs and Patents Act 1988

This is a work of fiction. Names and characters are the product of the
author's imagination and any resemblance to actual persons, living or dead,
is entirely coincidental

All rights reserved. No part of this publication may be: i) reproduced or transmitted in
any form, electronic or mechanical, including photocopying, recording or by means of
any information storage or retrieval system without prior permission in writing from
the publishers; or ii) used or reproduced in any way for the training, development or
operation of artificial intelligence (AI) technologies, including generative AI technologies.
The rights holders expressly reserve this publication from the text and data mining
exception as per Article 4(3) of the Digital Single Market Directive (EU) 2019/790

A catalogue record for this book is available from the British Library

ISBN: HB: 978-1-5266-9218-4; TPB: 978-1-5266-9222-1;
eBook: 978-1-5266-9224-5

2 4 6 8 10 9 7 5 3 1

Typeset by Six Red Marbles India
Printed and bound in Great Britain by Clays Ltd, Elcograf S.p.A

To find out more about our authors and books visit www.bloomsbury.com
and sign up for our newsletters
For product-safety-related questions contact productsafety@bloomsbury.com

For Andrei

'Sometimes the strength of motherhood is greater than natural laws.'

Barbara Kingsolver, *Homeland and Other Stories*

PROLOGUE

Murmurs drift from the living room into the kitchen where I stand clutching the countertop. In front of me, a drink is fizzing innocently in one of our best glasses, saved for special occasions. In the pocket of my dress the pills sit heavy, vibrating against my leg as adrenaline sends tremors through me.

I can hear Dad insisting people take more mince pies, and the rustle of the paper hats from the crackers. Justin flicking through a playlist searching for the least cheesy music. Delighted gurgles as Max crawls around batting at the torn wrapping paper scattered on the floor. He's in full sensory overload today. I should take him upstairs for his nap; it's overdue, but I wanted to let him enjoy his first Christmas. For us to enjoy it as a family.

Because we don't know how many more we'll have.

I wish I could smile at the sounds of my family in the next room. I wish I could enjoy the simple delights of a normal life. I wish so much that it hadn't come to this.

A mother's love is said to be the fiercest there is, born of the bond grown within one shared body. That thought has captivated me. Tantalised me. A love I never knew until the day my son was placed in my arms. But now it's being tested. Here, in my kitchen, on what should be the most joyful day of the year. I glance over my shoulder at the kitchen door. My hand sneaks to the pills in my pocket.

I stare down at the flute of bubbles, thinking of the people in the other room, all with no idea of the precipice I'm standing on. I can't possibly go through with this. Can I?

'Liv, come and look! You'll never believe it.'

Justin's voice is closer. I freeze. There's an excited babble from down the hall.

'Coming!' I call, stuffing the pills away.

Everyone is gathered by the window, Max perched in Justin's arms. Through the glass the sky seems an unremarkable grey, but as Dad steps to one side I see what they're all looking at. Outside, it's started snowing. Crisp, pearlescent flakes drifting down.

Justin beckons and I cross the room to his side. I can't remember the last time we saw a white Christmas. Even as we're watching, the snow falls thicker and thicker.

'Magic,' Justin murmurs as he pulls me to him, Max sandwiched between us.

'Magic,' I agree. Max is staring in slack-jawed bafflement, like the falling snow is sorcery in action. It makes me ache to see his pure fascination with this new world when I'm in a different place altogether.

'Let's go out!' Justin says, already making for the coat hooks. 'Just for a minute, so Max can see properly.'

I wrench myself away from his excitement.

'Right behind you,' I call, backing away down the hall. 'Let me just finish the drinks for everyone.'

In the kitchen, I shut the door with clammy hands. There's a prickle at the back of my neck, that animal sense of being watched, as if I'm being judged from on high. What would my family think if they knew where my mind has led me these last few weeks? I look back down at the fizzing glass in front of me. This opportunity has arisen, and it could be the only one I get. There's no other choice. I must try. I can't let them lose me, let Max lose me. Whatever the cost.

So, I harden my heart.

'I'm sorry,' I mutter, though I don't know to whom.

Then the pill is no longer in my fingers. It plinks to the bottom of the glass and begins to dissolve.

Part One

1

I've heard it said that having a child is like tearing your heart out and watching it walk around outside your body for the rest of your life. Perhaps to some people that sounds terrifying, but not to me. I say cut me wide open.

My folded hands shake in my lap as I sit on the edge of our bath, like a prisoner in the dock. I can't count how many times I've been here before, waiting, hoping. Two years of injections, weight gain, mood swings. Bruises flowering across my skin. Two years of yearning for those blue lines to appear. For that faint flutter, the soft drumbeat of life inside me.

Recently I've been feeling strange. Different. At least, I think so. Like everything is taking a bit more effort. New sensations. A low-level nausea and heaviness. I dare to hope what it might mean. Justin and I agreed to take the tests together, but this time I can't wait. He often gets stuck dealing with patient paperwork at the GP practice, and I honestly can't stand another moment of not knowing if this feeling is real or just another reverie. I hope he'll forgive me.

I replace the cap on the stick. Even after all our negative tests, my heart still beats double time, like it can't help entertaining the hope that this one will be different. I try to add up how long I've spent enduring this wait. This limbo. Hours of my life?

A familiar fantasy fills my mind. A little face peering up at me from the bathtub, suds on their head, a wide, gummy smile. A wobbly head, at bath-height, a hand presenting a forgotten cotton bud to me as treasure. Taller now, pretending to brush their teeth over the sink with a wicked giggle. A teenager preening in front of a steamy mirror, oblivious to me staring at how beautiful they are, wishing they knew it better. I'll be there for every milestone, I won't miss a thing. I'll make up for everything she never did.

Sometimes, when I'm at my lowest, I wonder if all this is a sign. A reminder that her blood runs in my veins, that I'm not made to be a mother; it's written in my DNA.

It's harder than you think. It takes and it takes, parenthood. You believe I failed you, but you don't understand what has to be sacrificed for a child. You don't have it in you.

Her voice bubbles up in the quiet moments like this. It's a struggle not to listen.

My hand presses against my abdomen, just below the belly button. Technically, I have been pregnant once. We felt that full-throttle rush of adrenaline, joy. But that was as far as it went. A 'chemical' pregnancy; such a painfully clinical term. The doctor said it was a good sign; it meant conception was possible, but if anything that made it all the harder. Fertility treatment is like an addiction. Putting money down on chance after chance, sinking further into debt but convincing ourselves to try just one more round. Just *one* more could do it.

Last night Justin and I had a rare fight about it. He's wanted us to stop trying for a while. This last round of treatment has cleaned us out.

'There's my father's care home, Nick's university fees,' Justin said, pacing around the kitchen, hands shoved deep into his pockets. 'Where do you think we're going to find enough money, Liv, with you working part-time? I think we—' He paused. 'My love, we have to accept it.'

I looked at Justin, the new lines drawn around his kind eyes since we met. The way he's started to hunch forward fractionally, under the weight of everything he carries. Perhaps the chaos of a baby will be too much? He is forty-nine. I know he just wants to see an end to my torture. But he's got what I long for already; he has Nick.

It's true their relationship is strained; they haven't seen each other since before our wedding three years ago. Nick has never forgiven Justin for his parents' split, his fury a misplaced loyalty to his mother. Justin's ex, Louise, doesn't feel hard done by; their separation was amicable. Long overdue, she once said. They stayed together too long, for Nick's sake. Parenthood may not be idyllic for Justin by any stretch, but our failure to have a child will never feel the same for him.

I know that a future without a baby has its charms; freedom, stability. My friends Nadia and Sinead are both happily childfree. Nadia is a successful management consultant approaching partnership. I can see it fulfils her, but my own patchwork career of dead ends and false starts can't hope to do the same. Sinead has a huge family. I lose track of the number of cousins, nieces and nephews in her Christmas Instagram posts. She and her partner Edie have concluded their lives lack none of the warmth and beating heart of family. I do know all that. And yet I cannot give up.

'Maybe we can... look at the finances again,' I said, blinking rapidly, not meeting Justin's eye. 'I could... I could sell my mother's ring.'

I've always meant to have it valued. The small diamond Dad bought for the engagement that she refused to commit to, convinced it was the worst of all institutional evils. Another means to tie her down. I can still hear her saying 'Collars are for dogs', even though at eight years old I didn't understand what it meant. She never even wore the ring, but Dad kept it for me. Sentimental fool that he is.

He asked me once if I missed her. I'd started my period, just after my fourteenth birthday, and he found me, red-faced, stuffing bedsheets into the washing machine at seven in the morning. For years he stretched himself wider and wider, trying to cover the hole that she left, but this was a corner he couldn't reach. I knew my answer had the power to break his heart.

'No,' I said, as firmly as I could muster. 'You're as good as two Mums.'

A smile broke across his face like sunshine through storm clouds.

'Three!' I cried, my arms around his shoulders, rubbing my cheek on his salt-and-pepper sideburns and knocking his glasses off.

The truth is I don't even know what to miss. When I was a teenager, I tried to track my mother down but she left no forwarding address, no clue as to where she was going. She didn't want to be found. We didn't even hear that she'd died straight away. For a few weeks I moved through the world believing I still had a mother, if an absent one, when I no longer did.

Opening my eyes to a view of the bathroom ceiling, I mutter a reprimand under my breath. Yet again I've let myself get my hopes up. Stupid. Get it over with. I'll suggest something to take our minds off it this weekend, a spontaneous trip to the countryside somewhere. We haven't been away all year, and I've always loved travel planning. Maybe a change of scene is just what I need, a break from the pressure of all this. I gather some toilet paper ready to wrap the test up. Finally, I look down at it.
There's a second blue line alongside the first.
I blink to check that I'm not hallucinating, then check with the instructions in the packet, though I've done hundreds of them. The test vibrates so much in my hands that I have to put it down to read it. To confirm what I think I can see.
It's faint, but unmistakable.
I sink to the bathroom floor. My legs feel weak, my heart is pounding. No. It's probably wrong; the tests before were all negative. False positives are rare, but they do happen with fertility treatment and changing hormone levels. But even with this knowledge a fragile hope is blooming through me like a sugar rush.

In a daze I tug on my coat. I'm late for my shift at Justin's GP surgery. When my fifth job interview came to nothing, he suggested I take some hours on reception duty there. It was meant to be a stopgap, something to fill the growing hole on my CV after I burned out as a lawyer in the City, but somehow almost three years on I'm still there. Since starting the fertility treatment I've been too scared to introduce any new stress into my life. Convinced myself it's best to stick to something low pressure for now.
As I leave the house, a picture propped on the mantelpiece catches my eye; the photo of my friends from my best friend Billie's baby shower, all hugging her as best we could around her ginormous bump. My eyes are shining with excitement for her.
The golden light of the winter early afternoon floods over the terraced houses on our street in Harringay, North London. In

that hue they look a little less tumbledown. Most of the houses haven't changed for decades, with slowly peeling paint and faded net curtains, but scaffolding has started to appear on a few. A sign of more affluent people moving in and extending. I wonder how long it will be before this road becomes unaffordable. How many people it's already unaffordable for.

The sun's fading glow illuminates traces of the families who live here. Three brightly coloured balloons tied to a door knocker. A tiny stripy sock lost halfway up the road. A mother with a buggy. There are several primary schools nearby, which once seemed lucky, but now serves up the personalised torture of children's gleeful shouts and clamour every morning. Maybe soon it won't sound so painful. Superstition kicks in and I squeeze my eyes tight shut.

Christmas is fast approaching and festive trees have appeared in the windows of those who can't wait any longer. In one house, a little girl dances around as her brother tries to lasso her with trails of tinsel. The cosy scene stops me in my tracks. I gaze through the window, like I used to as a child on the walk home from school. When their mother comes and closes the shutters I hurry on, berating myself. My God, don't be *that* weirdo.

But even as I walk away, my heart is thudding with a brewing, bubbling excitement. Has fate smiled on us finally? No... nope. I can't let the hope take root, not yet. Not until I'm totally, completely sure. I'll buy some more tests as soon as I can get to the chemist.

I turn onto the high street past the locksmith's, the Turkish bank and the carpet shop. The main road is thronged with delivery riders and trucks unloading goods; it's a world away from the quieter tree-lined roads near Crouch End where Billie lives, surrounded by boutique bookshops and pastel-painted coffee spots. I speed up past the temptation of the kebab shop where many a wine-soaked evening with Nadia used to end up, before I started the fertility treatment. Giving up alcohol has been harder than I imagined, when for me one of life's great pleasures is a glass of house red by the roaring fire in our local pub on quiz night, feeling the warmth spread through my veins.

I'm nearly at the bus stop when my phone buzzes with a Gmail notification. Another email from Al. I've seen one popping up already, but I haven't read it. We haven't spoken since his leaving drinks and it's been weeks now. He called the next day from the airport, but I was too angry for a protracted goodbye. I just wanted him gone. Off around the world; his long-delayed dream. Once, a long time ago, when we were students, we planned to take that trip together, but that was another lifetime.

I swipe the notification away and look for a minute at the photo on my phone background. A group shot from our trip to Paris last year: Nadia wearing the beret that only she could pull off, Billie and I clutching whipped cream-topped hot chocolates, the first hint of her bump showing, and Sinead crying with laughter at the less than flattering caricature she'd just had done outside the Sacré Coeur. The four of us have gone on our annual European jaunt ever since we graduated. In our twenties it was island hopping in Greece, knocking back ouzo, or sunning ourselves in Southern Spain. These days it's a cheap and cheerful city break with dinners out and a quick peek around a gallery as the nod to culture we've used to justify the trip. We haven't got around to planning this year's, the others conscious of my budget and how preoccupied I am with simply getting through the cycle of hope and disappointment each month.

The bus is hurtling towards the stop and I break into a run, panting within a minute or two. I really must exercise more. If it's true, if I am actually pregnant, I'll redouble the health kick which has slipped these last weeks. I'll swim in the mornings again. I used to go twice a week, relishing how the water seemed to wash worries away, even if the chlorine smell lingered. No more takeaway pizzas from the moreish place around the corner. I'll cook my fish pie. Frankly, there are only about five recipes I can actually make edible. Justin has the culinary flair though he indulges my feeble attempts with good grace.

I'm sprinting towards the bus stop, realising that in all the turmoil I forgot to water the wilting plants in the kitchen, when it happens. My chest tightens and it's suddenly hard to draw breath. The world starts to blur. One minute I'm about to step up onto the bus, the next I am crumpling to the ground.

Then my head slams into the kerb.

2

The ambulance feels like overkill, but I'm too dazed to convince the bystanders not to call for one. I try to stand up but my head swims and the kindly older man who made the call sits beside me on the pavement until it arrives. The paramedics are firm when I protest that it was just a dizzy spell; the laceration on my head needs stitches and head injuries have to be monitored.

I'm wheeled into A&E feeling guilty for wasting time they could be spending on more serious cases. A nurse takes my blood and I look away from the vial filling with wine-dark liquid. I've never been good with blood; it turns my stomach to see what's inside me on the outside. They give me a local anaesthetic to numb my forehead as a junior doctor carefully laces three stitches through the cut above my temple.

'How are you feeling now?' asks the tired-looking on-call doctor.

'Like an idiot?' I give a wry smile which she returns generously. 'No, um, okay really. Just tired. I guess a bit nauseous and slightly short of breath.'

'Have you been under any unusual stress lately?'

I look down at my hands. 'Maybe. I suppose things have… been a bit tough.'

Her eyes flicker briefly over my paperwork. 'Is there any chance you could be pregnant?'

I hesitate. I don't know how to answer. It feels *so* wrong to tell this stranger before my husband. Especially when I don't know for sure. Lying to a doctor doesn't feel any better, but I can't bring myself to say it out loud, like the pregnancy might evaporate if I dare to claim it as real. I find myself shaking my head.

'Right, well, your blood pressure is a little higher than we'd like so I'm going to have a listen to your heart.' She readies a stethoscope. 'It'll be a bit cold.'

I try to take slow, deep breaths as she listens.

'Okay. It's likely the breathlessness is from the shock and the nausea from a mild concussion, but you should monitor that head. I'd like to run a few more blood tests to be sure, but I don't see any reason to keep you here,' she says. 'If the pain gets worse or doesn't go away, or you experience confusion or memory loss, come right back in.'

'I will, thanks.'

As the doctor reaches to pull back the curtain of my cubicle, her sleeve slips down revealing something on her forearm, faded, as if she's not had time to wash it off. A child's scribble in bright pink pen.

Outside in the waiting room, I spot Justin. He's on the phone, pacing, clutching his briefcase; the old-fashioned one I tease him about, like he's playing dress up at being a doctor. It was his father's and, while there's no love lost between them, perhaps it's impossible not to sentimentalise. To want to reimagine a more nostalgic version of your childhood.

His dark curls are blown back from his forehead as if he's been running. The bags under his eyes look deeper. He's the GP who goes the extra mile, runs the internal meetings at the practice, does the home visits. It makes him something of a local celebrity. When I first moved into his house it took some time to adjust to him being greeted in the street. Even our disagreeable neighbour, Irene, a brusque woman in her early sixties who is only ever content when complaining, breaks into a smile when she sees him. But his role can be a heavy burden too. Having to be the one to break the bad news; reveal the test results no one wants to hear.

His eyes dart over my face. Though we called a truce, the aftermath of our argument from last night still lingers between us. I press myself into his arms, cheek against his neck. We hold each other close for a few minutes in the waiting room.

'What happened?' He examines my forehead tenderly.

'It's nothing. Stupid really. Let's go. I just want to get home.'

'Shall we cancel tonight? I can call Amir now, he'll understand.'

I forgot; we're meant to be going to his friends Amir and Rebecca's for dinner. It's been in the diary for weeks and I know he's been looking forward to it. As much as I can't stand Rebecca, a stalwart ally of Justin's ex Louise, who always behaves as if it's her job to make me uncomfortable, putting them off is only kicking the can down the road.

'No, it's fine. Really, I'm okay.' I take his hand. 'Just got light-headed. Didn't have breakfast.'

'*Olivia*,' he chides me in his GP voice. Concern etches lines deep into his forehead.

I think back to meeting him that summer five years ago. How, after so many uninspiring dates or brief, disappointing relationships, with him it was different. I'd just moved back in with Dad after my career divebombed. Though in my twenties I'd mostly avoided North London because the streets still echo with memories of my mother, I was happy to be closer to friends; Billie lived nearby, and Al was a bus ride away.

One warm midsummer evening Billie had summoned me to the pub to vent about Tom's latest misdemeanours, though they would go on to get engaged only a few months later. I needed the company after another terrible interview. It was like the law firms I was meeting could tell my heart was no longer in it. That the thought of returning to days spent logging every minute of my time as I switched between client accounts sent a sickly dread through me. But I'd trained as a lawyer, and it was all I knew. It was always my plan. Work hard to get a good, steady, respectable job and make Dad proud, after everything he'd sacrificed for me.

I was bringing our drinks back to the table when someone turned from the bar and knocked my shoulder, sending our white wines to the floor via my shirt. Justin was mortified. He and Amir helped mop up as best they could while I protested with reddening cheeks and Billie, watching from the table, snorted into her hands.

Ever the eagle-eyed wing woman, she spotted the spark between Justin and me and invited them to join us, then commenced a one-woman sideshow to entertain Amir. For the next two hours I had Justin's undivided attention and it felt like sitting beside a roaring fire in the depths of winter. He shared the difficulties of his recent divorce, and I found myself talking about the burnout from my career. The years sunk into being a corporate solicitor; trying to make a success of myself translating to never seeing the light of day. How I was temping instead because it was flexible and undemanding.

Before I knew it, I had mentioned my mother.

'God, sorry. Really bringing down the mood,' I said, quickly swigging my wine.

Justin held my gaze gently. 'I lost my mother too, when I was a child,' he said quietly. 'I understand.'

While I doubted he did, I think it was that moment when something lit up within me. Like some primal part of me had already detected the future. Read the stars and identified that this connection would mean something. When he invited me out for a meal, a rarity in the age of dating apps, I felt a flare of delight and said yes without hesitation.

Rebecca serves dinner at 7 p.m. on the dot. She is devoted to punctuality as if it's a religion. At least it means that not staying late won't feel rude. Her eyes slide over the stitches on my forehead, but she doesn't mention them. I'm not sure if it's bad manners or complete lack of interest. She works at a charity as an HR manager and displays a barely disguised relish at getting to lead the hiring and firing. She's never warmed to me, as if it's somehow my fault that Justin and Louise's marriage ended, years before I'd even met him. She's never forgiven Justin either.

I made the mistake of trying to face the coldness between us head on once, trying to be the bigger person, but she only looked at me like I was making it up. A wide-eyed innocence at the suggestion of any frostiness, like I was imagining the way she barely made eye contact when we were around the same table, as if I didn't exist. I realised there would be no truce between us; she'd made her mind up about me and that was that. Afterwards I stopped bothering to be polite and now I only really speak to Amir when I see them.

As we pass the sides around, I nod along with the small talk, but really I'm looking around their house. Plain walls. Cork coasters on every surface to prevent rings on the polished wood. A muted, floral scent hanging in the air like smoke. All Rebecca's various fussy touches. The house betrays none of its inhabitants' desire for children. I stare at Rebecca, wondering how she managed the strange, private grief of failing to have a family. I try to smile but yet again she doesn't meet my eye. My very presence seems to be an insult to her. As if me being thirty-six, over a decade younger, is intended to rub salt in the wound. The cliché about marrying an older man hasn't escaped me. I'd rather have met someone my own age, someone who would be fit and healthy enough for us to share a long future together as parents. To travel the world in retirement. Become grandparents one day if we were lucky.

'Yes, it was a lovely trip, York is a wonderful place,' she's saying when I tune back in. 'So much history. Nick seems to be enjoying it up there. He really is turning into an impressive young man.'

She pushes her fork into a restrained chunk of the bland grilled chicken. I bristle. Amir clears his throat. Justin takes a slow sip of his wine.

'I'm glad to hear it.'

His reply is calm, measured, betraying nothing of the pain her comment will have caused. Amir is Nick's godfather, so Rebecca knows full well that Justin hasn't seen his son since he went up to university in York, despite paying half the fees. Though she'll never admit it, she can't resist a dig, relishing the unspoken power play. I raise my eyebrows, expecting Justin to say more, but Amir smoothly changes the subject.

'How's work?'

Justin rolls his eyes. 'The usual underfunding nonsense. We're so pinched it hurts.'

'Don't we know it,' Amir replies. 'Been a bloody headache but the juniors seem to be making some headway with the strikes.'

He's a surgeon. He and Justin met at medical school and lived together during their training. I've got a lot of time for Amir. He's the sort of person who can always summon a smile, which makes his choice of Rebecca for a life partner all the more baffling.

After we've finished eating, I help Amir load the dishwasher.

'Nasty scrape, hmm?' He's eyeing the wound on my forehead. 'Looks like they've patched it up properly. Nice neat stitches. Shouldn't leave much of a scar.'

'Thank you.' I smile at him. I can imagine his presence is a great comfort to families forced to endure time on the ward.

Finally, Justin and I collapse through our front door, tugging off coats and shoes and spilling towards the living room. My head throbs with a dull ache.

'Thanks for coming, love,' he says. 'I know it's something of an ordeal to endure Rebecca without wine…'

I've promised myself no more drinking. Al's leaving do a few weeks back was a moment of weakness. Drinks I should never have had. It was a one-off.

'I had a nice time,' I say lightly. 'It's always good to see them.'

Justin raises an eyebrow. He knows I'm being generous. He tucks me up in our cosiest throw blanket on the sofa, the one with sleeves that I flounce about in, like a queen in royal robes. He examines my dressing carefully, then folds my hand tight in his.

'We have a nice life, don't we?' he asks quietly, pressing his cheek to my forehead, and rubbing my foot with his. He's thinking about our argument. The fertility treatment, not carrying on.

I flush at the thought of the test from this morning. The stick tucked in my bag, wrapped in paper towels, heavy as a sworn secret. The shimmering potential of what it might mean. I sit up as words form on my lips, ready to tell him, but what he said yesterday still hangs in the air. *'We have to accept it.'*

There had been an unmistakable note of relief in his voice. In all the chaos of the accident, I haven't made it to the chemist for another test so I'm not sure it's real yet. I lie back against him, my head resting on his shoulder.

'We do,' I say softly as he flicks the TV on to the latest episode of a post-apocalyptic series we've been hooked on. Reaching over, I switch to a historical drama I know he's been enjoying. He raises his eyebrow.

'Just need something lighter than fights for survival tonight,' I say.

'May I remind you that things don't end well for poor old Cromwell.'

I poke him in the ribs and he laughs. Taking his hand, I absent-mindedly twist the wedding band on his ring finger. It sits looser than mine, thanks to the indentation from the years wearing his last one.

'It's not going to fall off,' he murmurs into my ear.

I remember his expression the day I threaded it onto his finger in the wood-panelled room of the register office. His eyes said: *Finally*. Like he'd come home. That's what he is to me: the first time I have felt truly at home. He is safety. Stability. Concrete foundations to our life. All I want is for us to build our family on top of them.

I had this vision when I was a little girl. Nothing fancy. Not a mansion with a pool and a hot tub, or stables, or a ball pit, just a house with lights on in every room. With bright wallpaper and toys strewn around the floor. Siblings cavorting around, jostling for attention. Brimming with noise and life. A space where I could prance around the living room in clothes from the dressing-up box, performing to an audience applauding indulgently from the sofa.

As I've grown up, the fantasy has never evaporated, like most childhood dreams do. Instead, rather than the child performing, I have become one of the figures on the sofa. The adoring mother in the heart of her home, eyes aglow to witness the pure imperfect beauty of her family.

I would give anything to be her.

3

I wake to find a cup of tea on the bedside table and smile. From its colour I can see Justin has capitulated to my taste for oat milk, and from the few stray tea leaves I can tell he's used the fancy looseleaf kind I bought to cheer myself up after one of the negative tests. He's even popped a coaster under it, to save the cover of my current read. Overcome by nostalgia and the need for comfort, I'm rereading *Northern Lights*, my favourite book as a child. It's the same copy Dad bought me back when it was first published, well-thumbed and well-loved.

Justin's left for work, not wanting to wake me, so the house is silent. I watch the shadows from the tree outside dance on our sage green walls. I'd never have set foot on any property ladder were it not for this place. Justin bought it in the nineties when the area wasn't desirable at all. He's still got some of the mortgage to pay off, but he doesn't let me contribute now I'm not earning much. Every time I see the steep-pitched roof, like a child's drawing of a house, it reminds me just how lucky I am.

I sit up gingerly. The pain in my head has waned, though my chest is still tight, as if my body hasn't managed to relax since the fall. I take a sip of tea and grimace. It's cold. I glance at my phone and see it's already 8.15 a.m. There's a notification. A third email from Al. Sent at 4.05 a.m. from who knows where. I swipe it away then stuff my feet into the slippers Dad got me last Christmas. Somehow they feel tighter.

Halfway down the stairs a head rush leaves me bent double. Unnerved, I sit down heavily, listing off the symptoms. Low energy and nausea are familiar friends from the IVF treatment, but the swelling in my feet and this breathlessness feel new. I remember Billie complaining about it when she was pregnant; her body working twice as hard to accomplish the same things. I picture those blue lines. I need to go and buy another test.

As I'm stashing my empty mug loosely in the dishwasher, knowing Justin, who is tyrannical about stacking efficiency, will rearrange it when he gets home, my phone vibrates with a call. An unknown UK number.

'Ms Hargreaves?' enquires a professional-sounding voice. 'I'm ringing about your recent blood test results.'

'Oh,' I mutter, blindsided. 'Right, yes.'

'We'd like you to come into the hospital to discuss them with the doctor.'

Anxiety tightens my throat. 'Wow. That's so fast. Is... is that normal?'

'The doctor will talk you through everything,' the voice says, refusing to give anything else away. 'We've actually had a cancellation for one-thirty today, if that can work for you?'

'Okay... yes. I'll be there.'

After I hang up, my pulse fizzes with an adrenaline jolt. Why would they want me in? I think again about the exhaustion, the nausea. Breathlessness. Could I be...? Could the blood test from the hospital have confirmed it? I let the fantasy play out. Maybe I'm anaemic or something. They'll say I need to eat right to keep my iron levels up. Keep the baby growing well.

Or something worse. They've found something that means it's never going to happen for you.

She is my every insecurity on loudspeaker and I don't know how to shut her off. I force myself to ignore her voice. I can get over to the hospital during my lunch break. Brian, the other receptionist, will kick up a stink if I'm late back but he'll just have to manage.

There's a note of concern in Justin's voice when I call him. 'I'll come with you.'

'Honestly, it's fine, really. You don't need to.'

'I want to, Liv,' he says. 'One of the others can cover for me. I'll meet you outside the hospital.'

I'm glad he'll be there. That we'll be together when we get the news. Anticipation surges inside me but I talk myself down. Just wait. There have been too many disappointments. Wait until it's real.

In the consulting room, Justin and I perch awkwardly on the uncomfortable blue plastic chairs, examining the doctor's face for tells. She clicks a few times on the computer, then turns to us.

'You'll remember we did a blood test after your high blood pressure result and the syncope.'

My forehead wrinkles. 'Syncope?'

'The fainting,' Justin mutters.

The doctor nods. She is talking slowly, as if I might struggle to understand what she's saying. 'Well, I'm afraid the results are suggesting that there's an issue.'

I blink.

'There are some raised levels which indicate that your heart may not be functioning normally.' She pauses, letting her words sink in.

I stare at her.

'Given your other symptoms, I'd like to refer you to a cardiologist. They'll request some more diagnostic tests to get to the bottom of your condition.'

Silence falls over us as her words register.

'But... I haven't had any problems before now,' I say.

The doctor nods. 'It's not uncommon for a sufferer of your demographic to only experience mild symptoms. Let's just do these further tests and get clarity. I'm going to request an ECG, that's an electrocardiogram, and also an echocardiogram. Do you know what those are?'

'Yes, I'm a GP,' Justin says, sitting forward. 'I can talk her through them.'

'Good. We'll get you booked in as soon as possible.'

As she turns back to her computer, I look at Justin. He's staring at his hands. I want him to lean over and tell me everything's going to be fine, but he knows better. I have to tell them about the positive test, but this isn't how I pictured doing it.

Here in this sterile room, where people receive bad news from strangers.

Anyway, it makes no sense. People with heart problems can hardly walk across a room or fill their lungs. I'm far too young. Surely all this is a mistake? My symptoms, the fatigue, nausea, breathlessness, are all things that would be explained by a pregnancy. Maybe the extra strain it's putting on my heart is skewing the results, making things seem worse than they are. That must be it. This is all a misunderstanding.

On the way out of the hospital we pass the pharmacy.

'I just need to grab something,' I say to Justin, and duck inside.

Scanning the familiar shelves, I pick up a box of pregnancy tests. We stopped buying the expensive tests months ago, the ones that say Pregnant or Not Pregnant and how many weeks, but today I need to know for sure. I hurry to the till, trying to ignore the conspiratorial smile on the face of the woman behind the counter.

When we get home, I scramble straight up the stairs, my heart pumping hard. By the time I reach the bathroom door I'm panting. I rip open the box, take the tests, one after another, and then lay the sticks face down on the bathroom floor. Cross-legged, I wait, watching the timer on my phone count down. The doctor's words play in my mind and for a moment my confidence wavers. What if I'm wrong? Could I actually be ill? What if… The timer beeps jauntily and I shove the thought aside gratefully.

Finally, one by one, I turn the test sticks over. Hairs raise on my arms.

Three identical words stare up at me and I forget about everything that was said at the hospital.

Pregnant. Pregnant. Pregnant.

Downstairs, Justin is sitting on the sofa with his head in his hands. He looks up, eyes shot through with an unfamiliar distress.

'Liv, I think… I think maybe it's for the best. That we didn't… that we couldn't…' He can't finish, but I know what he's saying. 'If there's a problem with your heart, if… if you're not well… it would be so dangerous for you—'

I hold my breath. The conversation we have been putting off is rearing up now, like lava spewing up from a crack in the ground, before I can share my news. *Our* news.

'Justin—' I start softly.

'I'm serious, Liv. You need to take care of yourself. The IVF process has – it's a tsunami of hormones. You've put your body through so much.'

'*I've* put my body through so much?' I interject with a frown. As if he had no part in it.

'I just mean… I think… Well… maybe this is a sign.'

I bristle. 'A sign?'

'That it… wasn't meant to be. That we should move on. I'm sorry.'

My stomach flips. The jubilant words dry on my lips. I feel sick. It sounds like he doesn't even want it. Our baby. Our future. I start to panic. If he finds out now, what if he says it's not safe to proceed? We've spent *years* of our lives trying to get here. My eyes start to sting as I realise that I can't tell him.

I can't tell my husband that, after all this time, I am finally pregnant.

As I stand there biting my tongue, I'm scrambling to form a new plan. I'll have to wait until I've had the other tests. Once we have the results and we get the all clear, that's when I'll tell him. When I'm sure he'll be pleased, not worried. It feels mad not to say anything but it's just for a few weeks. Then we can finally celebrate the miracle we have yearned for without this shadow hanging over us.

Just as it's finally coming true, my dream of a simple life, a family of my own to cherish, a chance to heal old wounds, is threatening to unravel. I need to hold the stitches together before they come apart in my hands.

4

Each morning when I wake up I lie quiet for a few moments, as though, if I'm still enough, I might be able to feel the alchemy going on inside me. Wondering how big the baby is; the size of a seed? A pea? A grape? I look at myself in the mirror, fascinated to see if my reflection will give away my secret. The life taking shape inside me. Now that I've acclimatised to the guilt of not telling Justin, there's a sort of thrill in being the only person to know about the baby. My body, my secret. Fortunately, the nausea doesn't get worse, as long as I remember to eat, so I stash my pockets full of snack bars ready for the first pangs of hunger.

It's a strain not to tell Billie everything when we meet up for coffee in the park. Ever since we met at university in Bristol, a week hasn't passed without us speaking. Usually just her name flashing up, with the picture of us pulling stupid faces in sombreros on her hen do in Andalucía, makes me grin. Now she gives me a funny look when I ask for a decaf.

'Already had one this morning,' I say hurriedly.

We trundle around, bent double, as her twin daughters' little hands clutch our fingers for support. They're just starting to walk and so the whole world is an adventure playground.

'So, how's work?' Billie's been back at her job in PR for a few weeks since the end of her maternity leave.

'Oh, you know, always some client drama. They don't like the campaign font or whatever. But it's nice to talk about things other than teething and comparing soft-play spaces.' She grins, rolling her eyes. I detect a hint of exaggeration in some of the challenges she recounts. Tom being neglectful, Daisy and Poppy hitting a particularly exhausting stubborn phase. She's careful to play down the pure joy I know she's found in becoming a mother, eager to minimise my pain.

We sip our drinks in a silence which would be comfortable if there wasn't so much I want to say.

'You look... tired?'

It's a question; she's giving me room to disagree. It's something I love about her. She doesn't know how to insult anyone; she's too empathetic. She's one of those women who seems to exude sunshine. People just want to be near her, to bask in the glow of her, and yet she never steals the limelight.

I hadn't had the same privileged education as many of the others at Bristol University. From day one I realised I lacked some other language which seemed to matter. The casual references to top-tier banks and corporate firms where people's parents worked sailed over my head. But with Billie it was different. From the moment we met, shaking pinkie fingers with our arms full of boxes, she made me feel like I belonged. Every euphoric drunken night, and every cosy, hungover morning after was shared with her.

'Just a bit rundown,' I mutter.

'Well, at least you escaped the double whammy of 'flu and Norovirus. The girls lob germs between them like it's a tennis Grand Slam. I swear, Liv, I've never seen so much vomit. Not even when the rugby teams at uni had that competitive session. I think we're going to have to get the carpets replaced in the living room.'

I smile feebly.

'Have you heard much from Al?' she asks, eyes on the girls as they examine twigs on the ground with forensic focus.

I swallow. 'Not really, the time differences are so hard.'

'Yeah. I tried to FaceTime him, but the connection was terrible, so we mainly email. Seems like he's having a great time. Forgotten all about us boring trads.'

I feel a pang. They're in regular touch when I can't bring myself to reply to him. It's surreal that he isn't here for me to talk to. For a moment my chest aches at his absence, then I push it away. There's just been too much going on.

I think back to the echocardiogram last week, the feel of the sonographer's probe on my chest. How much I hope to feel that cold shock of the gel again; this time the probe placed gently on my swelling abdomen. The diagnostic tests don't seem to have betrayed us.

We have become an 'us' already in my head.

Work is a respite, a brief spell where other people's problems are a welcome distraction from my own.

'Morning,' Brian says dryly, with a side-eye scan of my appearance as I sit down behind our reception desk. He never fails to find a new way of letting me know how awful I look. 'Nice weekend?'

'Yes, thanks,' I say briskly as I switch my computer on. 'And you?'

At the best of times I tolerate Brian, and the feeling is mutual. He's never forgiven me for not inviting him to our wedding despite half the practice making the guest list. Perhaps I pushed my luck by saying it was just 'family and friends'.

Given it was Justin's second wedding we decided to keep it small. We didn't have money to burn and I've never been one for the spotlight. Justin insists the silver strands in my hair make me look distinguished, but I'm no fool. Past a certain, unspecified point, the big white wedding somehow becomes distasteful. A consolation not a celebration. I was happy with our register office ceremony and small reception upstairs in a local pub.

I spend the rest of the day sorting out test samples which need to go to the lab so I don't have to talk to him.

When I let myself into the house after work, wondering what I'm going to cook for dinner, there's a letter on the doormat addressed to me. I tug off my coat and snatch it up. It's from the hospital. For a moment I just hold it, staring at the neutral wording visible through the transparent plastic panel. Then I tear the envelope open and unfold the letter. I scan it hungrily for news of results. Something to confirm everything is okay, and that there's been an error. It reveals nothing; just details for a further appointment with a cardiologist in a week's time. Disappointment overwhelming me, I sit down heavily at the kitchen table.

Then I pause and read it again, more slowly. Something written in the small print has caught my eye. Looking at it for a second time makes fear flare inside me.

'*We recommend you bring someone with you to the appointment.*'

There's something headmistress-like about the cardiologist, Dr Mirza, which makes me feel like a criminal for withholding news of the pregnancy. Justin sits beside me. I didn't show him the letter. Even now I'm clinging on to the hope that it's a mistake. That all this has been down to the baby.

'So, Ms Hargreaves. You'll remember we gave you a series of further diagnostic tests to get to the bottom of some unusual results.'

She looks me in the eye. That must be in her medical training: always make eye contact with a patient when giving results. I nod stiffly.

'Well, the echocardiogram has revealed that your left ventricle – one of the heart's chambers – is enlarged and the muscle is weaker than it should be.'

Justin's hand tightens on mine, but I don't know what this means.

'When the ventricle is enlarged, it's harder for the heart to pump blood around the body, hence the symptoms. It's a condition called dilated cardiomyopathy.'

She pauses, letting what she's saying sink in. My throat is dry. Justin's eyes are locked on the doctor's face.

'It's not uncommon that this diagnosis comes as a surprise; fatigue, shortness of breath and swelling in the legs can be attributed to several conditions. The symptoms can be mild, but it is something we need to treat as soon as possible.'

Her words ring in my ears. *Diagnosis. Condition.*

I blink again and again as if clearing my vision might wipe all of this away. In my lap my fingers are white where Justin's grip is squeezing the blood from them. I've never imagined it would be me sitting opposite the doctor, being handed the grave diagnosis.

'In the first instance I'd like to start you on a series of medications to address the blood pressure and any fluid retention…' Dr Mirza continues.

I drag my attention back to her. She doesn't know about the baby.

'… And then we are going to refer you to our tertiary-care centre to discuss further treatment.'

Justin interrupts. 'So, it's… advanced?'

The doctor nods. 'I'm afraid so. More than we would expect to see in someone of your wife's age.'

They are talking about me as if I'm not here, but I'm struck dumb. It's all so… medical. Like we're talking about the anatomical model standing in the corner.

'Is further treatment really necessary?' I start.

'Ms Hargreaves, your heart is not functioning as it should. Given the weakness showing up on the echo, we recommend proper intervention now before any further deterioration. In many instances things can improve with the right medication, but we do need to act to minimise the risk of complications.'

My pulse rate starts to ramp up. I have to tell them about the baby. I can't take any medication without saying something. But I can't do it now, here – it's too public. Too cruel. Not when I already think I know what he'll say, what the doctors will say. Words I never want to hear.

Dr Mirza sits forward in her chair. 'I'm very sorry to be the bearer of this news. I know it must be a shock, and difficult to hear.'

'What… what caused it?' I manage.

'It can be hard to determine; sometimes it runs in families. Do you know of any family history of cardiac problems?'

'There's… nothing on my dad's side,' I murmur. 'But my mother wasn't around. I don't know her full medical history. She… she died a long time ago. Cirrhosis.'

'I'm sorry to hear that,' Dr Mirza says quietly. 'So, then there is the possibility you have could have inherited the condition.'

I absorb this. It would be one of the few things she left me.

The doctor unfolds her arms. 'Do you understand everything I've told you?'

I realise that, despite the shockwaves still reverberating through me, our time is up. She has other patients. Other lives to save or raze to the ground.

'I… I think so,' I say.

But I don't. I don't understand how this can be happening. My body has finally worked the indefinable alchemy I've wanted for so long, the magic of conception, only for me to learn that I won't have the strength to stay the course.

Life's not fair, my girl. You ought to know that by now.

She would call me that: 'my girl'. Empty words. She never wanted me. I was never hers.

Then Justin and I are standing. We find ourselves thanking the doctor, shaking her hand as if she's just done us a favour rather than breaking the news which threatens to unravel our lives.

5

At home, the living room feels airless, stifling. Justin sits down next to me. Neither of us knows what to say. The warmth of his hand on mine is a shock. I'm a lifelong sufferer from poor circulation, 'a case of the chilly fingers' Dad calls it, but now I wonder if that's all it is.

How long has it taken for my heart to become distended, weakened? Was there a cause, a moment that started it? Was it that day? The day she never came back. Did she do this?

Or did you?

'We should tell your dad.' Justin's good sense drags me from my spiralling thoughts.

Oh, God. Dad. Dread pulses through me at the thought of going over to my childhood home with the news. 'Hello, Olive!' he'll say; his customary greeting. 'Nice surprise!' Making his day, then breaking his heart.

But first I must confront the conversation I've been putting off with Justin. I fumble for words. It's all wrong. It's not supposed to be like this. Pregnancy reveal reels on Instagram are all of tearful women holding up positive tests; overwhelmed partners shouting in disbelief, delight. Today has derailed that possibility for us.

'Justin, I… I took another test.'

He looks up at me, frowning in confusion. 'For what?' His mind is still in the hospital room, hearing the diagnosis.

'A pregnancy test,' I say slowly. 'It… it was positive. It's positive.'

His face is a chaos of emotions doing battle. I squeeze my fingers, wringing them so hard it hurts, waiting to see which will win.

'How… how long?' he mutters eventually.

'Nearly seven weeks. I think.'

I see him take in the significance of that. Over five weeks passes the risk of chemical pregnancy. A huge milestone. It should be a triumph. He presses his fingers to the bridge of his nose and closes his eyes for a second.

'Liv, you need to tell them right now. It will affect your treatment—'

'I know. I just… didn't believe it.' I'm trying to soften the blow. *The blow.* How can this news which we have longed for be a blow? 'I thought if I just waited… I didn't know if it would… last.'

My voice cracks over that word. He softens.

'My love, this is…' He tails off.

It's fucked. That's the word he's searching for. The only way to describe our situation.

'I booked an ultrasound scan,' I say. 'To check it's… okay. Tuesday next week, after work.'

I need to see that tiny squirming mass inside me. To confirm this mistimed miracle is real. And I hope that seeing it might have the power to stop Justin's inevitable suggestion in its tracks. Because I can't make that choice. I can't even think about it.

He is silent for a while, staring at the floor, then he nods. 'Fine.'

As the ultrasound machine is prepared, I lie down on the bed. The image will be projected in cinema format on the blank wall in front of us. Supersized for our viewing pleasure. Justin sits beside me. I reach for his hand. It's clammy.

We're at a private walk-in clinic; a shop front on a local high street sitting surreally next to an off-licence and a post office. Couples who emerge after hearing world-ending news will have to step back out into this mundane normality. I press my nails into the flesh of my palm, praying that we aren't one of them.

The cold gel makes contact with my skin and I flinch. There is silence as the sonographer swipes around, with a gentle pressure. My lungs seize up. Like I can't breathe until I've heard it.

Then... *Thrum. Thrum. Thrum.*

'Is that it?' I whisper. She nods.

A heartbeat.

It sounds like wingbeats. A great flock of birds in flight. Like a wild stampede across a plain. I stare and stare, watching the pulsing on the screen. It sounds like nature. Like life. So very alive.

Then the tiny form writhes before us in black and white and I am transfixed.

'I'd say we're approaching nine weeks along,' the sonographer says.

My mouth falls open. It's longer than I thought. Warmth flushes me; another few weeks closer to the twelve-week milestone after which the risk of miscarriage is said to plummet. If only I could fast-forward time between now and then.

'Can we hear the heartbeat again?' I whisper.

The sonographer smiles. 'Of course.'

The probe comes back to rest over the heart, its four tiny chambers, and the percussive beat echoes around the room.

'Is it... it sounds so fast?' I watch the pulsating shape. 'Does it look okay? Healthy?'

'Yes, it's a very normal heartbeat. Lovely and strong.'

She smiles at us, no idea of the stakes at play, seeing just another happy couple. Justin still hasn't spoken. While I wipe off the gel, the sonographer prints the black-and-white image and holds it out to him. Justin hesitates, then takes it. He gazes at the photo, cradling it in his palm, like he's afraid of squashing it.

After I reveal the pregnancy, we are summoned back before Dr Mirza. I shrink from her unspoken criticism as she makes the relevant changes to my treatment, now obstetrics and cardiology combined.

'Olivia, let me be frank with you. Had you not conceived, we would have cautioned against it as this does make things much more complicated.'

Something in the core of me clenches and Justin shifts in his seat. His expression darkens.

'You'll need thorough monitoring throughout, and to have a planned Caesarean section before your due date. But women with your condition have brought pregnancies to term and delivered babies.'

I grip the sides of my chair.

'But... so... you'd recommend...' Justin pauses. He can't even say it. 'Would you recommend... not proceeding with it?'

Dr Mirza leans forward. 'I know this is extremely hard. Medically speaking, terminating would... improve Olivia's situation as pregnancy does limit medication options for managing the illness. I can't pretend that bringing a pregnancy to term and delivering won't put her body under a great deal of strain. We don't know what long-term impact it might have. But this is an unenviable choice. I do appreciate that.'

Once we get home, Justin drags a chair out in the kitchen and sits down. I stay standing, arms crossed, by the door, as if I can run away from what he wants to say.

'Liv,' he starts softly, 'I know you don't want to hear this—'

'Then don't say it,' I beg.

'Please. We have to discuss the options. We have to think this through. Objectively.'

'How can I be objective? There's nothing objective about this. There's no dispassionately taking the emotion out of it. This is a *life*.'

'No, it's *your* life, Olivia!' he shouts. 'Your *life*. That's what matters to me. Our life together!' The force of it makes me sit down next to him.

'You can't ask me to do that. You *can't*,' I whisper, voice shaking. 'You heard the doctor. Women with my condition have had babies. She said so. I'll take all the medication to manage it, and they can monitor me, and I can have more treatment after the birth if I need to.'

I pull my knees up to my chest, shielding my abdomen, the place we have fought so hard to make a safe space.

Justin drops his head into his hands. 'You don't know if the medication will work. You don't know how it might progress.'

His medical brain is whirring. He only hears about the problems, it's the nature of the job. It makes him see the challenges before they appear.

'There's two of us affected here, Liv,' he whispers.

I realise with a jolt that he is crying. I have never seen him cry before. Not once in the five years of our relationship. I shuffle my chair forward until I can reach him and cradle his head in my arms.

'My love,' I murmur.

'I couldn't bear it… if…' he whispers thickly into my sleeve.

There is something else in his eyes too. A pain years-deep. Barely concealed fear that history is repeating itself. The memory of hospital wards. Of hushed voices, IV drips and false joviality. That he will have to watch my life fade away, drop by drop, like his mother's did. But this isn't the same. That's not going to happen. He doesn't know how I feel. All this is happening to my body and I feel good. There are stories of pregnancies repairing all sorts of ailments. The body works in mysterious ways. I feel hopeful. I feel alive. This is the start of a new future. The chance to get it right this time.

I've seen him staring at a photo of Nick on his phone, thumb hovering over the call button. I've never understood the full extent of the rift between them, how such a loving man has been unable to resuscitate the relationship with his own son. I'm still holding out hope that when Nick is older, he'll forgive his dad for whatever occurred in the past. But this baby, our longed-for baby, is a chance to do it all again. Justin must see that. Sun-flecked family holidays. Cosy fairy-lit Christmases. Cheering at school sports days. Tiny, tangled limbs sprawled over picnic blankets in the park, mouths smeared with ice cream.

As I sit holding him, I feel a rush of anger. It's not fair. Life has served me up ambrosia and poison in the same meal. I think it will be the end of us, of everything we've built, if he says he doesn't want to keep our child.

Out of nowhere I'm hit by a deep urge to call Al, the friend who has known me almost all my life. He doesn't know about any of this. How could I tell him, casually in a catch-up email?

If we did speak, I'd hardly know what to say. I try to remember where he is now, but I've totally lost track of his travels. I still haven't found the words to reply to his emails. As it turns out, he's disappeared just when I need him the most.

'The diagnosis isn't a death sentence,' I whisper into Justin's hair. 'I'll be monitored so closely. They'll plan out absolutely everything. They'll be two steps ahead. More.' I pause, trying to read his expression as he sits up. 'Please, I won't be able to live with myself if—'

It's inconceivable to do anything other than keep this growing life safe. This life I have longed for. Hurt for. Bled for. Our baby, with its tiny, powerful heartbeat and its wild wiggling limbs.

Wiping his eyes, Justin gets up and walks slowly over to the mantelpiece where I've put the sonogram photo. He picks it up, as delicately as if it were an egg hatching, and stares at it. I hold my breath. Time stops with us right there, in our living room, my fingers clutching the sofa beneath me, my husband's eyes on the image of the life we have finally created together.

Justin turns to me.

'We'll be okay,' I say. 'We can do this.'

Then, very slowly, he nods.

I cross the room and throw my arms around him, and we cling to each other, like survivors to the bones of a shipwreck.

Part Two

6

A sound reaches my ears across the operating theatre. It's both brand new and so familiar. Air escaping tiny, wet, fresh lungs. The sound of life beginning.

I close my eyes and for a moment I'm back in the chaos of the last few hours. The scream of the ambulance siren as it raced through the streets. The coil of pain tightening around me over and over. The strobe of corridor lights above my head as I was wheeled into surgery for an emergency Caesarean, several weeks before we'd planned. The white-hot fear flowing through me.

Then the baby cries out again. A call. A call for me.

He's here.

Today my son is born, and I am born anew with him.

He is placed carefully on my chest. This hot, floundering, magical creature. His hands starfish against my skin, as if against a reef in the current, reaching for something to anchor him in this new world. I try to hold him steady amongst the tangle of wires, the drips in my hand, the violent tremors shaking my arms.

'He's so warm,' I gasp, and laugh. It's all I can think to say in the face of this profundity.

'Yes,' says Justin in a breathy murmur. 'Well done, my love. He's… he's incredible.'

The baby's waterborne black eyes struggle to make out my face. Here he is, my body, my heart, beating outside of me, just like they said. The very fact of him the most ordinary miracle. Despite my condition, the fears throughout the pregnancy, we are here now, together. We've made it safely to shore.

Surges of electric love pass through me with such high voltage I'm forgetting how to breathe. It is only his tiny body, rising and falling on the ebb and flow of my breath that reminds me.

'Do you have a name?' the midwife asks gently as she slips a white woollen hat snugly over his head, making him look ready for the first snow, though it's still summer.

Justin and I lock eyes. We nod.

'Max,' I whisper. 'After my favourite children's book.'

Then, without warning, exhaustion rears up, crawling across my body and claiming my limbs one by one. My muscles judder and then I'm going limp.

'Justin, you... have to... I can't hold him,' I say urgently, feeling the strength draining from my arms. 'Take him!'

'Let's give Mum a rest now.' The midwife swoops in and helps arrange the baby in Justin's arms. He gazes down at the face which represents his past, his present and his future entwined. I wish I was in the centre of that embrace, absorbing the nuclear energy from the heart of our new family. Everything I've ever wanted.

Then the faces of midwives and obstetricians start to go in and out of focus. People move faster around the bed, hushed exchanges, efficient shorthand. Everything starts to fade. I hear a word muttered and a new urgency. *Haemorrhage.* I scan their expressions through the haze of sensation, but it's as though I'm submerged, looking up through a fragmented surface at forms blurred by the waterline.

The last thing I see is Justin standing, helpless, holding our son tight to his chest as the noises around me drift away into a whiteness until the only sound is the blood pumping in my ears. Then I hear her.

Be careful what you wish for.

When I come around, we're out of the operating theatre in a private room. Justin is caressing my face with an urgency that tells me the time since I lost consciousness has been tense.

'W-what happened?' I mutter groggily.

'You needed a transfusion,' he says, taking my hand and pressing it to his lips. 'There was a haemorrhage. A big one, but they patched you up brilliantly.' His face is battle-weary. Tears track from the corners of his eyes, staining the hospital scrubs.

'I'm sorry,' I murmur as our foreheads touch.

Next to me, in a transparent swinging cot, Max lies bundled in his white swaddle and hat. I reach out for him with a clumsy hand and feel the hummingbird rise and fall of his chest. We look up as a nurse comes into the room to do some checks. As she stoops over our scrawny, squirming son, a thought hits me.

'Do you test him? For any heart problems?' I ask.

'No,' the nurse says gently. 'Genetic testing is a conversation to have later down the line – there are ethical concerns around testing babies. But don't you worry about that now, your little one's heart sounds lovely. He's fighting fit.'

'Thank you,' I say. 'Thank you all for everything you've done.' She smiles and squeezes my shoulder as Justin and I clasp each other's hands tight.

Hanging on the wall beside us is a framed print; a tranquil blue pen-and-ink sketch of a mother and baby swimming underwater, surrounded by fish. I stare at her beatific expression and suddenly I feel like everything is going to be okay. We are going to be okay.

After three long weeks in the hospital, the medical team is finally convinced that I'm strong enough to leave. My medication plan has stabilised me, so we are discharged with strict instructions that I am not to exert myself or carry anything heavier than the baby.

Back at home, the living room becomes our world. Upstairs feels like another country I fondly hope to visit again. Every morning a flood of pills spills out of bottles into my palm. The science has all been explained to me, but I can't hold on to the detail of it. My body recovers, achingly slowly. Time divides in half. BM and AM, we joke – before and after Max. After a few weeks where night and day bleed together, Justin has to go back to work so soon it's just the two of us, clinging to each other through the dusks and the dawns.

There are moments that I want to sink into and never return. Pressing my cheek to the silken whisper of hair at the back of Max's head, the softness at the nape of his neck. In the lonely hours, I find myself humming songs I didn't know I knew; the haunting melody of 'The Skye Boat Song' bubbling up from deep in my memory. Dad's beard against my forehead, his voice in my ear; the lullaby he sang to me, passed down through the years.

They have recommended against breastfeeding though I refuse to stop trying. The sight of Max's tiny, gaping, wanting mouth is so painful that I have to look away as I reach for the formula to top up his feeds. I'm told we're lucky he takes a bottle; it gives me some flexibility. But I want to be unbending. If ever I were to be pulled from him, I want to snap back, like elastic at its tension point, and bite the person trying to part us.

Even when he sleeps, I choose not to, lying beside him, nose to nose, watching his chest rise and fall. I take so many photos of him that my phone starts to slow down. Deleting even the blurred shots feels impossible, like I would be erasing a part of him.

Dad moves in with us for a while to help out. He stumbles through the door, glasses ever askew on the bridge of his nose, his beard unruly, like he's forgotten to trim it. His arms are laden with suitcases and gifts for us both. With an awed reverence he takes Max into his arms.

'Oh, Olive. It's bringing it all right back,' he murmurs, his cheek pressed to the top of the baby's head. His first and only grandchild. He spent his whole career as an educational psychologist working with children and he's missed it since retiring, so this is a moment he's been waiting for.

'Thank you for staying, Daddy.' I can't have called him that for years, decades even, but it slips out. I lean against his shoulder as I close my eyes, Max safe in his arms.

My friends visit, creeping in with cartoon caution while Max sleeps. They whisper their congratulations with shoulder hugs and moist eyes. Billie curls around me on the sofa, arms wrapping around mine holding the baby.

'So *tiny*!' she breathes. 'I can't believe how fast you forget.'

They bring flamboyant presents, going overboard to show their love. Their relief. Sinead's is a huge soft teddy bear with a tartan bow tie and a blue glass bottle of Neal's Yard Rosehip Oil.

'For the stretch marks,' she explains. 'Not a tiger stripe left on my sisters from all five babies.'

'Thank you.' I kiss her on the cheek, though I see the silvery-red lines that cross-stitch my stomach as a badge of honour, acknowledging service.

Billie's gift is a beautiful hand-painted keepsake box with Max's name engraved on it.

'For all the things you don't want to lose. The outfit he wore home from the hospital, the first tooth. All that.'

'Thanks, B.' I squeeze her hand, throat too thick with emotion to say more.

'Mine next. Best till last.' Nadia hands over her present with a grin.

The accompanying note reads: *I've heard these come in handy ;)* Inside is an expensive-looking device that looks worryingly like a sex toy. I raise my eyebrows at her as Sinead and Billie fling hands over their mouths. Then we realise what it is. A pelvic-floor trainer.

'Screw the baby getting all the good stuff,' Nadia cackles.

Billie swats her with the wrapping paper as I snort into my tea, sending it down my chin. It feels so good to laugh.

'You are ridiculous,' I say.

As I mop myself with kitchen towel, the doorbell rings. Nadia answers it, returning with a big bouquet of colourful flowers and a package.

'Got a secret admirer?' she says with a wink. 'Promise we won't tell Justin.'

I roll my eyes at her as I dig out the card. There's a funny feeling in my stomach because I think I know who this is from. How has he heard? I never found the courage to reply to his emails from the various far-flung places on his route. Jakarta, where the airport was as capacious and hectic as a small city. Cape Town, where from the top of Table Mountain you could see almost to the ends of the earth. Each with the subject line *Sorry*. They stopped coming after a while.

'Aw, they're from Al!' Billie says, reading the simple card over my shoulder.

'When's he back?' Sinead asks as she arranges the blooms into a vase.

'I think it's December, right, Liv?' Billie says. 'That's what he said to me.'

'Something like that,' I say vaguely.

Of course. Billie will have told him the baby came. She's not asked me about him, so he's not told her about the fight. The last words we exchanged. I don't remember exactly what we said, the alcohol put paid to that, but I do remember the expression on his face as I closed the door.

I open the parcel. Inside is a book.

'Oh, the girls love that one,' Billie says. 'One of your favourites, isn't it, Liv?'

'Yeah.'

I gaze at the iconic cover. The illustration of the little boy in a wolf suit, off on an adventure in his red-and-yellow boat. *Where the Wild Things Are*. The book that has inspired my son's name. When we were children, Al and I used to read it together religiously, delighted by its anarchic spirit. We would insist that his mum, Annette, read it to us again and again, testing her patience.

Inside the cover there's a handwritten message.

Welcome to the world, little one. You are already off to a head start with a mum as terrific as yours. From your pal, Alistair.

I close it too abruptly.

'Right, time for bubbles.' Nadia pulls the cork from a bottle of champagne. 'Wet the baby's head and all that.' Uncharacteristically, she's kowtowed to my medical advice and has bought a non-alcoholic brand.

'To our Liv, postpartum and with a dodgy ticker, but still looking delectable. I pay good money to the man with the needle for that level of glow.'

Nadia raises her glass with devilish grin.

'It's so good to see you all,' I say as our glasses clink. 'To the fairy godmothers.'

I asked the three of them just before Max was born. I feel so lucky to have all this love surrounding me. Ever since I was a child, since the day my mother left, I've struggled to feel like I deserve any.

After the others have gone home, I sit staring at the flowers in the vase. Vivid yellow dahlias and purple-blue salvias. Though they are fresh and about to be in beautiful full bloom, I quietly open the front door and throw them in the garden waste.

As the season shifts and the chill of autumn begins to take hold, I tell myself I'll be feeling stronger soon. It's only a matter of time until I'm back on my feet. Recovery isn't linear. It can take up to two years for the body to adjust postpartum. But however hard I try to explain it away, as the days pass it's becoming impossible for me to ignore that I'm not getting better. It feels like I'm constantly jetlagged, as though my body sprang a leak during Max's birth and the blood has been *drip, drip, dripping* out ever since.

Then, one afternoon when I'm alone with Max, I take the stairs too fast and my head starts to swim. I clatter to my knees on the landing, my chest aching, struggling to take a full breath. Fear billows through my veins as I realise I'm too weak to get back downstairs. I crawl to my phone and call Justin at work.

'Can you… can you come home?' I manage, the tone of my voice telling him all he needs to know. I wait on the floor, lit by the glowing red womb-light of Max's sound machine as it emits the strong, rhythmic heartbeat that my body can't.

Justin thunders up the stairs to find me there, Max nestled into my arms.

'Liv!' His face pales as he kneels at my side and takes the baby.

We drive to the hospital as night falls, streetlights strobing over our faces. Max sleeps in the car seat. It's a Friday night and outside people spill merrily from pubs, end-of-the-week jubilation in their blurry expressions, their teetering gaits. I stare at them, my face pressed to the glass. Another world.

My skin is probed, measured, punctured. Cannulas. Drips. The relentless beeping of monitors. A bed for the night for observation. Results in the morning. They bring a cot up from the postnatal ward so Max can sleep next to my bed. We pull the blue pleated curtain around us, recreating the days after his birth. Justin dozes fitfully in the hard plastic chair, twisting his height into its ungenerous dimensions.

Though I dim the lights, I can't sleep. The electric glare dances gleefully, the series of beeps is a discordant chorus. Max whimpers and I turn, draping a hand over him to feel the bird thrum of his fluttering heart. Then I lay a hand on my own chest, feeling its struggling beat. I close my eyes.

Please. I beg my body. *Please*.

Dr Mirza appears at the chink in the blue curtains, the threshold between our little low-lit corner of the world and the rest. I scour her face. No trace of a smile at the corners of her mouth. But have I ever seen her smile? She clears her throat, and in that sound I know. In that split second pause as she gathers herself, I know that it's bad news.

She talks quietly so our horror is not shared with our anonymous neighbours in the adjacent beds. She talks calmly, so we are not alarmed by what she is telling us. The bald facts. Delivered grave-faced.

'I'm afraid the efforts of pregnancy and labour have weakened your heart much more than we'd anticipated. As of now, the medication is no longer enough to stabilise your condition.'

We stare at her, unblinking, as if we are both praying for the words to turn around, apologise and jump back into her mouth; they got the wrong bed. Max makes the first sound, a plaintive gurgle that tells us his stomach is growling. Justin reaches for him and bundles out a bottle, fumbling over the formula.

'What does that mean?' I ask, over the baby's satisfied gulps.

Dr Mirza looks down at my notes, as if a second or third glance might alter what she has to say.

'Based on the recent results and the severity of these worsening symptoms, it means that we're going to need to take more drastic action. Usually there is an intervention we would try first, but I'm afraid the scans have shown some aortic abnormalities that make you high-risk.'

Justin falls silent, a question half out of his mouth.

'So, what we're recommending, Ms Hargreaves, is that you are assessed for transplant candidacy.'

Her words hang in the air.

'It... It can't be that bad?' I hear the plaintive note in my own question.

'I'm afraid given the speed of your decline over the past eight weeks since the birth, we don't feel confident that medication alone would be sufficient to stabilise you for long at this stage.'

I try to wrangle her words, find other ways for their meaning to fit. Stare at her, wanting to say: *You told me I could do this! That other women had before me. I believed you!* I search her face for a trace of emotion. In vain. Of course she won't be feeling my pain, she wouldn't be able to do her job if she did. No one in the medical profession could keep their head above the rising tide of pity if they let themself feel for every patient. Yet now it's happening to me, I want to believe that she cares. That the world gives a damn.

Backing apologetically out of our blue fabric chamber, the doctor leaves us sitting in silence in the ashes of the conversation. It is only now, in the quiet, that I understand what she's said. Just how bad things are.

The truth is that, slowly but surely, I am dying.

7

After weeks of assessments, physical and psychological, I'm put onto the transplant waiting list. The term seems so ordinary. So everyday. The waiting list. As if it's for a nursery or a gym class. A throw of the dice which has landed me in the company of strangers.

I have been added to the Urgent tier and, as it stands, there are two others alongside me, and one person above us on the Super Urgent list. I try not to think about how ill they must be to earn the top spot. Or how, even if a heart that matches becomes available within range of my local centre, I'm not first in line. Recipients are chosen by a range of factors from location to severity of their condition, so the list is in constant flux. It feels so crude to ask how many organs become available each year, but the question burns inside me.

How many people need to die for me to live?

The clinician hands me a leaflet for a support group. 'It's run by fellow patients, both pre- and post-operation,' she explains.

I take it, along with prescriptions for my new medications; more pots of pills to keep my heart functioning while we wait.

'Do consider going,' the clinician says as she stands up. 'They can really help.'

'I'll… think about it,' I say, but the idea of sharing such raw emotion with total strangers seems too much to endure.

She rests a hand briefly on my shoulder. Her kindness makes it worse.

Billie comes over as soon as I call her with the news. I open the door and she folds into my arms.

'I'm so sorry, Liv,' she says into my shoulder. 'I just can't believe it...'

Within seconds we're both in tears. Her pain is somehow worse than feeling the devastation myself. This is almost harder for Dad, Billie, Justin; they're on the outside looking in, wishing desperately that they could do something, anything, to help.

We pull ourselves together and curl up on the sofa under a throw, with cups of chamomile tea, while Max sleeps in the bassinet at our feet. Billie digs in her pocket and brings out a tiny gift bag.

'It's only a little thing,' she says quietly.

Inside is a pair of tiny stud earrings embedded with translucent white stones.

'I know you think it's all bullshit,' she says with a wry smile, 'I'm not sure I believe it myself frankly, but they're made with clear quartz. It's meant to be a "master healer" according to my friend at work – she's got a crystal side hustle.'

I look at her and grin and we both suddenly dissolve into giggles.

'Oh, my God, I'm such a prat,' she gasps. 'I just thought, you know... you could wear them to your appointments and everything. All the tests. And maybe in hospital when...'

The depth of sentiment stops my laughter. 'Oh, B.' I reach out for her hand. 'I love them, thank you.'

She's started to cry again, silently this time.

'Sorry, I thought I was off the hormone rollercoaster but there's a crash when you stop breastfeeding. Be warned!' she says, brushing her cheeks dry.

I look down at our hands, still entwined. The silver lightning bolt ring on her first finger that I got her at graduation; the rose-gold bracelet around my wrist, her gift for my thirtieth. Symbols of our love for each other. And now another to add to the collection.

'Liv, I want you to promise you'll call me whenever it all gets too much. Any time.'

She knows I'll struggle to tell Justin when I'm finding it hard to stay hopeful, or Dad. How cruel it will feel to subject them to my own pessimism.

'I will.'

'I mean it,' she says. 'I've been thinking... how hard it must be for you, going through all this without... well, without a mum.'

I look at her. We rarely talk about my mother; Billie knows there's very little to say.

'It's *such* a lot to be dealing with... Max, the diagnosis. I know how much I lean on my mum. I mean your dad's amazing, like *seriously* someone knight Terry for services to parenthood, but... I suppose I wondered if you've been thinking of her. And if it might... help to talk?'

My gaze drifts to the window. I think of the voice I sometimes hear. I was ten when she left, and just starting at uni when I heard the news that she'd died. At nineteen I was still stubborn in my conviction that I didn't need her. But, much as I wish I could stop, I do think of her. More often now I am a mother, haunted by what she might have thought of me. Wondering how she would have felt to know that the daughter she erased from her life is fighting to hold on to her own. The daughter whose life was an accident in the first place.

Dad was always honest about that. He's shielded me from as much as he can, but he's never wanted to lie. Pretend the picture was rosier. He did all he could to try and build a family out of a mistake but those are weak foundations to start from.

For a moment I wonder darkly if we had the same blood type; if she'd have been a potential donor.

Billie doesn't say anything more. She understands my silence means it's something I don't know how to put into words. Instead, she picks up the earrings and gently threads them into my ears.

'Gorgeous,' she says, and pulls out her phone for a selfie of us. 'High time I had a new background. The photo of the girls is from when I was totally hormone blind to the fact they resembled aliens more than babies.'

'Thank you,' I say, leaning my forehead into hers as we smile up at the camera.

Justin grows quiet in the weeks that follow. Tender, attentive, but silent. I know what's going through his mind. His mother died when he was fourteen from a degenerative illness that took her spirit long before it took her body. Perhaps it brought us together, this knowledge of a motherless life. Part of me wonders if marrying someone younger was Justin's subconscious way of protecting himself from having to go through that again. While my dad more than made up for the absence, Justin's did not. He's now an ailing octogenarian battling dementia in a care home that Justin pays a huge whack for but can't bring himself to visit.

One evening, when I pause at the door of the bedroom, I see Justin sitting by Max's crib, his head bent, silent tears on his cheeks. My hands clench at his despair, which I can't soothe. I need to call in reinforcements.

'Liv, I was so sorry to hear,' Amir says quietly down the phone. More than most, he knows what we're going through.

'Can you... speak to Justin for me?' I ask. 'I'm worried. I don't think he's dealing with it. Processing it. He's not got many people to talk to and it's happening to him too.'

'Of course, whatever I can do. For you too. Any questions I can help with, anything I can talk you through. I might be general surgery, but believe it or not, I do remember most of medical school.'

'Thank you. They've given me lots of leaflets. They're pretty... vague.'

'Like almost all patient information leaflets,' he says wryly.

So many questions have formed since my appointment. I was too blindsided to ask them all in the room. There's a helpline, but that feels so horribly impersonal, like a customer service line.

'They told me... that the average wait for a donor is eighteen to twenty-four months.'

He sighs. 'That sounds about right. Every year will be different, and I understand it's improving with the new Opt Out system – now that everyone has to choose *not* to donate – but a wait is to be expected for a blood-type match.'

'I'm A negative, is that... common?'

There's a pause.

'Right,' Amir clears his throat. 'So that's not the rarest. About eight percent of the population have it.'

'But it'll take longer to find a match?'

'I'm afraid it's possible. Unless a universal donor comes up. O negative can match all blood types. Then the HLA markers need to match too. Did they explain those?'

'...Yes?' I cringe at how little detail I've retained.

'They're protein markers that your immune system uses to tell which cells belong in your body and which don't. They need to be compatible too or your body will reject the donated heart. It's very hard to predict. I'm sorry, I know that's not what you want to hear.'

'It's okay...' I murmur. 'Thank you for helping. I... we really appreciate it.'

Amir's words linger after I hang up. Eighteen to twenty-four months. That's how long I have to wait. That's how long I need to fight. And while I do, I will take every pill, every test. Follow every bit of medical advice to the letter. I need to look after myself with the same voltage of love I look after my son.

Rifling through our miscellaneous kitchen drawer, I dig out the support group leaflet. I'd stuffed it away, but now I want to know who these people are. These others for whom life has set the same brutal trap. It's only been a few weeks since I joined the list, but already I'm beginning to understand just how much energy it will require not to lose faith. The Transplant Centre number is saved in my phone. I know it's too soon for them to call, but my eyes still flick constantly to the screen. Just in case.

8

The morning of the group meeting my stomach lurches as Dad drops us off outside the pub where it's held, a few postcodes away. A man in his fifties holds the door open for me and I wrestle the pram inside. His face lights up as he sees Max.

'They grow so fast. Everyone says so, but you don't realise how fast until they're yours.' He smiles at me. 'Enjoy it. Even the tough days – before you know it, he'll be grown.'

'I will,' I say, forcing myself to return his smile, while pressing down the sharp pang of pain he had no intention of inflicting.

In the back room, people cluster around a table with tea urns and stacks of white cups and saucers. The air of familiarity and gentle conversation suggests the others have met before. My face flushes as I park the pram in the corner, hoping Max won't wake up. As people start to sit down, I follow. An older woman with straight amber hair swept up in a clip makes for the same chair. We do an awkward dance of silent gestures. She laughs and the skin around her eyes crinkles like crepe paper. Her smile reveals a gap between her front teeth that gives her the look of a little girl, though she must be in her sixties.

'Please, you have it,' I say, turning in search of another.

Max squawks and I hurry over to get him, digging out a bottle with one hand while I sit down. He gulps the milk too fast and possets down his onesie. I lurch around for a muslin. Without hesitating, the woman gets up, reaches for the patterned square from the pram and hands it to me. I flash her a grateful smile.

'Thanks so much...'

'Junie,' she says, and we shake hands over the baby. In the look that passes between us, I know she understands. She must be a mother too.

Once we are seated, a woman in her fifties stands up. I blink at the incongruous slogan on her rumpled T-shirt. *Second Heart, Third Husband.* She introduces herself as Cathy, the Group Chair, and explains she received her donated heart two years ago. I gaze up at her, a prophet of hope. The others stare too. Living breathing proof that we might be saved. Her eyes fall on me.

'We have a newcomer today, I think?'

'Yes, hi… I'm Olivia,' I say with an awkward wave. 'And this is Max.'

Sympathy ripples around the circle as they take in the hand I've been dealt.

Conversation is stilted at first. The others have mostly met before, but I feel like I'm at some painful speed-dating evening. They jokingly ask my name, age and diagnosis, then where I'm being treated. People compare hospital canteen food horror stories and wait times. It's a group for patients of the two transplant hospitals in Cambridge and London, so everyone is fairly local. Before long the small talk transitions into rawer territory. We share our symptoms, brittle hopes and yawning fears. What it might feel like to go under the knife. To exist with part of someone else inside you. To survive because of it. Grappling with the terror of leaving our families bereaved. All the things we can't bear to say in front of our nearest and dearest.

As the hour concludes, I feel drained, thin-skinned and vulnerable. When I look around the room, a thought flutters into my mind. Any one of these pale faces, frail, hopeful smiles, might share my blood type. Sit alongside me on the list at the same London centre.

A horrible notion: one of them could be my competition.

'It's lovely to share but it does take it out of you,' Junie says kindly, one eye on my face as we walk slowly out of the pub. Her pace is even slower than mine and I can feel the effort it takes her to move. 'Which way are you headed?'

'I'm waiting for my dad. We're just over in Harringay, but he's insisting on playing chauffeur. Can we give you a lift anywhere?'

She smiles, understanding the need of those around us to be doing something to help.

'I'm in Elstree so a bit out of your way, but thank you,' she says. 'I don't drive but I'm lucky, the trains are really reliable. And on a bad day a taxi gets me to Harefield Hospital in half an hour.'

I look away. We're being treated at the same hospital. For a moment I feel a wave of nausea, then I remember the joke she made earlier. *A positive*, she'd said, with a laugh. *Full marks.*

We're not the same blood type. I swallow my relief.

'Well,' Junie says brightly. 'It was lovely to meet you. Until next time?'

We embrace, carefully avoiding the question of whether there will be one.

The weeks march doggedly on. This year the approach to Christmas feels different. When I walk back from the park with Max in his pram, the daily trip I take no matter how weak I'm feeling, I don't look in at the cosy family scenes all around. I hurry home.

The practice has offered Justin some family leave, sympathetic to our situation, but we've agreed to save it until we really need it, whatever that means. Now that my three months of maternity pay are up, Justin's salary alone isn't enough to keep us afloat so I have to start some shifts back at work. Just two days a week, spread over half-days.

'I'm not an invalid,' I say when Justin suggests we should rethink. 'The new medication is really helping. Besides, it's not like I work in construction. I sit at a desk all day. I can cope. I don't even feel that bad.'

There's a silent 'yet' at the end of that sentence which we both ignore.

Justin examines my face. I know he wishes I didn't have to work, but he can hear in my tone that I need it. A reason to get out of the house, comfortable that Max is happy with Dad, being read all the stories I was read as a baby.

All through this I want things to stay as normal as possible for our son. Every morning when Max wakes, I tickle him, joy flooding me at the sound of his hiccupping gurgles. I need to teach him that the world is full of warmth. That, though I have been dealt this terrible hand, it is just bad luck. I cover the walls of his room with stickers of whimsical images; whales flying through the stars with castles on their backs. Justin thinks too much time dwelling on the fantastical only leads to disappointment in real life, but I think filling Max's world with things that aren't possible will give him the ability to imagine they might be.

Dad is over to help almost every day so I can work or rest. Billie drops in most evenings bringing shopping and frozen dinners. Sinead and Nadia keep up a bombardment of messages, visits and deliveries. Quietly, tactfully, they have all stopped using the heart emoji. I'm so grateful for our tiny village, holding us up, even if Al's absence is growing more apparent by the day. I haven't thanked him for the flowers, the book. It's been so long now, I don't know what to say. Where to start.

When his dad fell ill, Al had to come back from his gap year early, his dream of a life-changing trip cut tragically short. Warm, effervescent Phil died of a stroke, out of nowhere. I never asked about the details at the time, not wanting Al to rake over them as they smouldered. Now I know the pain of other people's silence, however well intentioned.

Al and I planned to resurrect his gap-year trip after university. Then I got an unexpected job offer, one of the fiercely competitive internships that were the only gateway into a career as a solicitor. All the other firms rejected me and it felt like a tipping point so I panicked and pulled out of the trip. I felt terrible – Al would never go on his own – but I couldn't turn my back on the chance of securing a stable job. Growing up in a single-parent household had given me a powerful desire for financial stability. Al understood, but he didn't go without me. Annette clearly felt I'd abandoned him, messed him around. Really, though, what his mother hasn't forgiven me for is changing my mind about the brief, misguided relationship which bubbled up between Al and me after university.

When it started, I remember feeling like it was so obvious, like he must be the one because he'd always been there at my side. For a few weeks there was a heady sense of fates aligning, until the knot in my stomach wouldn't unclasp and I realised that I'd got it wrong. No matter how much I wanted to, and though I loved him deeply, I just didn't feel that way about him. He was a life raft as we struck out into the big wide world, but only in the way a friend is. In the aftermath of me ending things, when Annette came to help Al move out of our shared house, she gave me a look that hasn't left me. A look that told me she had expected nothing less.

Al was the only witness to the reality of my childhood. To avoid the hours after school when it was just my mother at home, I would cross the road to his house where Al would scoot up on the sofa, chucking me an N64 controller. Mostly Dad came to get me, but a few times a loud, slow, unfamiliar knock would sound on the door. I would drop the controller and fumble to gather my things. Annette would watch with narrowed eyes as I bolted without saying goodbye or thank you for the dinner she'd made. When I would throw glances back, Al was always there at the window.

All of a sudden, I find myself reaching for my phone and dialling his number. It rings a few times, an international dial tone, but then I hang up. What the hell am I going to say, calling him out of the blue after so long? Who knows what time it might be wherever he is. I picture him snoring in some hotel bed in another time zone. Perhaps not even alone.

I stuff the phone into my pocket and press on. The Second Hearters are hosting another meet up. I'm eager to see them again, this fragile collective; people who understand how it feels to be a time bomb, praying desperately to be defused. Justin is trying. Billie is trying, Dad too, but none of them will ever know what this is like.

9

Junie is at the social. With a smile, I slide into the seat next to her while peeling off my coat, waiting for my breathing to calm. She nods in solidarity.

'Always takes me about ten minutes to get the heart rate under control,' she says, and I give her an appreciative smile. 'No little one today?'

'He's... with my... dad,' I pant.

'Lovely. Nice for them both to get that precious time together.' She looks uncomfortable for a moment. 'I didn't mean precious like—'

I hold up a hand to release her from her verbal knot. 'It's okay. Is it too early for mulled wine? I've been looking forward to the first of the season.'

'Just orange juice for me.' She forces a smile. 'I don't drink.'

I nod, wondering what is behind the uncharacteristic stiffness in her face. I get a round for the other six people who turn up. We toast to another group member, George, a man in his fifties from Knebworth who has just had 'the call'.

People's good news is shared jubilantly in the WhatsApp group, photos of patients holding up wavering thumbs from their blue-blanketed hospital beds as they are wheeled off through the double doors towards the rest of their lives. Bad news is reserved for in-person meet ups when it can be broken sensitively. I know after talking to Ravi, an accountant from Reading, that he's been denied a heart twice; the first was considered a bad match, the second didn't make it to him in time. He's waiting for the lucky number three. The news tightens my throat and I retreat to Junie's side.

She nods towards the others around the table. 'It's a great community, but sometimes we're all hearts, hearts, hearts.'

I smile; she's sending them all up to put me at ease. The balm of gallows humour.

'It's nice... to have somewhere to go.' I look around at the motley crowd, from all backgrounds, walks of life. Disease doesn't discriminate.

Junie leans forward. 'Can I tell you something?'

My stomach churns, fearful of more bad news. 'Of course.'

'You remind me of my daughter.' She says it quickly as if it's difficult to get the words out. 'It's your eyes, I think. Hers were just like them, that lovely blue-grey medley.'

Junie is gazing at her lap, fiddling with a ring that I took for a wedding band. Now I realise it's on the wrong finger. Her eyes have dulled, like a light has been extinguished within her. She's only mentioned her daughter in the past tense.

'Oh, Junie... I'm so sorry,' I mutter, at a loss for what to say to a stranger, even one who is being so honest. 'I...'

She waves away my fumbling. 'It's been a long time now. Years. Hard to believe how long actually. I... well, I got very low after we lost her. Drank a lot. Got rather too reliant on opiates. But I'm on the straight and narrow now. So just the OJ for me.'

She raises the glass of juice to her lips. A faint tremor rocks it. Now that she's said it, I can see the tell-tale signs on her face. The gossamer skin, sunken eyes. All those layers of hardship; an addiction on top of grief, and now failing health to round it off.

'It's nice,' she says, 'to meet you. People always try to make sure I'm not reminded of her, but of course it's all I want. They don't need to worry; I think of her every day of my life.'

For the rest of the social we chat on lighter topics, trying to get to know one another outside of our respective diagnoses. Weekend plans, what we've been enjoying on TV, books we've loved.

'What are you up to for Christmas?' I ask her.

'Oh, just having a low-key one. I'm normally with a friend but she's having her first Christmas as a granny, so she's otherwise engaged,' Junie says, trying to sound cheerful. 'I'm due a quiet one though,' she assures me. 'Important to rest, as we know.'

My chest convulses with pity. Before I recognise it, I find an invitation spilling from my lips.

'Come to ours.'

I haven't even asked Justin, but he's already invited Amir and Rebecca to join us after their usual travel plans disintegrated. He can hardly argue Junie isn't in need of the company. The thought of someone so ill spending what might be one of their last Christmases alone is intolerable, so I double down. She graciously refuses, but I insist.

'I can't bear the thought of you on your own. Please at least come for lunch, then when we get too irritating you can peel off, no questions asked.'

I smile encouragingly, while wondering how it must feel to have your late daughter's eyes shine back at you from a stranger's face. Or perhaps we aren't that anymore, now we've shared so much of ourselves.

Junie smiles. Her face is lit with a new glow. 'That's really very kind of you, Olivia. I should like that very much.'

Christmas is upon us in an instant. Usually, I am straight out of the gate; decorations up as soon as tradition allows, stockings over the fireplace, cards hung up on strips of ribbon, candles scented with cinnamon and orange on the table. A house full of the sparkle and glow of fairy lights fills me up in a way I can't quite articulate. I've always loved that frisson of goodwill as thoughts turn to presents and ice rinks and mulled wine and festive markets.

But this year I keep putting it off. The boxes of decorations sit there, but I can't bring myself to open them and dress the house in its usual finery. So, the morning I emerge from our bedroom to find the banisters laced with tinsel and baubles covering the tree, I have to stifle a gasp of delight.

'Thank you,' I murmur, pressing myself to Justin's chest and breathing in the reassuring woollen scent of his favourite jumper. It's starting to wear at the elbows, so I've bought him a new one as a present. Identical, just as he'd want.

I've not said anything, but I can feel a faint disconnect between us since all of this. As though, for all his medical expertise, he just doesn't know how to feel, how to be, now his work has come home with him. He'd hate to think that's how I feel. I know he's doing everything he can. I have no idea how I'd cope without his support.

'Let's do this one,' Justin says later that day, pointing at the most complicated-sounding roast recipe in the cookbook.

'Sounds ruddy delicious,' I say encouragingly.

We're choosing a recipe for the goose we've opted for. We don't often make such an effort to cook anything fancy, but this year Justin seems to have a fire in his belly. I want to put it down to the joy of the baby, the start of new traditions for our family, but the unspoken fact remains that just as it's our son's first Christmas, there's a chance it might be my last.

'Junie's asked what to bring,' I say, as I start jotting down a shopping list of ingredients.

'She really needn't bother, we can manage,' Justin says, full of the optimism of an infrequent Christmas host.

'I know, I told her, but I think... Well, I think she needs to,' I say quietly. 'So it doesn't feel like charity.'

'It's good of you to ask her,' he says, stroking my back.

'I had to. I couldn't bear to think of her alone. Not after she said I look like her daughter. I told you she died? So awful. Junie really struggled after that. Developed an addiction, she said. Painkillers. She's been through it. She said she's lucky she's still on the waiting list – apparently, they're very strict on substance abuse. Poor thing.'

'Awful,' Justin repeats, eyes already drawn back to the recipe book.

For such a warm man, his well of sympathy for strangers doesn't run deep, not when he needs to keep his emotions in check for work.

On the 22 December, as I'm sitting in front of my to-do list worrying that I still haven't decided what to get Dad as a present, my phone rings. It's Junie. I rush to answer. Is she calling to cry off? Or to tell me her condition has deteriorated?

'Olivia?'

'Hi, Junie, is everything alright?'

There is a pause.

'Yes. Well... yes, it is.' There's a note of something in her voice, some emotion I don't know her well enough to identify. 'I've... I've had a call,' she says. 'I've had the call.'

I go still.

'They said... They said I've got one.' Her voice catches. 'They've got a heart for me. A universal donor.'

The phone is suddenly heavy in my hand.

'Wow. Oh, my God. Junie. I... I... thought there was someone more urgent?'

'There was.' She pauses. 'Until a few weeks ago...'

She doesn't need to finish the sentence. The person at the top of the list didn't last the wait. Nausea pulses through me. I swallow back an acid-sharp pang. We're being treated at the same transplant centre. The heart they are giving her is from a universal donor.

That means, were it not for Junie, this heart would have been offered to me.

'That's... that's... wow. Um. Wonderful.'

My thoughts spiral as I fumble for congratulations. Of course I'm pleased for her. I am.

'I hope you don't feel I'm calling to gloat,' Junie adds quickly. 'It's just that they've said to be ready because I could be called in any day now. They did say it's very unlikely to be before the twenty-seventh because...' She pauses. 'Well, because the family want until then... to say their goodbyes.'

We both fall quiet as the words sink in. A flash of that terrible scene, a family gathered at a deathbed as the world around them celebrates the festive season.

'So, you see, I didn't want to be rude, it's not likely, but just in case I get the summons when I'm with you,' she continues, moving briskly on from the horrible truth of her good luck. 'If it's still alright for me to come...'

'Of course.' I force myself into gear. 'Of course, Junie. It's absolutely brilliant news. I'm so very happy for you. We'll have to celebrate with some bubbles over lunch. There's this nice non-alcoholic fizzy white I can get more of—'

'There's no need, really,' she interrupts me gently. 'You have enough on your plate.'

After a few more stilted pleasantries we hang up. Then, slowly, I slump to the floor, propped against the kitchen cupboards. Max gives me a quizzical look, peering down from his highchair like a miniature monarch staring at his subject. He's only just started sitting in there now he's stable enough. His eyes are bright with excitement; with both of us at home over the holidays he's in heaven.

Justin comes back into the kitchen and finds me on the floor. He rushes to my side, but I hold up a hand.

'It's okay. I'm fine.'

When I tell him Junie's news, he sits down next to me and pulls me close, pressing his cheek to my forehead.

'There'll be another one,' he whispers forcefully. 'It'll be okay. It will, Liv. Don't lose hope.'

That night I can't sleep. Every time I close my eyes, I see images of the family whose loved one will be ending their life in a few days' time. Face the reality that a heart for Junie does not mean that a heart for me is any closer. Before long I can't help myself; I start imagining that I'd had the call. That the heart was destined for me. What Christmas would look like if that were the case, if our wait was over. A gift no present could ever match.

I imagine Max, on his fifth Christmas, vibrating with excitement at the presents in his stocking; things we've agonised over, not wanting to spoil him but at the same time wanting to give him everything. Sneaking the chocolate decorations from the tree when he thinks we're not looking, Justin and I dissolving into silent hysterics at his attempts to be stealthy. Breath steaming in front of us all as we walk around the park to visit the ducks and run off Max's sugar rush. My glorious, ordinary family.

All I've ever wanted.

I try on the masochistic fantasy time and again, watching my future light up like the tree, before reality bites back. I dig my nails into the soft skin of my palm, thinking about how Junie has been waiting longer. How she's in a worse state. She needs it more. Then, with a guilt thick as tar, I wonder how old Junie is. She must be nearly twice my age. If, really, she has many years left... An appalling, twisted thought. Bitter like bile. But if that heart had come to me, I would have half my lifetime with it. See my son grow from toddler to teenager and beyond. Be there for parents' evenings and exam results. Drive him to swimming lessons, or off to university. Meet his first partner. His children.

Junie told me that I remind her of her daughter. She knows I have Max. So much to live for.

So much more to live for...

My mother's voice is visiting me more and more. I force my eyes shut. It's just the envy. The pure, ice-cold fear of leaving my baby without a mother. My time will come. My time will come.

My time must come.

10

I spend the next day distracting myself. Wrapping gifts and ticking them off my list, writing cards. Justin and I have bought Max a little activity cube now that the days of the dreaded tummy time are behind us and he's sitting all the time. It's a nightmare to wrap. After floundering with torn paper, I settle on using material in the Japanese Furoshiki fashion which makes me feel pleasingly worthy. I finish the day by checking everything's ready for the Boxing Day blood drive event run each year by the practice. As I get into bed I'm feeling good, but sleep doesn't come. In the dark, lonely, small hours, as I lie staring at the ceiling, the twisted thoughts return.

An anger rears up in me. At the world for dangling the dream of a family before me, only to snuff it out. At my mother for failing in every capacity: to be a parent to me, to stay with us, to warn me about my own broken genes. With myself for my actions all those years ago which pushed her away. Most of all I am angry that death and life can be such close bedfellows. That I have to imagine not living to see my son grow up. That, as things stand, every day is a gift.

Then I think about Junie's addiction. How people with substance-abuse problems are disqualified from the waiting list. She will have faced a battery of tests to prove she remains clean. To get her second chance.

Then a new thought comes to me. An image.

The GP surgery. The cabinets in the pharmacy adjoining the reception area which are locked and carefully inventoried by Krish, the pharmacist. Rows and rows of little cardboard boxes sitting inside, waiting to be prescribed. Medications. The monthly check, due this week, to clear out those which are no longer in date. I think about the names of the medications. The variety. Analgesics, depressants, stimulants.

Opiates. Painkillers.

I've seen enough prescriptions, I know which is which. Pethidine, Tramadol, Oxycodone. Morphine. Tablets, topical creams, vials. Liquid capsules.

No.

It's a fantasy too dark to entertain. Brought on by insomnia, by the shock of Junie's news bringing my own dire situation into clearer focus. I thrust the thought away.

What a good girl.

When my eyes open on Christmas Eve morning, the thought is still there, lodged in my brain like a nail I can't prise out. I stand at the window, my breath fogging the glass, watching the street as the night slowly lifts, lit by the soft glow of fairy lights inside every living-room window. There in the quiet of the predawn I unshackle my thoughts, even the darkest ones. Let them creep out and see the light.

It's said that babies don't consider themselves separate from their mother until well into their first year of life. So, right now, my son believes me to be a part of him. For me to die would be for him to lose himself.

How can I let that happen?

Once it's light enough, I wake Justin gently. 'I'm going to take Max around the block,' I whisper. 'He's not going down.'

Justin rubs the sleep from his eyes. 'I should do it—' he says, starting to get out of bed.

'No, no. It's early. I'm up anyway. I won't go far. I could use the fresh air.'

'Liv...'

'Please,' I whisper. 'You're shattered and I need to get out. I'm climbing the walls. I'll go really slowly and stay close to home.'

He nods, eyelids already heavy again. My illness is taking its toll on him. The countless early mornings and late nights are visible in his face. For a moment the bags under his eyes remind me how much older he is than me. That he's done all this before, a long time ago.

Was he really happy to do it all again? Or was it just for me?

As I go carefully downstairs, I feel a flash of shame for blaming Max when he has been quiet and peaceful virtually all night, while my eyes were wired open. He's sleeping better now we've introduced a little soft toy rabbit which he's taken to and rubs between his fingers and against his cheeks in his crib. A transitional object, they call it. Something to comfort him when I'm not there. I felt a strange stab of jealousy when he first started to reach for it after we put him down for naps.

I check my phone. It's 6.30 a.m. I have about an hour. My palms are slippery as I strap Max into the carrier on my chest, the comforting weight of him bound to me, like another pregnancy. It won't be long before I can't manage to carry him anymore. I hold a hand protectively over him, stuck again between the wish that I could go back in time to when he was safe inside me and wanting to fast forward to a donor, the operation that would save me. To being able to look head on at the future.

I'm just going for a walk. That's all. I'm meant to take it easy, but not to spend my days horizontal. I'm just a tired, harried new mum doing whatever she can to get her baby to sleep. If it takes me past the surgery, fine. I can maybe pop in, check everything is in order for the blood drive in two days. Check that Brian hasn't forgotten the biscuits for the donors.

It's not real. It's just a game. A fantasy.

The surgery is in darkness. The waiting room still and quiet behind the glass screen. No one comes in this early. Brian barely scrapes in before the doors have to open to patients. On Christmas Eve he'll be pushing it to the wire. A CCTV camera covers the entrance, but I know for a fact Brian hasn't changed the hard drive. I hurry behind the reception desk.

From my pocket I pull out two hair grips. I watched a YouTube video on my walk over. 'How to Pick a Lock'. Trembling like I'm holding a power drill, I slot the grips carefully inside the keyhole and press the pins up until it clicks. The sound makes

Max startle and I murmur reassurances. The pharmacy cabinet door swings open, revealing rows of identical white cardboard boxes. It worked. I was almost hoping it wouldn't, then I'd have to stop. I don't even know what my plan is. I don't have a plan.

Max makes a curious chirrup, a sound he has just started to make, like a baby dinosaur, and reaches for the boxes. I clutch him tight, pulling his arm away, holding his soft head against my chest. With my other hand I rifle quickly through the boxes, checking the date for the oldest, which will be due for a cull this week. Very carefully, I tease one open. I've seen Krish do this cataloguing, one of his least favourite tasks. A missing box would catch his eye, but he only gives them a cursory check inside. There are often a few single pills cut from the foils to make up precise prescriptions, easy to miss. No one will notice.

I slip a couple into my pocket and slam the cabinet shut too hard. Max whimpers in fright. 'Hush,' I whisper, kissing his head. 'Hush.' Adrenaline courses through me and my breathing is starting to get laboured. I'm about to wipe my fingerprints from the cabinet until I remember they will be there from months past.

Outside, the morning air stings my face. The street is still cloaked in the light mist of a winter dawn and I can't see more than a few metres ahead. Headlights appear like helicopter searchlights, seeking me out. I shrink back into the overgrown hedge of someone's front garden, shaking.

What the hell have I just done?

Better get off your high horse now, little Olive.

Back home, I open the door to the smell of scrambling eggs and coffee. Justin is already up, preparing breakfast. The stolen medication feels instantly heavier in my pocket. Justin kisses us both on the forehead then takes Max and sits him on his playmat. He began to sit unaided at five months, and now he insists on it, though he needs our help to get up. Justin shows him a real egg, next to his white squeaky toy ones and Max crows in fascination.

'Merry Christmas Eve,' Justin says softly. 'No luck, eh?'

I look at him, confused.

'Getting him to sleep.'

'Right, yes. No,' I manage. 'Maybe it was too cold.'

'You look done in. You go back to bed, I can hold the fort till your father gets here.'

He's right, all my energy has evaporated. I drag myself up the stairs. In the bathroom, I slip the pills into the bag where I keep my medications, then crawl into my bed, melting into the covers and closing my eyes. As I drop off, I wonder if the last hour has been a fever dream.

I wake up to the sound of Dad singing to Max downstairs.

'Zoom zooom zoooom, we're going to the moon!'

Listening, I smile, until I remember the events of earlier this morning and head straight for the bathroom. I stare down at the foil-wrapped pills, pressing them into my palm, feeling the sharp metal edges against my skin. I can't believe I actually took them. Could I really ever do anything with them? Even if I could do something so cruel, so deranged, so *criminal*, Junie's new heart may not come to me. There is another person out there somewhere on our Urgent list. It's a universal heart. It could go to someone else.

Or you can sit here and waste this opportunity. Wait as your life drains away.

A new fear flares inside me. Is she now the devil on my shoulder, poised ready to voice all my very worst thoughts? I shake her away. She never earned the right for me to imagine what she might think.

On the kitchen table is the goose Justin collected from the butcher, our Christmas lunch for tomorrow. In the morning light it has the look of a naked baby. The pale, plucked flesh turns my stomach.

Sometimes people have to be selfish to survive.

No. This isn't who I am. Who Dad brought me up to be. I can't continue to indulge this insane idea.

I must keep believing in miracles.

11

Christmas Day starts with so much joy that I forget what I was considering just the day before. Justin and Max bring me a ginger-spiced tea, the warm, festive scent filling the living room. Even though it goes against his every instinct, Justin has dressed Max in the red festive onesie I found on Vinted, sweet but not twee, with three embroidered penguins, in hats and scarves, skiing. We all lie together on the sofa, wrapped up in a blanket, tantalising smells wafting in from the oven.

'Here,' Justin says, reaching for one of the wrapped gifts under the tree.

'Already?' I raise an eyebrow. We're usually a presents-after-lunch family.

'Before everyone else gets here,' he says softly as he hands it to me.

I take the present and unwrap it. Inside is a framed print. An illustration in Quentin Blake's inimitable style. I gasp. It's the pale blue sketch of the mother and baby underwater, from the hospital ward. One of the midwives told us that Blake had done the series of illustrations especially for maternity departments. Justin has tracked a print down.

'It's… It's *beautiful*,' I murmur. 'I love it. Thank you.' I lean and press my lips against his over Max's head.

For a moment I feel bad about the simple jumper wrapped under the tree for him, but Justin is constantly saying that he has everything he needs.

For the rest of this blissful morning I am immune to my own dark thoughts. We are just a family enjoying our first precious Christmas.

Later, I hold on to that memory.

Dad arrives to help us cook lunch. He can't help but fuss around me in the kitchen, asking for jobs and grimacing whenever I carry anything. I know it's how he expresses his love, but right now it's too much.

'Dad, can you take Max down the road? The supermarket on the corner should still be open. We need a couple more non-alcoholic bottles for Junie and me, and lots more tonic.'

'Of course.' Dad jumps up, thrilled to have a task. 'Maxy and I are on the case.'

'Will you go with him?' I ask Justin quietly. 'I don't want him carrying it all himself plus the baby.'

He nods and squeezes my hand.

As soon as they're gone I sit down heavily on the sofa, my head in my hands. The guests are arriving at 1 p.m. I still need to get dressed. The black shift dress I wear for work isn't exactly festive but it's pretty much the only thing that fits me from my smarter clothes. I spent the early months after Max's arrival exclusively in tracksuits or leggings. I'll have to try and jazz my outfit up with some earrings. My thoughts wander from the inside of my wardrobe to the bathroom cabinet, and into the pocket of my medicine bag, to the pills which might change my future.

Justin's laptop is open at the kitchen counter. I click on a search window, hesitate before typing, then switch to incognito. I'll just play out the what ifs. Just so I know what would happen if someone ingested only a small amount of the drugs I took. I have a sense of dosages from work; most prescriptions tell the patient how much and how many times to take the medication. I have seen countless scripts for opiates, and I know what too much might do. I scan the screen until I've found the website I need.

It tells me the medication I've stolen is slow release. Just half a dose would show up on blood tests but wouldn't make anyone feel any worse than a bad day with a failing heart might otherwise do. I sit back. So, it definitely wouldn't be life-threatening.

Just immoral. So deeply wrong that my fingers grow slippery on the mouse as I hurriedly close the web page. Then I roll up my sleeves and start dusting icing sugar over the Christmas cake.

Junie arrives first.

'Hi, welcome! Come in, come in,' I say as brightly as I can, making a show of bringing her inside, taking her coat.

We sit down together in the living room as Justin and Dad finish laying the table and debating exactly when the bird should come out of the oven. They've taken over all the food preparation, so I've had little to distract me from my thoughts, apart from Max intently examining his stacking pots and drooling copiously.

As Junie sits down heavily on our sofa, I notice that she can't take her eyes off him. She retrieves something from her coat pocket.

'I hope you don't mind...'

It's a little present, wrapped in jaunty paper with robins on it. My fingers dig into my palms. She's got a gift for Max.

'That's so... so kind of you.'

I let Max rip the paper away, revealing a teething toy in the shape of a Christmas tree.

'It's just a little thing,' Junie says, with obvious delight that he starts to gnaw on it immediately and with gusto. 'It's silicone so free from any nasties – I checked.'

'It's really wonderful.' I try to keep my voice steady. 'He loves it.'

Before I know it, I'm offering him up to her. 'Do you want to hold him?'

Junie's eyes light up as she takes him, clucking and bouncing him gently on her knee. Max smiles and coos at her beaming face.

'He likes you.'

'I... I never got to be a grandma,' she says softly.

I nod, blinking rapidly. Pain stabs at my chest. What am I *doing*?

Once Rebecca and Amir have arrived and we're sitting around the table strewn with torn crackers, wearing those flimsy paper crowns, Justin brings the goose out of the oven. As the carving knife slices through its tender, steaming flesh, everyone around the table cheers – but all I can see is the scalpel sliding across Junie's chest, ready to pry her open. Ready to start her anew.

The others watch as we give Max his ceremonial first taste of solid food. He's not quite six months but he's been sitting up so confidently over the last few weeks and following the progress of food to our mouths with such fascination, we've decided to start today. A Christmas treat. Justin has prepared an unappetising-looking medley of pureed roast potatoes and Brussels sprouts which he's dubbed 'festive mulch'. We watch with a nervous anticipation as Max launches himself open-mouthed at the spoon. His expression transitions through surprise, bewilderment, and finally lands on approval. His little legs kick vigorously in the chair as he smacks his lips. Even Rebecca cracks a smile at his verve.

'I'm surprised,' she said wryly. 'I wouldn't have thought he'd go for it. They're very bitter.' She eyes a Brussels sprout warily before spiking it with her fork.

'We're going to use this book Liv found,' Justin explains. 'It says to front-load him with all the boring, strong-tasting vegetables while it's all a novelty, and the idea is he'll then eat anything. Isn't that right, love?'

'That's the theory,' I say distractedly. We're nearly at dessert already. My window of opportunity is closing.

I find my gaze drawn to Junie again and again. She is making polite conversation with Dad, telling him about her days as a teacher. That goes some way to explaining her natural instincts with the baby. She understands children. I think about how hard it must have been to continue working after losing her own daughter. To pour her love into other people's children day after day, knowing she will be going home to an empty house. Her marriage didn't survive it. Dad is laughing at a joke she's made and I realise Junie can't be much younger than him, though she looks a decade older.

Max starts to fuss in his highchair so Justin hands him the spoon. I can see from the jerkiness of his limbs that he's verging on overtired. His movements are so erratic that he shoves the spoon too hard into his mouth, catching his top lip. His face flushes and crumples, his bottom lip folding down cartoonishly. Justin picks him up, but Max fights against his chest as he sobs. He is turning his head side to side, straining for something.

For me. To see me.

I leap up and he reaches for me. It's the first time he has done this so unmistakably. In his anguish, he wants only me.

'Hush, hush, my sweet, you're okay,' I murmur, pressing him to my chest. I make apologetic faces to the others before walking away down the hall, shushing his wails. Once we're alone, he calms as I stand at the window, his favourite vantage point.

'Look out there,' I say, pointing. 'A red car. And over there those people are walking their dog.' His eyes are alert, jumping from movement to movement, taking in the world as the red blotches on his skin from crying start to fade. Then he rests his head on my chest and I sway from side to side. I watch as a huddle of teenagers moves en masse down the road. Their barely concealed social anxiety, the jostling for supremacy. These adolescents, whose lives have only just hit double figures, have already been through so many selves. The tantrums, the sleepovers, the school reports, the house parties. What will Max be like at thirteen? What book series will he sink into at bedtime? What game will he clamour to be bought? It's not just the downy head and milky breath I want. I want all of it.

My eyes fill as I press my face into the creases of his neck and his eyelids start to droop. In that moment, as I stand wrapped up in my love, my son calm in my arms alone, something shifts inside me. Another heart could take months, years to appear. It could be too late.

What if this is it? My only chance.

So, what's it to be?

A sob burns at the back of my throat but I force it down. I force Dad's face from my thoughts too. Slowly, my mind is making itself up.

For once I need to be like *her*. I need to be cold-blooded.

The glasses rattle like chattering teeth as I carry the tray of drinks in from the kitchen. A whisky cocktail for Dad and for Amir.

Another glass of Nyetimber for Rebecca. Non-alcoholic fizz for me and Justin. And non-alcoholic fizz with elderflower cordial for Junie.

Thick, sweet, overpowering elderflower cordial.

New bubbles adding to the torrent in her glass, like snowfall in reverse.

Justin is upstairs putting Max down for a nap. I think of the photo he took earlier of the three of us standing out in the street, in the brief flurry of festive snow. He said he wants to print it out. A milestone to remember; the first time Max saw snow. I hope he forgets to.

'More drinks!' I say, summoning a false note of cheer from somewhere. 'Old Fashioneds for Dad and Amir, no offence!' My voice is high, cracked. Teetering on the edge.

Dad smiles indulgently. He doesn't know it's a desperate front. That I'm overcompensating, praying my exuberance will distract everyone. I was heavy-handed with the cordial, hoping its cloying sweetness will cover up the other taste. The other substance lurking in the bottom of Junie's glass.

My arms start to shake as I cross the room. Dad winces and gets up to help.

'Don't worry, I've got it!' I say quickly.

I keep my eyes locked on the bubbles in Junie's drink. They fizz up in the glass with an accusatory hiss. *Traitor*. I pray with everything I have that it's not too much. Then I pray again, with the devil on my shoulder, that it's enough.

'Here, shall I be mother?' Junie leans forward and starts to hand out the drinks to the others one by one.

Her words echo around the room. My pulse hammers through me and my breathing gets shallow. There's only one drink left on the tray.

Then Junie is reaching for her glass.

12

For a fleeting moment I see a life ruined, at my hands. The guilt I would have to live with. Junie has endured this half-life for so much longer than I have, and after all she's been through. How can I declare my life worth more? How could I hold my head up in front of my son, tell him that I played God in his name?

Then I lunge forward.

'Oh! Silly me, I forgot the cordial for yours,' I say brightly, sweeping Junie's glass out of her reach and turning back for the kitchen.

'Don't worry, I don't mind,' she says warmly. 'Happy to live without it.'

'No, no. It'll only take a second,' I gabble, already at the door to the hall.

Standing over the sink I brace my arms, bend forward, breathing hard. My heart is protesting as if a gavel is striking against my ribcage. It beats so hard I can feel my whole body flinching. As if a pointed finger is jabbing me in the chest. *How could you?*

Madness. A fleeting mania. That's all I can say to explain it. As though I've been sleepwalking since this morning in the surgery.

I thrust the drugged glass onto the counter, snatch a fresh one from the shelf and pour in the ingredients for a new drink. I'm trembling so much that the syrupy elderflower cordial spills over my fingers, coating them.

By the time I go back into the living room they've moved onto the cheeses. Justin keeps shooting me glances because I can't sit still, getting up to bring the biscuits nearer, going to check on Max. Anything to avoid talking to Junie. For once I'm grateful for the constant barrage of questions Rebecca considers good conversation, which Junie is weathering gracefully.

'I'll do it,' Justin murmurs as he sees me getting up again to fetch more cheese. 'Put your feet up.'

I nod and sit stiffly next to Dad who pats my leg affectionately.

'That was a really lovely lunch, Olive.' We share a smile. For years Christmas was just the two of us and now my home is full of life. Just like I always wanted.

As the afternoon wears on and Junie begins to look tired, I feel a flush of relief; the day is almost over. When she stands to go to the bathroom, Justin reaches up instinctively to help. He knows the regular spells of weakness we both have to endure. She smiles back, gripping his arm gratefully.

'I must stop standing up too fast,' she mutters as the others glance over.

'Easily done,' Justin says.

I go into the kitchen to start cleaning up, searching for something to do. Occupation for idle hands. But Justin has beaten me to it. The dishwasher is already on. The counters and table clear. I smile faintly, remembering Billie's complaints about Tom.

'It's like he thinks there's a washing-up fairy who comes overnight, and by magic the kitchen's clean in the morning,' she'd said. 'I mean, I love him but he's like a child. His mother still goes round picking up after him.'

I may not have Justin for as many years, but I am thankful for his maturity. If I am lucky enough to get the chance, I'll try not to be the kind of mother who spoils her son.

In the living room, Junie is leaning back in her armchair. I stare at her, at the fragility of her. The spectre of who I nearly became, just an hour ago, lingers in one corner of the room and I feel numb.

Parenthood is all sacrifice. It's no surprise that you don't have it in you.

I clench my hands tight. No. I can't let her goad me. I've made the right decision. Of course I have.

'I think it might be time for me to make a move,' Junie says, sounding worn out.

'Of course,' I say quickly.

'Well, Junie, it has been a real pleasure,' Justin says, getting to his feet. 'Let me drive you home.'

Junie's face is steeped in gratitude. 'Do you know, normally I would protest, the fresh air does me good, but I am feeling rather wrung out. All the good company and good cheer.'

Dad helps her on with her coat and shakes her hand warmly. 'It's been lovely to meet you, Junie.'

'And you, Terry.' She smiles back at him.

For the first time, I wonder if Dad is lonely. If he wishes he had someone with whom to share the dusk years of his life. He's thrown himself into grandparenthood with such vigour and is so brilliant with Max, I've hardly stopped to think about what it must feel like when he goes home to a quiet, empty house where nothing has moved unless he's moved it.

'See you on the other side,' Junie says, her arm tucked in the crook of Justin's. 'A whole new me for a whole new year!'

My chest swells with the sheer horror of what I almost did, like it might burst me from the inside.

'Good luck,' I say, forcing the words out.

'Say hi to the others at the New Year's knees up,' Junie says over her shoulder. 'Raise a toast to me!'

I nod, trying to imagine sitting amongst the support group at the drinks in a few days' time, knowing everything I've thought. Everything I nearly did.

'Back soon,' Justin calls. 'Don't let Amir loose on all that Stilton. Just say "cholesterol" if you need to rein him in.'

I crowbar on a smile. He winks and for an instant I'm dazzled by the glow of my wonderful husband. The blessing I was granted before the curse. If only he realised that he doesn't really know his wife at all.

After they've driven away I linger in the doorway, looking up and down the road at the warm light shining from every window. I'm about to close the door when I notice the neighbours across the road have a skip.

Darting another glance in both directions, I cross over to it. With one quick movement, I pull out the broken foil and the remaining pill and stuff them under a splintered floorboard. Then I tug my jumper closer around me and turn back to the house.

This is not who I am.

13

As is our tradition on Boxing Day, we hold the annual blood-donation drive in the community centre next to the surgery. For the past two years I've manned the door, logging the donors, keeping them hydrated and fed with biscuits to stave off the blood sugar crashes. This year Brian is enlisted to help. He sits beside me, huffing about having to work on Boxing Day, shooting resentful sidelong glances at me. He hasn't been told the full picture about my health and feels hard done by because he believes that it's my choice to procreate which has deprived him of half his Christmas break. After yesterday I haven't got the energy for my usual spiky ripostes, every ounce of my brain power is required just to fill in the volunteers' details. I bury myself as deep as I can in the practicalities, anything to distract myself from what I almost did.

The morning has already served up the withering disdain of our next-door neighbour, Irene. She was first in the line to donate and impatient with it.

'Some of us have places to be,' she muttered under her breath as I fumbled for the forms. She has a knack for putting me on edge. Whenever she sees me with Max she tells me he looks hungry, that his clothes are too small, or that he should be wearing a hat. I can see her casting an eye over my lank hair and dark-ringed eyes. I have to resist shouting the truth at her. Justin says to let it wash over me; she's from a different generation.

I sink into my work routine behind the clipboard. Name? NHS number? Blood type? Fill out this form, take a seat. Though the few hours away from Max feel like two days, there is something satisfying about being useful. I think about what my life might have looked like if I'd stayed the course in law. Would I be on track to make partner by now, with the lavish holidays and wardrobe which come with the salary? I think of the smart Reiss suits hanging in my wardrobe collecting dust, the uniform of my old life. Would I have had time to help out with something extracurricular like this? Would I even have met Justin, with every day and night spent chained to my desk?

Rebecca and Amir arrive. They come every year because Amir is loyal and Rebecca likes to be seen to be doing her civic duty, though she hasn't got a neighbourly bone in her body. Nadia pops in on her lunch break with her new boyfriend, a musician called Oz. It's the first partner she's been serious about for some time and she's had rough luck with men over the years so I really hope this one isn't a total prat. He's in a band which is the kind of thing that would once have made us roll our eyes at each other, but he's making her happy which is all that matters.

When Billie arrives, she pulls me into a tight hug. 'How was Christmas? Did the goose live up to the hype?'

'Just about,' I mutter feebly, remembering when something like whether the goose came out well felt important.

Billie has someone with her. A young woman with sun-kissed hair who I recognise but can't immediately place.

'Liv, you remember my cousin Steph? She's moved here.'

Billie's extended American family used to visit all the time, but it's been years. Steph must have been about fourteen when I last saw her. She's grown into a tall, athletic twenty-something with naturally highlighted blonde hair and hazel eyes speckled with hints of gold. An All American Woman.

Steph throws her arms around me like we're family. Says she remembers her cool older cousin's cool friend. I blink at this description and Billie hides a grin.

'Congratulations on your baby!' she says warmly. 'Max, right? Great name.'

'Thanks.'

As Steph signs the list for her blood donation I'm struck by her warmth and zest. It runs in the Elcott family, but her sunny Californian manner gives it an extra facet of brilliance. She tells me how she moved to the UK earlier this year after graduating in Tourism to put her studies into practice, spending the first six months in Edinburgh with a family friend. She speaks with the same wide-eyed enthusiasm as Billie.

The line is lengthening behind them, so Billie whisks her off to the health-screening queue and I turn back to the next person. So many people donating some of themselves for no reward, only to help. I wish I could join them. Some kind of penance.

Then, suddenly, a glimpse of a familiar face in the line. My stomach clenches involuntarily. I look down, then up again. Could it be? I want to rub my eyes, blink the vision away. The woman at the front harrumphs and I gather myself, take her details. I have to ask her to spell her surname twice, then try not to betray my churning stomach as the man I think I've recognised moves closer.

Five more people. Then four. I force myself to glance up again, hoping my mind has played a trick on me by conjuring up the face of someone I believed I'd never have to see again. Someone I haven't encountered for almost twenty years.

Dark brown hair with a slight curl. The arched eyebrow-raise that got him into and out of all manner of trouble. A smile that splays as a smirk to one side. Eyes of such deep blue they look artificial, made people double take. Made me double take.

'Never trust anyone with blue eyes,' my mother used to say, laughing at Dad and me. Brown eyes are more trustworthy, so studies say, though not in her case.

'I'm just going to the bathroom,' I mutter to Brian.

In the cubicle, I press my hands over my eyes. Thoughts of the day before, of Junie, are swept aside as a succession of memories takes hold. Those intoxicating years at university when the whole world seemed to be at our feet. Rushing hungrily to lectures, trying not to seem as excited as I was. The leafy streets by the faculty. Smoking joints in Brandon Hill at the foot of Cabot Tower, looking out over Bristol towards the sea. Our futures stretching as far ahead of us as the view. Other recollections are knocking at the door too – loud, insistent – but I will not let them in. Not now.

There's a knock on the toilet door.

'The queue is becoming unmanageable,' Brian calls loudly.

'I'll be out in a minute.'

I move in slow motion back to the rickety table at the front of the line, scanning my surroundings like prey for signs of a predator. My chest releases. He must have been processed and gone through already.

The final half-hour passes in a blur. When I'm finished, I gather up my things, dreaming of burying myself in Max's sweet embrace. I intended to wait for Billie, but I can't be in there a second longer.

Outside, the air has the fresh bite of winter. The sun is disappearing, lending the rooftops that honeyed golden hour glow, but today its glory is lost on me. I fumble for my gloves, trying to sidestep a couple kissing on the street outside the community centre. The woman steps back just as I pass, knocking into me.

'I'm so sorry!' she says, holding her hand over her mouth as I stumble.

'It's fine,' I say, waving away her apology. I turn to nod at them both when everything freezes.

It's him, looking at me, frowning with recognition.

I turn and walk away robotically, as quickly as I can. It's at least a hundred metres before I realise I'm walking in the wrong direction. I lean against the railings on the corner and catch my breath.

It was him. After all these years, it was Dan.

That afternoon I try to lose myself in Max and our beautiful bubble where all troubles are as simple as tiredness or hunger – easily remedied. But it's not long before questions sneak into my thoughts. What can Dan be doing here? While the rest of us spread out through London, I heard he had settled West, living in the basement of his parents' house. The thought that he has moved around here, perhaps only a few streets away, makes me feel invaded. My past descending on my present.

The tawny-haired woman with him is familiar too. The gleaming ring on her finger didn't escape me. A recollection bubbles up; her bouncing through the campus in tennis whites, a high ponytail dusting her shoulders. She was in the year below us, I think. Effervescent, confident, a woman in Billie's image. Already playing for the university squad in her first year. She makes total sense for Dan. A golden couple.

Those student days feel like another lifetime ago. Eighteen years *is* virtually a lifetime; enough for people to become unrecognisable. But, despite approaching my forties, despite being a mother, when I close my eyes I am still that awkward eighteen year old, so eager for approval. I feel an urge to call Al or Billie, share this blast from the past, but neither of them knows the whole story.

By the 27 December I've almost convinced myself that I dreamed the events of Christmas. Usually we spend this day leisurely grazing the leftovers, marvelling at just how much we've managed to eat, with, at the very most, a gentle walk around the nearby woods. This year I can't face leaving the house, but I insist Justin takes Max for some fresh air. All day I've tried not to wonder what Dan is doing back here. Or think about what is happening across London at the hospital with Junie. She's probably in surgery right now, at the mercy of a surgeon's deft hands.

For a fleeting moment I imagine that I had given her the drink. I picture her slumped, groggy, on the sofa, having not made it to her bed. No. I would *never* have gone through with it. It was just a brief spell of lunacy. The desperate longing to see another Christmas.

But you nearly did. You so very nearly did.

I put my head into my hands, palms pressing against my eyes. I can barely look at Justin. The man who willingly sacrificed his holiday for the blood drive, helping to save lives, while I very nearly destroyed one. The ethical code of his profession: do no harm. The stack of secrets I must keep from my husband is growing by the day.

When they return from their walk, Max has nodded off in the carrier, slumped weightless, his little feet dangling. This image of complete surrender makes my chest contract with love. His total faith that we will look after him, even in the depths of unconsciousness. He feels safe enough to let go entirely. I wonder if I'll ever feel that relaxed again.

Justin moves gingerly up the stairs to start the fraught task of transferring Max to his crib and I lie back on the sofa, trying to keep my mind away from dangerous territory as the sun dips behind the roofs opposite. It's only 4 p.m. but the day has already hung up its spurs. Soon our living room is lit only by the soft golden glow of the Christmas tree, but I don't switch on the overhead lights.

That's when the phone rings.

The words Transplant Centre flicker across my screen and, just for the briefest moment, I stop breathing.

14

'Ms Hargreaves, I'm calling with some good news,' comes a jaunty voice. It's the transplant coordinator. 'A belated Christmas present, you could say.'

My heart is hammering so hard I can barely breathe.

'Hello? Ms Hargreaves?'

I make myself drag in a shaky breath. 'I... I'm here.'

'Brilliant. Well, we'd like to invite you down to the centre as soon as you can get here.' The man pauses. 'We have a heart that we think will work for you.'

He waits, mic dropped, for the inevitable intake of breath, the speechless stuttering of shock and delight. But I can't summon the words to reply. I'm casting around for possible explanations. I would only get this call if there had been a problem with the intended recipient.

With Junie.

'But... I... I didn't think I was the most urgent case,' I finally manage, the words coughing out of me.

'Oh... well...' He's thrown by my reaction. 'There's... been a change in situation. I can't share the details, you understand.'

I'm replaying Christmas Day in my head. I see myself swiping the glass from the tray before Junie can grasp it. Taking it to the kitchen. Emptying it down the sink before making up a new one. Throwing the other pill away into the skip.

I didn't do it. I didn't go through with it.

But wait... Did I pour it away?

I can see the spiked glass sitting innocently on the counter. Looking fresh and ready to drink. I think about the clean kitchen and the dishwasher Justin dutifully stacked. I think about the drink on the coaster next to Junie's chair. How it seemed like she was drinking slowly. How often I was upstairs, seeking sanctuary on the floor by Max's crib, listening to him breathing to try and clear my conscience. How Junie might have been in the kitchen and seen the glass. How easily it would have been mistaken for a fresh drink when Justin was clearing up. Oh, God.

That glass. That fork in the road.

I let the phone clatter to the floor.

Justin comes in frowning, confused by the sound. I push past him into the hall as he picks up the phone, notes the caller ID and puts it quickly to his ear. In the downstairs bathroom I fling myself over the sink and retch. Nothing comes up but self-loathing. Against all odds, despite my change of mind, it has worked. Junie will have failed the tests. I have taken her place. Somehow my twisted fantasy has come true.

The heart meant for her is now mine.

When I return, pale and shaking, Justin is finishing the conversation.

'We'll leave now. We'll be with you as soon as we can.' He is all competence and quiet professionalism. He hangs up and turns to me, eyes burning bright.

'Merry fucking Christmas,' he whispers, holding his arms open wide.

I lean into them, hoping that his embrace will absolve me. As we stand there, locked together, I know for sure that he can never find out what I've done. What he might have done without knowing.

We are admitted to the hospital, quickly and efficiently. I hear Junie's words. *It won't be until the twenty-seventh... the family needs the time to say goodbye.* I swallow thickly. Only now do I have to confront the reality that for me to continue living, someone has had to die.

As I lace up my hospital gown, peel back the familiar blue blanket and climb onto the squeaky waterproof mattress, a sadness sits heavy on me. Dad has taken Max, and Justin has lined up his compassionate leave. I've stopped eating and drinking since we got here. We're as ready as we can be, not knowing how long my recovery might take, or how well my body might respond to the intruder in its midst. There are so many unknowns. Even now the nurse has taken more blood from me to perform the latest in the barrage of tests. She winces at the track marks along the inside of my arms.

'Been sucked dry, eh?' she says.

'A bit, yeah,' I say, mustering a smile, but my mind is blank. Disbelief that I'm here, prepping for major surgery, curls like smoke around the fact that I'm only here because of what I've done. And I'm going to have to live with that for the rest of my life.

My phone pings, a good luck message from Billie. Justin must have called her. I swipe away the notification, leaving my home screen blank. The background photo of Max beams up at me, his face daubed in puree. His expression is one of untrammelled joy. Pure and utter pleasure in this wonderful, overwhelming new experience called food.

I imagine his future. His wobbling form cruising along the walls of our house for support, toddling after a favourite toy and returning it to my hands as a token of love. I can see him right there, just a few feet away. Always just out of reach, disappearing around the next corner so I can't quite make out his face clearly. His features. Know how much of me there is in him. All this is so I can stay here for him.

It has to be worth it.

I'm roused from a half-sleep by the sound of the curtains peeling back. Dr Mirza hovers at the entrance to my cubicle. Justin sits up straight. She glances around then ducks out again and reappears with another chair. Perching on the edge of it, legs crossed, she finally looks at us.

'Ms Hargreaves, we've had some test results back.' She gestures at the piece of paper in her hand. It is scattered with numbers and letters. Justin comes to sit beside me on the edge of the bed, lacing his fingers through mine. We both know what is happening. Instinctively, we can both tell.

'As you know, we test the antibodies in both donor and recipient to ensure there's going to be a match.'

I nod gamely, as if it's a biology lesson and I am going to be tested on this information, rather than sitting in an urgent-care ward listening to the worst news in the world.

'Well, I'm sorry to have to tell you that, on this occasion, there isn't a match here.'

I droop back against the pillow. Adrenaline has been haring around my system since we got the call and it is finally too much. I can tell from the doctor's wince that she feels sorry for me, but this time I don't want her sympathy. I don't deserve it.

Justin's whole body is stiff, as if he refuses to bend to the truth.

'The antibodies didn't show up before? I... I... we shouldn't have come here.'

Dr Mirza nods.

'It's very difficult to hear this, I am sure. There's a chance these antibodies were formed during pregnancy, or...' She glances down again at my file. 'I see you needed a transfusion during your labour. Again, that could be the source. It's not uncommon, I'm afraid.'

I stare at her, then turn to Justin for confirmation. He drops his eyes and I know it's true. Having our baby is what has cost me this chance of remaining with my family.

They continue to talk in hushed tones, but I've stopped listening. I turn away from them, folding into a foetal position. I've heard all I need to. I will return to the waiting list, tail between my legs, no further forward than I was before the events of Christmas.

I have stolen Junie's chance at life for no reason at all.

Part Three

15

When we get home I lie awake as the sun falls and rises again, haunted by the sight of my phone beside me. I've managed a paltry text to Junie with clumsy condolences, but she hasn't responded. The desire to call her taunts me, as does the knowledge that I won't.

Dad is staying with us again until early January to give us more time together, but I can barely face him.

'Are you going to go to the New Year drinks?' he asks tentatively, as he lays Max beside me on the second day I haven't left the bedroom.

I look at him, confused.

'Those support group ones that Junie mentioned.'

'Oh... Maybe,' I mumble. It stings to hear him say her name.

I'd completely forgotten about the festive social tomorrow. It's apparently an annual tradition that they get together on 30 December every year and toast to good fortune and the future to come. It's almost superstitious, a liquid offering to fate.

'I'm very happy to Max-sit,' Dad continues gently. 'Some of them must have experienced this too. Talking could really help.'

The idea of sitting alongside the others on a pub bench as they commiserate with me feels impossible.

'Please, love. It'd do you good.' Dad reaches over and strokes my cheek like I'm a little girl again and I almost flinch away. My body telling me I'm not worthy of his sympathy.

I stare up at one of the people who loves me the most in the world and see how much he needs this. Something to ease the suffering which he doesn't know I've brought on myself.

'I'll think about it,' I say, turning back to Max who is babbling beside me as his tiny fingers explore my ear.

I try to occupy his growing attention span with flip books and felt flaps. Sing songs and pull silly faces. He's become fixated on a series of Peekaboo books where the swipe of a finger makes animals with cartoonishly large eyes appear. Another swipe and they vanish. I swipe up again (Peekaboo!) and Max thumps his fist appreciatively. I smile, turning the pages, until the final shape makes me falter. A large red cartoon heart. That anatomically incorrect ideograph which has become synonymous with love. I pull out the heart. Then make it disappear. Each time it appears, Max lights up and pain bites at the back of my throat.

My friends double down on their efforts to cheer me up. Nadia offers to revamp my entire makeup collection with the Chanel she swears by, her eyes flicking over my sallow complexion. Sinead offers her sister's services for a free haircut. They suggest a weekend away at a spa to take my mind off it all. Whatever they can think of to help. But adjusting my appearance, painting over the cracks, isn't going to cut it. Billie is the only one who understands. She's the only person apart from Justin who hasn't ever commented on my changing body, my papery skin, my sunken eyes. I believe she doesn't see them. I believe she just sees me, and I love her for it.

But when she comes over the next morning, I see the first flicker of concern on her face. It sends spasms of panic under my skin, right to the very core of me. That flicker behind her eyes says that I'm starting to look like I'm dying.

'Let's go out for lunch,' she says. 'Clear your head, get some air. Justin has Max and Terry said he'd give us a lift.'

Too tired to protest, I let them bundle me into the car. We drive through streets littered with the bone-dry corpses of discarded Christmas trees and the sight of them makes me shudder. Sitting in the back with Billie while Dad is up front driving makes me feel like a child again, being ferried between playdates. He's always been ready to drop everything to help me.

We pull up outside a pub and it's not until I've got out of the car that I realise which one it is. The pub where the support group socials are held. I whirl around and take in the faint glimmer of conspiracy in their faces.

'Junie mentioned when it was.' Dad looks a little sheepish. He dropped me off last time and remembered the location. 'We just thought… it might help.'

I wonder if Justin had something to do with this too. The idea they've all been discussing me behind my back, plotting some sort of intervention, is both touching and infuriating.

'We can just pop our heads in before we get food. I'll come with you,' Billie says, reaching out for my arm.

'No,' I say quickly. 'No. I'll go.'

Billie takes a table in the main room of the pub to wait, assuring me that the alone time with her Kindle is frankly a blessing. I clench my fists as I walk towards the familiar back room. I haven't been on the group chat since before Christmas so I have no idea who will be here. My pulse skyrockets as I push open the door.

As I move into the room there are warm smiles from some faces I recognise. I do a very fast sweep over them for Junie, but I can't see her. I feel a sickening relief. Cathy is there, reliably in her Second Hearters T-shirt.

'Olivia, hello! Welcome. Happy nearly New Year!' She pulls me into a hug.

I'm just disengaging from it when she drops her voice so the others in the room can't hear her. 'Listen, I heard what happened. With Junie.'

My mouth dries. I fiddle with the zip on my coat. 'Oh.'

'We spoke after… She said there'd been some mistake. She'd failed a drugs test that concerned them, what with her history. Nonsense, of course, she must have mixed up some pills or something, but they're extremely strict with these things if people have a history of dependency.' Cathy shakes her head sadly. 'Have you spoken to her?'

'I wanted… to give her space.'

'Of course. Well, she… I think she was wondering… if you got the call afterwards? She wanted me to ask. I know she wanted to talk to you but, well, I think she couldn't face telling you what happened. She's embarrassed. After you've been so kind. It meant a lot to her to be with you all for Christmas.'

The knot in my stomach coils tighter.

'I… I did get the call,' I murmur. 'But it wasn't a match.'

Cathy's face sets into an expression of intense pity. 'Oh, my dear. I'm so sorry to hear that. Junie will be so disappointed on your behalf too.' She clutches my shoulders tightly. 'Well… look. It isn't always first time lucky; we all know that. You just… hang on in there. Keep your chin up. Don't lose hope.' She squeezes my hand.

But there's a forlorn air to Cathy as she turns back to the others. This woman who has gone through the tunnel and emerged into the light, who carries the weight of all our dreams.

I sip an orange juice, the glass juddering in my hand, remembering Junie's fingers wrapped around hers as I make small talk with the few others I remember; Richard from Hertford and Anya from Ealing. They're on the Routine list and I can see their expressions shift when I say the word Urgent. The rapid scan taking in my pallid complexion and the grey bags under my eyes. I see off any probing questions with claims of post-Christmas exhaustion; I did too much. The lie burns in my mouth.

If they only knew the whole picture.

'You must look after yourself,' Richard says. 'Pace yourself, you know?'

I nod with a faint blush, thankful Cathy doesn't seem to have said anything to the others. It's her policy not to share gossip and rumours, they can be too damaging. As soon as I've finished my drink I start to make my goodbyes. I've endured enough time here to convince Billie and Dad that it's helped.

Just then the door to the back room creaks open and a woman makes her slow way into the room. My breath catches. She's here. I glance quickly around, wondering if I can hide myself amongst the others. Slip to the toilet as an excuse. Or leave before she sees me.

At least look at her, you owe her that.

I turn towards the door, biting my lip. What will she look like? How much will the disappointment have eroded her already failing body? What on earth will I say to her? My pulse is so fast I have to sit down on one of the chairs ringing the room. But when I eventually look up, it's a woman I don't recognise. She's dressed in black, save for the collar of a white shirt beneath a dark jumper, and for a split second I'm convinced she's a police officer. That they've come for me. Sniffed me out by the stench of my guilt.

'Hi. I'm...' The woman clears her throat and I can tell that emotion is tightening it. Under the low lights her eyes are gleaming, wet. 'I'm here for Ravi.'

There's a faint rumble around the room. A minute gasp only just audible. Ravi. The friendly accountant from Reading at the last meeting, waiting for lucky number three. I glance around the group. He's not here. I'd thought nothing of it.

'I'm Aditi, his wife. I just... I wanted to come and thank you all. For the strength you gave him over the last year. I don't...' She stops to compose herself. 'I'm not sure he would have been able to fight for as long as he did without it.'

Cathy steps forward and envelops Aditi in a hug. I can see the tremors in her chest as she breaks down. The others in the room gather around, but I press myself against the wall, away from the rawness of her pain. Like a magnet repelled from a pole, I back out of the door.

At home I make noises about seeing them being useful; sharing the load of our collective pain. All the things I think the others want to hear. Dad and Justin nod, reassured. When Dad has taken Max for a walk, and Justin puts a third cup of decaf next to me on the sofa then turns back to the study, I feel a flush of irritation. He's spending more and more time in there with the door closed, like he told me his father did when his mother was ill. I don't think he's even noticed the parallels. His facade of calm, steadfast strength was a huge part of the initial attraction for me, but now it seems like armour he can't take off. Now I just wish he would let me in. I need us to be honest as we face the future. Acknowledge that we must make some decisions. Especially now.

'Listen, shall we… we should talk about this.' I pat the sofa next to me. 'About me.'

Justin sits down slowly, alert to the seriousness of my tone.

'I think we should talk about Max. About what I want for him. If…'

'You're not joining the back of the queue. There could be another heart in a matter of weeks.' His voice is restrained.

'Or it could be months,' I reply slowly. 'Years even.'

Justin recoils. 'Where was this negativity before the baby came?' he snaps. 'You seemed to think everything would turn out fine then. All sunshine and roses.'

I stare at him. 'That was before. It's worse now, you know that.'

'Yes, and why is that?'

'Hey, Justin, we wanted this. We wanted him.'

He fixes me with a long look. He doesn't say what I know he wants to say. What he really thinks, deep down. That, while he loves Max wholeheartedly, he thinks it was the wrong choice to have him. My chest tightens. Have I done this? Have I made him have a child he doesn't want? Cursed my son to a future where his father can't love him without his mother being present? History repeating itself.

'Let's talk about this later.' Justin gets up stiffly and leaves the room.

The door of the study clicks shut. Again.

At the surgery that afternoon, I try to ignore everyone making New Year's resolutions. Dad thought I should stay off a few more days and rest, but I need the distraction. I've started catching the bus the few stops to get there, saving all my energy for Max.

Every time I glance at the pharmacy a shiver runs over me, but Krish has said nothing to alarm me. The chaos of the year's end has covered my tracks. I wonder how Junie is now. How she's coping. A knife twists in my gut.

Brian goes on his lunch break and takes his attitude with him. The quiet calms me a little. I turn back to my to-do list on the desk. Writing one out every day is a habit from childhood, crossing things off a simple satisfaction which never gets old. It always makes me feel better. I work through some mundane tasks: sending reminders for vaccinations and flu jabs, alerting patients to test results. When I see a set of results returned with bad news it strikes a chord of pity in me, but there's also a warped sensation of peace. Life is cruel to other people too, it's nothing personal.

Finally, I reach for the list of donors from the blood drive to make sure we have everyone's details on file correctly: names, addresses, NHS numbers. Check how many people attended so we can prove it's worth our while. I run my finger down the list of names, past the people I remember signing in. Irene, Rebecca and Amir, Billie and Steph, Nadia and Oz. Then I see them.

Daniel Wilkins. Emily Nelson.

A shared address on Oakfield Road. It's a leafy road ten minutes from us that I've often walked up wondering what careers the inhabitants must have to be able to afford such huge, beautiful houses in London. He's only ten minutes away.

I continue down the list, a slight judder in my finger now. As I tick off the other names and write in their sample bag numbers, I find my eyes keep leaping back up the list. They flicker again and again over a few names. A frown laces my forehead as I have to re-enter some details for the second time: name, date of birth, address.

I pause. Look again at the list of details in front of me. Then, quite suddenly, I realise the other piece of information this list gives me.

Blood type.

Amongst the thirty odd donors who came, there are three people with the universal O negative blood. Three more have A negative. My blood type.

Those six names gaze up at me. Two of them I don't recognise, but four of them I do. Rebecca. Our neighbour Irene. Steph; Billie's cousin. And, finally, like some sick joke, Dan.

As I stare at the list, I realise what I'm looking at. Written on the paper in front of me are the details of six people whose hearts could be compatible with my body.

16

As I'm walking up the front garden path towards the house, battling to stop my thoughts in their tracks, my phone rings.

'Liv, hi.' It's Amir. 'This a good moment?'

'Yes, sure,' I say, clearing my throat.

'Great. Look, I wanted to call and say how sorry I was that the donor didn't work out.'

'Oh… thanks. That's really kind of you.'

'But listen, I spoke to a friend in Cardiothoracics. He's had a proper look at the waiting list and there's a bit of good news. There are several other Routine cases waiting, but as it stands no one else Urgent. You'd be front of line for a heart that matches.'

I tighten my grip on the phone. I've looked at Junie's number over and over but never found the guts to call. She's still not said anything on the group chat. She was never a big talker, just added star emojis to good news – our accepted stand-in for the heart. But if I am at the top of the waiting list, it means that the heart which was meant for Junie has gone to the shadowy third person who sat alongside us.

And that Junie is no longer on the list.

'It may not stay that way, of course,' Amir continues. 'Patient conditions can change fairly rapidly, but as it stands, you're up there.'

'Oh…' I manage, wading through conflicting emotions. 'That's good to hear.'

'I can't give you any idea of timeframe, but hopefully it's a bit of encouraging news.'

'It is. Thank you, Amir. It's really good of you to take the time.'

'Not at all. And I'm in touch with Justin. About it all. We're… talking it through.'

I smile faintly. Amir is no better than my husband at emotional vulnerability, infected with the medical profession's coping mechanism of keeping things locked up, but he's trying. I thank him again and hang up.

I take off my coat, then go into the living room and switch on the light. I jump to see Justin is sitting there on the sofa, staring into space in the fading light. A glance at the monitor tells me that Max is asleep.

'I made him some vegetable soup for dinner,' he says quietly.

I sit down at his side. 'Did he like it?'

'Hoovered it up.'

We share the indulgent smile of new parents delighting in their child.

'I'm sorry. I… I can't stand it when we fight,' I say. 'I need us to be together in all this. I need you with me. I don't know what I'd do if—'

'I agree,' he says gently. 'And I am with you. I'm at your side for every step.' His voice quavers over the last words.

I squeeze his hand tight and my pulse rate finally starts to slow. I tell him what Amir said about the list and I can feel him stiffen, as if he won't let the hope in. Not until he's sure he can cope with it.

'Maybe… maybe it won't be long now,' I mutter, leaning into his chest.

'It won't,' he replies, whispering it into my hair. 'It won't.'

We stay like that until the monitor picks up a whimper from Max.

In his room, I creep to the powder blue rocking chair by his crib and reach down to press my hand over his little chest while he stirs in his sleep. One fist is curled up tight next to his chin, as if defending him from bad dreams. 'I'm here,' I whisper. 'Mama's here.' We've just moved him out of our bedroom now that he's coming up to six months old. Though Justin thinks Max will sleep better in the quiet, part of me didn't want to move him. He looked cocooned in the crib next to our bed. Safe. Enveloped, like he was back inside me.

As I sit beside my son, his soft skin beneath my hands, our heartbeats in sync, my life feels suddenly, hopelessly out of control. As though the hours are slipping through my fingers like sand. Each new dawn another struck out on the list of days I have left with Max. That Max and Justin have left with me. I blink back tears which fall, staining the material of his sleep sack. Then my thoughts drift back to the surgery. To that piece of paper in a file on my desk.

That list of names.

I can't help myself. A question turns over in my mind. Someone from that list could be a full match for me, HLA markers too, but I won't ever know without testing their blood. Then I think about the sample fridge. The blood-donation bags locked away inside, waiting to be transferred to the lab. It's unusual they're still there but pick up has been delayed with understaffing over Christmas.

I think about what just a few drops of each donation would tell me.

My final shift of the year is the following afternoon, New Year's Eve. The surgery is quiet. Brian is sullen and complaining about the cold, his Christmas spirit short-lived. I manage to summon sympathetic noises, but I'm totally distracted. My eyes keep drifting to the sample fridge. The idea that has been quietly unfurling is taking root. A crazy one.

A criminal one.

You've already broken the seal, what's one more crime?

No. It's not who I am. I couldn't even consider something so… dark. An urgent need to be alone washes over me, as if these terrible thoughts are so loud someone might hear them.

'Why don't I lock up today?' I say to Brian suddenly. 'You get off a bit early to your party.'

He looks at me suspiciously. 'Oh. Really?'

'Absolutely.' I smile, but not too hard, so he thinks I'm just looking forward to a quiet hour rather than actively trying to get rid of him.

'Okay. Well, fine,' he says, adjusting the stationery on his side of the desk. 'I'll do that.' He shoots me a sidelong glance, as though I might ask for something in return, then types with renewed vigour for the rest of the afternoon.

After he's gone, the GPs each sign out one by one. Justin is one of the last. He frowns when he sees me alone behind the desk.

'I thought Brian was closing up.'

'I said I would. It's fine, Justin. I'm sitting down,' I say, firmly. 'Seriously. Go home and help Dad with Max. Please. I won't be long.'

Justin gives me a look, clearly wanting to say more, but he purses his lips and leaves. Finally, the surgery sits empty. I exhale shakily.

With the computer screen angled safely away from the CCTV camera, I start to do some hurried online research. If I were to do this, how would it work? I search for a private blood-testing lab, not necessarily something unusual to search for from our work computers. When I find one, surreally, it's offering a January sales discount. I study it, chewing a nail.

I feel light-headed as I stand up and turn to the sample fridge.

Just get the answer you need.

I steady myself on the handle as I gaze in at the bags of dark blood. Then I tug the fridge open. The cold air hits me. Oh, God. Oh, God. What the hell am I *doing*? I take an involuntary step back, as if my body is warning me not to do this. If I were ever found out, if anyone ever saw me, I'd lose my job. Worse maybe. This must be a criminal offence. Another one. My crimes are starting to mount up.

But if I don't do this, I'll never know. Forcing myself forward, I rifle through the blood bags until I find the six matches, three exact, three universal. Concentrating hard to keep my hands steady, I scramble for some vials, the 4-millilitre vacutainer tubes, and begin the careful transfer. It's like I've become disembodied, like I'm looking down from somewhere and watching myself at work. My hands tremble so much with the first sample that I spill some. Swallowing down adrenaline, breathing shakily, I scrub the floor with an antiseptic wipe. A spectral red stain seems to linger behind my eyes, like a sunspot.

As I drip, drip, drip their blood into each tube, their faces flash up in my mind. Six people. Two featureless strangers and then those I know; Rebecca, Irene, Steph, Dan.

After I replace each bag, wiping my fingerprints hurriedly from them, I seal the vials carefully in a plastic pouch in my coat pocket. My stomach churns. It's like every new choice is turning me into someone else. Chiselling away another chip of my humanity. I hope there will be enough of me left to fight for, wherever this ends.

As I feed the padded envelope for the lab into the post-box, I try desperately not to imagine what Justin would say. If there were even a suggestion that he knew anything he'd be suspended. Our marriage wouldn't survive. He loves me with all his heart, but he's a moral person. His doctor's oath means everything. I have my suspicions that his job, helping others, is what saved him after the divorce and the breakdown of his relationship with Nick. But a drop from each sample will answer the question lodged in my brain which won't leave me alone. I have to know.

When I let myself into the house, Justin is laying out the glasses and bowls of snacks. My friends have abandoned their usual New Year's plans in favour of drinks at ours tonight. Billie is coming with Tom, though I dread to think how much a babysitter has cost them. Nadia and Oz are making an appearance before some raucous party in town. Sinead and Edie are bringing sparklers.

'Hi,' I say, trying to keep my voice level. 'Has Max eaten?'

Justin nods. 'Pureed courgette *à la Grandad*. He's just getting cleaned up.' He gestures to the kitchen where I can hear Dad chattering to Max.

'Great.' My body feels weak as I shrug off my coat. It's an effort to hang it up, the impact of the last hour's stress levels. The realisation sends a chill through me; I've got to be so careful.

'Listen, before the others arrive, I thought we might...' Justin tails off. I glance up at his tone. He's holding some paper and pens in one hand. 'I had this idea. I thought we could write Max letters. It could be a nice New Year's Eve tradition. Tell him everything we wish for him in the coming year.'

His vulnerability startles me.

'That's... a really lovely idea. Okay. Let's do it?'

He nods and we sit down at the table. But as I pick up a pen, a thought forms. If I don't make it to next year, Justin would at least have something to show Max when he's older. Words written by his mum about how much he means to her. I realise what this is. Consciously or not, Justin is asking me to write a letter to my son which will immortalise my love for him.

I pretend I don't know this, but each time my pen presses against the blank paper, I choke. I have no idea where to start. How can a letter take the place of my presence in Max's life? No words will do justice to that absence; I should know. Eventually I push the paper aside.

'I'll think on what I want to write,' I say to Justin as I get up and head for the kitchen. All I want is to hold Max close to me and inhale the scent of him.

Later, once Max is asleep, the living room is filled with my friends and family, all studiously avoiding talk of resolutions. When Big Ben begins its tolling, Justin turns to kiss me and, though I smile at my husband, my thoughts are elsewhere. Here, on the last night of the year that our son was born, it's impossible to think of anything but what the next has in store for me. All at once, fate, destiny, the fancy names we use for a future that is out of our control, seem laughable. The clock is ticking on how long I will be up and about. Carrying my son. My own weight. The sand in the hourglass started to fall a long while back and I have no way of knowing how much remains. How much time I have left.

The question is: what will you do about it?

The wait for the sample results is excruciating. Each morning I move as fast as I can down the stairs, my eyes on the doormat, ready to intercept the post. I paid for the fastest turnaround, a few days at most. It was more money than I've spent on anything in a long time, more than I can afford. I dipped into my meagre savings rather than using the joint account, to avoid having to explain anything to Justin.

On the third morning, I'm forced to abandon my watch to go to a hospital appointment. A routine check in on my medication. In the waiting room I catch sight of a familiar face. It's a man from the support group who I've not really spoken to. We share a fragile smile of recognition and then I pretend to be engrossed in my phone, praying my appointment will finish before his so we don't have to talk.

The doctor is new, a kindly man in his forties who seems harried, if empathetic. He asks after my symptoms and I look at my hands as I tell him that the breathlessness is getting more acute. The dizzy spells more common. He frowns as he checks my medication and my latest test results, then he turns towards me and leans forward in his chair.

'Ms Hargreaves, you've been breastfeeding your baby, is that right?'

I feel a flush of embarrassment, as if it was the wrong thing to be doing. 'Yes. As much as I can. Once a day really.'

He nods and smooths down his beard. 'Well, looking at the results and what you're reporting about symptoms worsening, I'm sorry, but I'm going to need to start you on a new medication which is contra-indicated for breastfeeding.'

My confusion must be evident because he explains. 'It won't be safe for the baby. I'm going to have to advise that you stop altogether.'

'Oh,' I say dumbly.

As he writes up a new prescription, I sit listening to the clacking of his keyboard and realise that this morning was the last time I would ever breastfeed my son. It stings like a fresh cut. I bite my lip or I'll break down right here in his treatment room.

'And how are you managing generally, with motherhood – your baby? Everything. It's an awful lot.'

'I've got lots of help.' I explain about Dad, at home with Max now. How Justin bears the brunt of it on weekends. The doctor nods but the concern doesn't lift from his face.

'Look, I don't want to seem alarmist, but you really ought to consider some further options.'

'What do you mean?'

'Well, as your condition is… deteriorating, you'll need plenty of back up. For the baby. In case you're admitted.'

'Admitted?' I realise my mistake a millisecond before he clarifies.

'It's not uncommon for those with later stage heart issues to be hospitalised. As time goes on…' He hesitates. 'If you need any further intervention, you may well end up waiting for your operation here, in the ward.'

On the bus home, salty tears sting my chapped lips. As I get off and start my slow walk from the stop, my vision is so blurred that it's a few minutes before I notice the man walking up the street towards me. His hair is longer. His skin etched with a thick coating of stubble he would never normally permit. A warm caramel tone to his skin. He's back and I didn't even know.

Al.

17

Everything we said to each other the last time we were together floods into my head. Even bits I thought I'd forgotten. Al glances up from his phone. He sees me and his face rearranges itself into an expression I can't decipher. He stops a few feet away. A plastic bag buffets against his leg.

'Livi...'

It's what he used to call me when we were little. It sounds at once so alien and so familiar.

'Hi,' I manage in a strangled voice.

'I would have called but I thought... I was just... dropping this off for you. I know it's late.' He gestures at the plastic bag. I can see the jaunty red ribbon of a Christmas gift inside. 'It's... it's great to see you. You look—' He doesn't finish the sentence, but he doesn't need to.

I pull my coat closer around me, suddenly aware of my clothes; one step up from pyjamas. My frazzled hair barely held back by a battered scrunchie.

Something brittle shifts in Al's eyes.

'I... I was so sorry... to hear,' he hesitates. 'I saw Billie when I got back. She...'

Of course. Billie's told him, trying to weave the strongest safety net she can muster around her best friend. His face has folded into a familiar expression. The one which was on his face when he told me his dad had died. Pain in every groove, every crease, every pore of his skin. We stare at each other and for a moment I hate that he knows.

We take shelter from the threatening rain in a café on the high street. As the waitress puts down the herbal teas, we both look at our laps. Now that we're sitting opposite each other, the months of silence between us are deafening.

He'd always wanted us to take that life-changing trip around the world together, just like we'd planned when we were younger. I'd told him the last round of IVF hadn't worked. That I didn't know where it left Justin and me, whether we could weather the agony together or if it would finish us. Al said I just needed a break from it all. To rediscover the joy in life. See the world anew, like I'd once dreamed of. Come with me, he'd said. I yelled at him for being selfish when I was just as guilty of it. I didn't want him to go. Stay, I said, fuelled by alcohol and existential disappointment. It didn't need to be the start of the end for us, but somehow it was. And then, of course, it only got worse.

'Can I see… a photo?' Al says hesitantly. I frown, confused, until I realise he means Max. He's never met Max.

'Oh, right,' I say with an awkward laugh. 'Yeah, sure.'

I wrestle out my phone, stuffed in my pocket alongside a crumpled shopping list and numerous scrunched tissues, and flick to my favourites.

'He's so big,' Al whispers. 'How old?'

'Six months.'

'Got you and your dad's eyes.'

I try to put the phone away, embarrassed to be one of 'those people' who coo over endless photos of their offspring and expect everyone to be interested, but his appetite isn't sated.

'Any videos?'

Softening, I pull up the videos from Max's Christmas lunch where he gets the 'festive mulch' in his ear and over both eyebrows. Al laughs out loud.

'He's… superb,' he says quietly. 'Well done, Liv. I'm so… I'm so happy for you. All of you.'

There's so much unsaid but it feels good to see him. I've almost forgotten about the wait for the results.

'When did you get back?'

'Three weeks ago,' he says. 'For Christmas.'

'How's Ben?' I ask, grasping at topics to fill the awkward space between us. 'And Annette?'

'Oh, you know Mum, ever the stalwart. She insists she's not lonely, but I can tell she's glad I'm back. I don't think waiting on Ben and the girls hand and foot when he deigns to visit is quite the treat for her he thinks it is. She adores them, but she's feeling like the help. She's let it be known though, no fear there.' He grins.

Annette is notorious for speaking her mind. She thought very little of my mother and even as a child I could tell she felt that apples never fall far from the tree. After my ill-considered tryst with Al, whenever I saw Annette it was clear she felt I'd wronged him. Changed the direction of his life for the worse. Perhaps I had, though I didn't mean to. That's the very last thing I wanted.

I've never told Al this, but when I was nine, Annette's disapproval got to be too much. At parents' evening, the first my mother had attended for two years, I was showing her around the classroom and pointing proudly at things I'd done displayed on the walls. Annette's eyes were on us and I could feel her judgement. I could feel that my mother was falling short in her eyes.

So, as I walked past Annette's table, I nudged it hard with my hip. A plastic cup of coffee tipped down her smart cream trousers, leaving a long dark stain. As I glanced back, trying to keep the triumph from my face, Annette was looking at me, her expression telling me that she knew exactly what I'd done. A look which told me I was as rotten as my mother.

Perhaps it's turning out to be true.

'How is it being back?' I ask Al. 'Do you miss the travelling life?'

'It's… weird. You know? I guess I always realised it would be a tough transition. I've started back at the ad agency, but the rent's gone up so I think I'll have to find a new place to live.'

He sounds gloomy. It's sad to think of him finally leaving that little flat in Finchley. He sublet it to some students while he went travelling, unable to let it go. It's a place that holds so many memories. Perhaps that's part of the problem; the rest of us have moved on but Al's still stuck, surrounded by echoes of the past. I try not to think about the last time I was there.

'I'm just going to ask for some water,' I mutter, getting quickly to my feet, but then a headrush hits me full on. A fizz of black dots dances before my eyes and I thud back down into my chair, lurching sideways towards Al.

'Jesus, are you okay?' He lunges to catch me as others in the café turn and look.

The hospital warned me about moving too fast, especially standing up. I've got to be so careful to not force my heart to jump-start from stillness.

'I'm… just… stood up too fast.' I press my hand to my chest. My heart is *thump-thumping* with a vengeance.

'Do you need to go home?' he says, bracing himself around me. Tension vibrates in his arm, concern alive throughout his body.

'No, not to mine.' I don't want Max to see me like this, or Justin.

Al calls an Uber to take us to his flat. In the car I rest with my eyes closed, forehead against the glass.

'Are you sure you don't need to go to hospital?' he mutters. I know seeing me like this will hit him. Bring back memories of his dad which stab like needles.

'I'll be fine. Promise. Just need to rest a bit.'

He's holding my hand tight. He hasn't let it go since the café.

At Al's flat I lie down on the sofa. The same faded rust-red corduroy throw under my cheek. The same green and blue scattered cushions. He's brought a few new touches back from his travels; a rug with a lion pattern from Ethiopia, a huge beaded giraffe from Cape Town. Al has never really been one for interior design so it's all pretty mismatched, but it's so cosy. Framed pictures of us adorn the walls: grubby and grinning at a music festival, crammed in the photobooth at Billie's wedding. We all look ridiculously young. So full of life.

My phone pings with a reminder to book Max's next vaccinations. Al sees the background of my screen, the picture of Max's elated face, smeared with food. He looks to the ceiling, I can see he's blinking hard.

'I'm okay,' I say softly. 'A bit tired but you know me, any excuse for a lie-in.' He ignores my attempt at gallows humour.

'How long is the wait? On the list.'

I shake my head. 'We don't know. It could be… It could be up to two years.'

Al doesn't need to say anything, I can read his thoughts on his face, just like he can on mine. *That's too long*, they say. *I know*, mine reply.

His eyes are wet. 'I wish you'd told me. I wish you'd called. I'd have come back.'

A rush of anger billows up inside me. 'Why? You didn't stay when I asked you to.'

'That's not exactly fair.'

None of this is Al's fault but suddenly his absence has become a betrayal. He hasn't been here when I needed him so much.

'No,' I say, my voice dropping low. 'You know what isn't fair? Fighting for years to have a baby, only to be told you won't live to see him grow up.'

Al looks down at his hands.

'You don't know what it's been like.' My voice wavers. 'You haven't been here! You haven't… You don't know what I've had to *do*.' I stop myself.

I want to tell him everything, just how bad things are. What I've thought. What I've done. How it's all eating me up inside. Words strain at my lips, pressing to be let out.

'What do you mean?' he asks slowly.

Before I know what I'm doing, they're out, the words tumbling from my mouth. A waterfall of guilt. Maybe it's exactly because he hasn't been here, because he doesn't know me as a mother that I can tell him things I could never tell Justin or Billie or Dad.

'I met this woman, at a support group. She was being treated at the same centre as me. It was just her and me on the waiting list for the area. They found her a heart, a universal donor, and when she told me I—' I swallow, close my eyes. 'She'd told me that she'd had a drug problem in the past. The hospital won't give a donated heart to someone with a history of substance abuse. So,

I... when I was with her just before the operation... I...' I drop my voice to a whisper. 'I drugged her drink.'

Al's jaw falls open.

I speed up. It's pouring out of me, a full confession. 'But I couldn't... I couldn't go through with it! I didn't give it to her. I switched the drink and tried to forget about it, but she did fail the drugs test. I realised she must have drunk the drugged glass by mistake and... then I got offered the heart meant for her. But I... I wasn't even a full match. They did more tests and I wasn't compatible.' Shame fractures my words. 'After all that, I ruined her chance at life for nothing at all.'

My hands are in my hair and I find myself tugging at the roots. I only just manage to stop myself talking before I mention the list of names from the blood drive, the results I'm still waiting for.

We sit in silence. Al's face is frozen, his eyes locked on mine. I search them for the familiar softness I know, but it's not there. I pinch the skin on my hands, trying to decipher from the twitch of his lips the exact moment that I lost him.

'I wish – I wish I hadn't,' I begin, in a feeble attempt to take it all back. 'I'm sorry. I shouldn't have told you.' I scrabble for my coat. I can hardly believe I've been so reckless. What must he think of me? His oldest friend slowly unravelling.

His face is set in a frown. He looks perplexed, as if he is turning it all over in his mind, trying to make sense of it. Then he speaks.

'No.' The frown deepens.

He looks angry. Fear floods my stomach. I freeze, wringing my hands, fingers turning white from the pressure. Then Al sits forward.

'You don't have to be sorry,' he says quietly.

I stare at him.

'You were only doing what you had to. You have a son to think about.'

Tears start to leak down my cheeks. Al leans over and hugs me with force, and somewhere within me the weight of it all eases just a fraction.

When we let go of each other and I wipe my face, I feel the cool metal of my wedding ring against my cheek. We've been here for over two hours. Justin will be home and wondering where I am. Max too.

'I need to get back.'

Al puts a hand over mine.

'Liv.' His voice is low all of a sudden. 'We should... we need to talk about...'

I bristle. My stomach churns. I thought there had been a tacit agreement between us when we agreed to duck into the café and 'catch up', that we wouldn't talk about this.

I gently pull my hand away.

'Al...'

'Come on. You ignored my emails for months. We can't just pretend—'

I reach for my coat, standing up. 'Please, just stop,' I say, my mouth dry. 'It was a mistake.'

My breathing is shallow so it comes out almost as a hiss. 'It was a mistake and that's the end of it.'

Then I stumble from his flat, down the hallway lined with framed group shots of our shared lives.

18

I think deep down, ever since I was a little girl, I had wondered in some part of me if I would end up with Al. With his gleaming green eyes, dimpled grin and floppy, dirty-blond hair, plenty of people think he's a catch. He's been one of the few constants in my life. It's hard to explain what it's like to be abandoned by a parent. Enduring the thousand tiny cuts of others' presumptions. The casual plural 'parents'. Losing my mother just before I started becoming a woman myself. It makes those that remained in my life all the more precious.

When we were at university it was feeling that way which confused me. Tricked me into believing that Al and I were somehow 'meant to be', because we'd always loved each other. It was the summer of my third year at Bristol, days oozing with stagnant heat. Al was down visiting from Manchester. Exams behind us, Billie and Nadia threw a goodbye party for our house which swiftly got out of hand. When my drug-fuelled elation morphed into crippling anxiety, Al guided me past the sweaty revellers to the sanctuary of my room. Inside, a semi-clad couple were draped over my bed. I recoiled when I recognised Dan.

I'd hardly seen him since the end of our fling the year before. I didn't think Nadia would have invited him, but I'd consciously played down just how painful our dalliance had been. I tried to back away, but Al kicked them out, tersely. As Dan made for the door, he saluted Al, his eyes flickering over me, and I looked away, hugging my elbows. When the door shut, the air still crackled with the charged atmosphere. I sat on the bed, my body tense, and tried to breathe.

'You should go back down,' I muttered. 'I'll be okay now. Don't miss out 'cos of me. You know Billie and Nads. And I think Lucy likes you.' I nudged Al's foot playfully.

'It's fine, really. 'S nice just to be Al and Liv.' Referring to ourselves in the third person was a game from childhood.

'Al and Liv,' I repeated with a smile. 'How long has it been Al and Liv?'

He sat down on the bed and was quiet for a moment. 'Fourteen years.'

I realised he was right; we were both five when he moved in across the road. 'Al-Liv,' I giggled. 'Al-Liv. Alive.' As I repeated it, it started to sound hilarious. 'You make me feel Al-Liv.'

I meant it too. His presence here beside me, after an excruciating encounter with my recent past, had reminded me how much I loved him. He met my eyes, the smile on his face so broad I thought he was looking past me at something. I turned to see if a photo on the wall had caught his eye, but there was just the window behind me. When I turned back, we were nose to nose. He'd been smiling at me. In his face I saw a truth that I'd not looked hard enough to see before. Then he kissed me and, overcome by some heady mix of gratitude, love, nostalgia and fear, I kissed him back.

It only took a few weeks for me to realise how wrong I'd got it. I didn't see him like that. So often when I looked at him, we were children again, playing Super Mario and squabbling over the controller. I thought he might have picked up on this disconnect too, felt the same way, but the shock on his face when I told him I wanted to end things told another story. I think it's the only time I've ever broken someone's heart.

We didn't see much of each other for some time after that. It was hard but it also meant I didn't have to face up to how much I'd hurt him. He started dating Nadia's friend Lucy and when they moved in together, I thought that was Al sorted. I was happy for him, busy with my own preoccupations, like all of us in our mid-twenties trying to work out who the hell we were.

A few years later when Al and Lucy's relationship ended and Al moved to his Finchley flat, we rediscovered each other.

Something seemed to have shifted. We could finally put the past behind us and just enjoy our friendship. There were Sunday movie nights at Billie's flat, pub quiz Wednesdays with Nads and Sinead and their partners. Al was there for me throughout my burnout, insisting I go swimming or jogging with him on the weekend so my days had some semblance of structure. Cooking me meals so I wasn't existing solely on takeaway food. Then I met Justin.

It moved fast. I'd been single for so long that I tumbled headfirst into this new relationship, forgetting how frustrating it is for friends to be abandoned in the first flush of a new romance. It must have been a shock to Al's system. He had spent the last few years talking in grand, dreamy terms about reviving 'the big trip'. That's what we'd called it when we were younger. I would nod along, feeling sure it would remain a dream. Looking back, I realise that he must have been hoping his excitement would rub off on me. Eventually his patience ran out and he booked his round-the-world ticket.

So, that rainy November evening, we got together for his leaving drinks at our old regular pub. The nostalgia from the scent of dried Guinness and wood panelling was as strong as a hit of hash. As we sat reminiscing, I found myself reaching for glass after glass of the house red. Billie glanced across her apple juice at me, knowing the bad news I'd just had from the fertility clinic, knowing that drinking alcohol sure as hell wasn't going to help, but she said nothing. Instead, like a true friend, despite being deep into her third trimester, she ordered us all another round. Eventually, everyone else had peeled off back to their kids and cats, and Billie pulled herself to her feet, energy levels finally exhausted, kissed us both and waddled off to her taxi.

'One more for the road?' Al said.

I could see that if I didn't agree, he'd have to face up to the reality of setting off alone on a trip which ought to be shared and I would have to go back home and face the reality of another failed cycle. The conversation which had been brewing with Justin; the truth that we couldn't afford to keep trying. We ordered another bottle.

Once we had finished it, Al pressed a glass of water into my hand.

'We should get you a cab home,' he said.

'I can't. Not yet. He'll…' Justin would know instantly that I'd been drinking after swearing off it. He'd be so disappointed.

Al gave me an odd look. 'What's he going to do, ground you?'

I caught the edge of steel in his tone. 'Stop it. I just can't yet. Need to sober up.'

'Come back to mine,' he said, hauling me to my feet. 'I'll make you a coffee.'

Al rattled around his tiny kitchen as I sprawled on the sofa. The coffee had started its work, but booze was still tripping up my tongue. My eyes were drawn to the noticeboard on his wall. The plastic see-through wallet sleeve with the routes and itineraries for his trip.

'You excited?' I asked as he nudged my legs aside and sat down beside me.

He hesitated for a fraction of a second. Then nodded.

'Wish I was coming too.' I mumbled it into my coffee cup but when I glanced up he was staring at me.

'You mean that?'

''Course.' I smiled. ''S always been Al and Liv against the world.'

Part of me really did mean it. I wanted to run away with him, just like we'd planned all that time ago. Forget about my troubles.

As our eyes met, time seemed to change its matter. It became liquid. Everything else fell away and in that one charged moment it felt like we were seeing each other for the first time. Like I was a student again, on my bed in our shared house, bass pounding up from below.

Then Al leaned in and I didn't pull away.

19

I lie propped up on the bed, staring at the ceiling as the sounds of Max enjoying his meal drift up the stairs.

'Mmmm, tasty pasta!' Justin is saying. 'Open up. Yum yum yum.'

Max babbles back. I can hear the excited slap of his palms on the highchair tray. A few days ago he said 'Dada' for the first time and Justin's face lit up. Though Max switched to repeating 'dididi', I said we should declare it his first proper word and Justin just hugged us both.

I close my eyes as guilt surges hot through me. There's no defence, only context. I was at my lowest, grieving the motherhood which was eluding me, lonely despite my caring husband, and deeply in need of escape. The truth is that it would never have happened with anyone but Al. I needed to be close to someone who knew me for more than what I was going through, who didn't see me as a failure. An alternative reality. Maybe that night signalled the start of my moral decline. The tipping point when my principles first started to decay.

What a pickle, Olive. What a pickle.

She sounds smug. Like she always knew I was on an inescapable trajectory towards her path. Dad never told me outright, but I am sure there were other men. The number of times she didn't come home left it hard to explain any other way.

But her life is not mine. No matter how hard things get, I will never give up on my family. I wish I could go back in time to our wedding, to the vows Justin and I made which, in one drunken moment, I broke. I want to swear them again from this vantage point, as a mother, with the knowledge of what it will really mean to betray them.

I briefly allow the thought of what could have been if Al and I hadn't been careful that night. Not for the first time I thank some unknown deity that we used protection. At least we don't have to look behind that door.

My phone pings. I roll over to see a message from Al. *Please call me. I need to say something.*

Fear flares up inside me. What if, after thinking over my confession about Junie, he's realised that he can't let a wrong go unpunished? If we all forgave our loved ones for breaking the law, where the hell would that leave society? He could get me arrested with what I've told him. Before I've had a chance to do anything. I can feel the beat of my heart like someone knocking on my ribcage from within. They're increasing some of my medication because it's stopped working as well. The doctors call it 'optimising' which feels like a strained, enforced positivity.

Then I hear the snap of the letterbox.

I sit up sharply, my vision swimming. Crawling from bed, I squint down from the top of the stairs and I see it sitting on our woven doormat. A letter with the test-centre logo, just under a leaflet for a window cleaner. Light-headed, I grip the banister and start my careful descent. Halfway down, Justin calls to me from the kitchen.

'Liv, that you? D'you want to eat? I've done some more pasta. Can make you a salad too?'

I freeze. 'Yes, please. Lovely!' I call, trying to not sound out of breath.

'Do you need a hand?' I can hear him approaching down the hall. The soft scuff of his slippers on the floorboards.

'No. No. It's okay,' I start.

He reaches the stairs and looks up at me. My eyes dart to the doormat but I drag them back. My knucklebones gleam white as I grip the banister rail.

'Are you alright?' His voice is laced with concern.

'Fine, fine. Just took the stairs a bit fast,' I say, waving him away.

'Please be careful, don't push yourself.' He gives me his grave General Practitioner look and I drop my eyes as if contrite. When

I look up, he's glancing at the post on the mat. Before I can think of a reason to stop him, he's gone towards the door.

'Hey!' I call lightly. 'I was going to get my post.' I pull a disappointed face. 'Light exercise and all that. Doctor's orders.' I salute jokily.

Justin straightens up, a letter in his hand. He holds up his other hand in surrender.

'These are for me,' he says, waving some envelopes. 'I won't touch yours. No sprinting though.'

I flash him a smile. 'Yes, Doctor. Could you bung the kettle on for me?'

He nods and turns back to the kitchen with his post. After I hear the click of the door and the hissing of the kettle, I let out a shaky breath before creeping over and snatching up the letter. In the safety of the living room, I tear it open.

Scanning down the results, I gloss through the text for the key information, the tissue type. HLA markers, the combination of proteins telling me how compatible each sample of blood might be with my body. The paper quivers in my hand. I blink again and again and again as I try to understand what I'm seeing. I wish I could ask Justin to verify what is written in bold type before me. That, except for one, the samples are all a tissue match.

Five matches.

In none of my fantasising did I imagine this. I thought I would be lucky – if I can even use that word – to find just one. That my choice would be whether or not I could ever bring myself to take action.

Whether I can decide that I deserve to live more than someone else.

I scan each result for a name, looking for who I can cross off the list. I reach a name I don't recognise, Ms Alba Perez. Not a tissue match. My stomach drops. Only one of the strangers is compatible. If only one of the strangers is compatible, that means that each of the four people I do know – Rebecca, Dan, Irene and Steph – is a full match.

Sitting down on the sofa, I can hear Amir's words ring in my ears; the next heart to materialise should be assigned to me. Then the doctor's words from my appointment; how the end of this road will leave me in a dimly lit ward, too ill to hold my own baby.

Don't pretend your mind hasn't gone down this path already.

Then I am up, crossing the room to the writing desk that was my granny's and digging out the notebook where I write out shopping lists and things I need to do. It doesn't mean anything. It's just to help process the chaos in my head. Lists have always helped me organise my thoughts. A diligent attention to detail which made me a good lawyer, while it lasted. The pen shudders in my hand as I write out the names one by one. When I get to Steph's, I can't even bring myself to write it down. She might be a match, but she cannot *ever* be on this list. So, I write out the four remaining names: the stranger – a man called Michael Kendall, Irene, Rebecca and Dan. Then I stop and stare at them. What on earth do I write next? Their virtues and vices? Pros and Cons? How they are deserving or undeserving? How would I even know? How would I begin to decide whose life is worth the least? I don't even know one of them.

I pull out my phone. With the same frenzied energy I Google each of the names, scouring their online lives for clues. There's hardly anything useful. Irene's search shows nothing. Dan's that he's run a marathon for charity. Rebecca's LinkedIn tells me where she went to university and how long she's been employed. I flick over to socials; Irene's name doesn't show up, Rebecca's only got a long-dormant Facebook page. I trawl for anything about Michael Kendall, but there are several profiles matching his name and all are set to private. Dan's are too. Then I stop and frantically clear my search history. Slam down my phone, revolted with myself.

Max and Justin are literally next door.

Even if I could pick a candidate, how on earth would I even do it? I've watched my fair share of true crime shows. I know covering your tracks is a fine art. It would have to seem like an accident. Something innocent, causing minimal damage to the body. Is it even possible? Do I have the guts to find out? I swallow. Simply entertaining these thoughts with my family down the hall makes me feel sick.

All of a sudden there's a cry from the kitchen. I recognise the rising swell of Max's wail instantly. Strength washes through me as if from some supernatural force; my body responding to his distress of its own accord. I'm in the kitchen before Justin.

'I only left him for a minute,' he says quickly.

'It's okay,' I say, pressing Max's tear-drenched cheek to my shoulder. He's banged his head on the cupboard and there's a faint red welt rising on his forehead.

I rock and hum and bob my legs, swaying him gently as I walk around the room, calming the hiccupping sobs wracking his tiny body. As soon as he's in my arms, his heaving chest starts to slow and the sobs turn to sighs. I rest my chin against his head and he presses into me, as though he wants to fuse our two forms back together. As I stand here with my precious, fragile family, at the dawn of a new year, on what should just be any other Saturday afternoon, I realise I've set something in motion and I don't know if I can stop it now.

I think about the letter in my pocket. About the list of names scribbled in my notebook. Four people that, should they meet with an accident, could give me my life back.

What if waiting, like a good girl, a patient girl, a good patient, isn't enough?

20

All I can glean from Michael Kendall's NHS patient profile is his age and that he must be in good health because he rarely visits the GP. Once Brian has gone to get his sandwich, I leave a halting voicemail telling Michael he is due a blood-pressure check. When he calls back to say it's a mistake, I almost drop the phone. Thinking on my feet I tell him he needs to come into the surgery, just in case. He sighs in frustration but agrees to pop by that afternoon; he doesn't live far away. For the next few hours I jump every time the door opens, scrutinising the faces of every man who comes in for an appointment. Could this be him?

Eventually, just as my shift is finishing and I'm giving up hope, the door clangs. A man in his late forties, with salt-and-pepper grey at his temples, strides in. He has a friendly face, though it is currently concertinaed into a frown.

'Hi, I'm Mike? Kendall.'

My hands clench.

'Yes, hi, Mr Kendall. I'm really sorry about the confusion. I wonder if you might just take your blood pressure now with our machine over there? Then I can make sure everything's correct on the system. It won't take long.'

It's the only thing I can think of to keep him here. He shifts his weight and checks his watch, clearly irritated but too polite to voice it.

'Alright.'

He sits by the blood-pressure machine and squints at the faded laminated sign before pulling up his sleeve. As he waits for the plastic cuff to contract around his arm, he looks around the room, one leg juddering impatiently. I have to force myself not to stare at him. When he comes over with the result, I ask him to fill out a form with his name and address. As he picks up the pen I see there's no wedding ring on his finger and feel a flutter of relief. During our brief exchange I try desperately to glean what kind of person he is. What his impatience might mean. Is he a pillar of the community? A nightmare neighbour? Has he done things he's not proud of? Things he regrets, things he ought to pay for?

Would he deserve it?

He hands back the form before saying a clipped goodbye. It was too brief. I've barely had a glimpse of him. I hurriedly search his address. It's about a ten-minute bus ride away. That's the limit of my energy levels. Following a stranger home is verging on psychopathic, but I have to know more about him. Anything.

As I leave the surgery, I call Dad to tell him I need to pick up a few things on the way, so could Max stay at his for another hour.

''Course, Olive. Just take it easy, alright? No heavy lifting.'

I make my promises and message Justin saying Dad will drive Max and me home. Then, before I can change my mind, I set off.

Mike Kendall lives in a narrow, terraced house not unlike ours, on one of the many suburban roads in the borough. Some houses on his street still have their festive decorations up, though it's now well into January. Junie's face appears in my mind. The warmth on her face as we raised our glasses together over Christmas lunch. The gratitude. Emotion catches my throat. Can I really consider this?

You're damned in any case.

I walk slowly along the road, wishing I had Max in his pram as an ironclad excuse for this nervous pacing. There's no sign of Mike and only a faint light on in the back of his house; he might not even be home. I feel deranged going back and forth, keeping my scarf pulled up around my face in case he emerges. I glance at my watch. It's 5.30 p.m. I need to get back soon before Dad starts to worry. Enough. I'm about to turn for the bus, wondering how I'll find an opportunity to come back here, when the door to Mike's house opens. He comes out with a coat on and a football scarf flung around his neck. My pulse thumps out of time as I fall into step a few metres behind him. He nods at a neighbour as they come out to their wheelie bins. So he's known to people, civil, perhaps even friendly.

He ducks into a corner shop and re-emerges with a blue plastic bag which looks like it contains a can of beer and some crisps. Preparing for a night with his mates watching the game? Or just a lonely film night at home? I'm starting to form the picture of an unremarkable sort of man who lives alone, has his simple pursuits. Probably well enough loved by a family but no one nearby. Though the thought makes me shudder, I let myself play along with this image of someone who the world wouldn't miss a whole lot.

He stops abruptly to cross the road and I turn away instinctively, fearful he might see me. He's sped up, reading something on his phone as he walks. All the cars which pass seem to be family estates or hatchbacks; after-school pickups. I look at the houses, my old habit of peering into the windows rearing up. It's a decent area. Quiet. Not somewhere people get murdered.

Suddenly, I look up and Mike is gone.

I panic. Stop, glance around. There are no houses on the side of the road he was on. Just a school. I double back. Walk past the iron gates with their intercom system. Through the barrier I can see a few figures in the playground. I freeze. One of them is Mike. He is talking to a woman wearing a cardigan who has a distinctly teacherly air. Behind them, the doors to the school burst open. Two girls tear out into the playground hooting with delight. They throw themselves at him.

At their dad.

He bends down and pulls out some fruit snacks from his plastic bag. The girls cheer. Squabble over who gets which. The older looks about five, the younger must be in the nursery, she can't be much older than three. Mike produces two juice cartons which they tear open thirstily. Finally he takes out a can for himself. Flicks open the ring pull. As he stands up and turns to the light I see the label. Red Bull. Much-needed energy for an evening with his daughters.

As they approach, snippets of their conversation drift across the playground.

'Have you had a good week with Mum?'

The older girl nods as the younger one beckons him over. She reaches up and 'takes his nose' with her hand – enclosing her thumb in her fist and sticking out her tongue. She yells gleefully and runs off as he pretends to chase her.

'No, no, not my nose! I need that for smelling!'

They're coming towards me. I turn away, moving as fast as my heart will let me as I head back up the road.

'Oh, my God,' I whisper under my breath.

I take a few gulping breaths to slow my pulse. He is divorced. These are his two young children. If I hadn't followed him, I'd have assumed he lived alone. I wouldn't have known. The horror of it bubbles in my blood.

How close I might have come to destroying the lives of two children, on a hunch.

As I walk back towards the bus stop to Dad's house, it hits me. I will never know the full picture of a stranger's life. It would be so much easier to consider this with someone I know nothing about. Not to have to witness the collateral, their friends, their families, their responsibilities, but I can't. Not after what I did to Junie. I *have* to know the full extent of the damage this deal with the devil would inflict. Most of all, I have to be totally sure that no children would lose out in my fight for survival.

With a thick, black pen I score Mike's name from the list in my notebook with such vigour that it's barely visible. I stare at the other names. My crude columns of Pros and Cons. Now there are only three left.

Irene, Rebecca or Dan. Three people. Three chances.

With an acquaintance, I could find out everything. I could be totally sure of what damage I'd be doing. If, somehow, I can bring myself to go through with this, then it would have to be one of them. If I could ever work out how the hell to choose. I swallow as my eyes jump down the names. The candidates. The pragmatist in me says Irene. She's the oldest, with the least family, which surely makes her the fairest option.

If you're going to all this effort, make it worthwhile. There are four matches left, not three. Choose the youngest.

I stiffen. No. I could never... I won't even write Steph's name down. I shove the notebook back into my bag and stare out at the embers of the day. People commuting home, dreaming of takeaways and Netflix and another glass of the wine. I squeeze my eyes tight shut. How did I even get here? On the way home from stalking a stranger. Weighing up in my mind if I could *kill* someone? It's as if all this is happening to someone else and I'm in an audience behind the cameras, jeering and cheering. Could I actually do this? If it came to it, could I ever take a life to save my own?

21

The question will not leave me alone. It seems to haunt every day. Lingering in the corner of the waiting room at work when an anxious three-year-old boy in for his MMR booster holds fast to his mother's hand. On walks in the park when I see young parents swinging their toddlers effortlessly up on their shoulders. In next door's garden when a nest is violently dismantled by a storm, the birds clinging desperately to the branches beside it, squawking in distress. In the morning there is nothing of it left. Life and death in discord.

I throw myself into something positive. Justin's fiftieth birthday is at the end of January. He hates a big fuss, but I talk him into having a small gathering. Still low key, but a marking of the occasion. He acquiesced faster than I expected. We both know the subtext of why. Billie jumps at the chance to help organise, taking on the food, with Nadia volunteering the music (an offer accepted with caveats), and Sinead, the decor. I make them promise to keep things simple, but I realise they need this too; a chance for us all to get together in happy circumstances.

One afternoon, I tuck Max into his pram and head for the bakery to order Justin's cake. Billie's meeting us there for coffee and a pastry, our monthly ritual. Max is mesmerised by the outdoors, eyes wide as the sky offers up its unending delights. Squirrels darting across branches, birds swooping overhead. These brief walks work for us both: he gets to see things he has never seen before, while I get room to think. The slow, rhythmic pounding of the streets a metronome accompaniment to the list running over and over in my head. The awful choice in front of me.

As I wrestle the pram into the bakery, the door jingles and Billie looks up from a table by the window. It's only when I glance up again that I realise she's not alone. Al is sitting next to her. My grip tightens on the pram handle. We've not spoken since I saw him. Since I told him everything. Almost everything. I feel my face flush hot. I didn't reply to his text, instead I buried my head in the sand, and now he's here and I've got no idea what he'll say. Billie springs up to give me a hug and strokes Max's cheek.

'I invited Ally too, like old times!' she says brightly, oblivious to the atmosphere.

'Great,' I say quickly.

As soon as she's at the counter ordering me a drink, I look at Al with pleading eyes. *Don't bring it up again, not here.* He leans forward.

'Livi, I'm sorry to ambush you like this,' he mutters. 'I just… I wanted to say, I'm sorry for everything you're going through. I'm here and I want to help. With anything. Whatever you need.'

He holds my gaze and inside that look is another message saying something deeper, something unsayable. It says: *I will stand by you*. Despite everything I've told him.

'Thank you,' I whisper.

Then I lift Max from the pram and hold him out. A peace offering. When the baby sees it's a new person, he wriggles and kicks his legs excitedly. Al's expression melts. He takes Max from me confidently. An uncle twice over, he's done his time around babies and it shows.

As I sit there, watching my two best friends play with my son, my thoughts turn to the future. These two people I hope will be role models to Max; Billie's his godmother, and Al is as close to a godfather as I could wish for him. If I don't make it, if Max is left to navigate the world without me, it will be them who keep me alive to him. I picture Billie taking him to the cinema with the twins to see the kinds of superhero movies or neon-lit animations that Justin wouldn't be able to stomach. Al taking him to water parks or Go Ape; adventurous days out when Justin's age starts to make itself felt.

I blink back the sharp pain of imagining Max's future without me in it; trying to cling on to the scant comfort of my friends' presence in his life. I wish there was some simple solution to my situation. Some eject button I could press which would conjure up a new heart, without me even having to consider going to such wildly extreme lengths. And then I hear my mother's voice again.

You can find anything if you know where to look.

The next day I'm sitting on the faded carpet of our local library while one of the librarians sings an energetic 'Row, Row, Row Your Boat' in a cracked baritone. Max is in my lap, utterly entranced, but my eyes keep drifting back through the hushed atrium to the everyday tableau beyond the glass doors. A man with two boys choosing some new story books. An elderly woman picking out her next read. A man in his fifties squinting at a computer.

A bank of anonymous computers.

Seven more nursery rhymes later, we're released. I try to look busy packing our things into the pram. Usually I make an effort to smile at the other parents and grandparents, grateful for the relative normality of sharing teething troubles and sympathy about terrible nights' sleep. There are one or two mums I've struck up a loose companionship with, but today I avert my eyes. I push through the doors, ignoring the friendly smile of the librarian, my eyes tunnel-visioned on the bank of computers. I sit down awkwardly, posting Max's dangling legs between mine, and dig out a bottle for him as I try to interpret the instructions on the faded paper by the monitor.

With one hand I tap in the username to login while the other holds Max's bottle. As he gulps contentedly, I open up a search engine before glancing around. I've probably only got ten minutes before Max grows restless. Shifting closer so that my head blocks the screen from people behind me, I stare at the search bar. All the mad thoughts I've been keeping at bay start to pour out. The question *who* has preoccupied me so much, I've hardly given any time to thinking about *how*. How I could even pull this off. An accident that would put someone in a coma but keep their body functioning. A fall? A car crash? A serious head injury? The irony doesn't escape me that the perfect person to ask, the person closest to me with an intimate knowledge of the human body, is my husband.

My thoughts race on to new dark, desperate places. Maybe I don't have to do it myself? Maybe I can... find someone else, somehow? Put out a contract. Pay someone else to go to hell on my behalf. You hear stories about those things being arranged on the dark web. I throw a look over my shoulder. The librarian is occupied with a queue of pensioners and the remaining Rhyme Time families are still causing enough chaos for me to be of no interest.

I click open an incognito window and then, with a clumsy finger, I type 'accessing the dark web' into the search bar. The results talk about a Tor Browser which will cover my tracks as I ask the questions I never thought I'd need to ask. For a minute the insanity of the situation hits me. As other people browse our local library for their next bedtime read, thinking about what to make for dinner or if there's enough milk in the fridge, I'm sitting here, with my baby on my lap, asking an anonymous computer to help me commit a murder.

Another thought springs out from deep in the worst places within me. Maybe I don't need to kill anyone at all? Can't you buy anything on the dark web? Even a heart? That would put my list to bed. I wouldn't need to do anything other than find the money...

'Liv?'

I frantically click the X on the search engine. It's one of the mums from Rhyme Time. I haven't seen her for a few weeks, since before Christmas. Before Junie.

'H-hi,' I splutter, almost dropping Max's bottle as I half-stand up.

'Good to see you!' she says, smiling warmly. 'Hi, Max!'

In my panic I've totally forgotten her name.

'How was Christmas? Feels like ages ago!' she says. 'We haven't made it out to Rhyme Time since last year, this one's been on a non-stop carnival of germs.' She grins, flicking the cowlick curl dangling over her little girl's forehead.

'Oh, poor you!' I say, jiggling Max as he starts to wriggle. I dart a look back at the computer screen to check I closed the window but it's still there. Shit. I try to nod and make the right kind of vague comments about being tired, but Christmas being good.

'Wow, he got his first teeth!' The other mother is beaming at Max who is grinning gummily back.

'Right, yes! Just last week,' I say, trying to unearth my 'proud mother' voice from beneath 'freaking the hell out'.

I straighten up, sweating in my coat in the heat of the library, pinning my cheeks into a friendly smile, hoping she can't read anything untoward on my face. Finally, she peels off, waving goodbye to us. As she goes through the doors, she throws an unconscious glance back over her shoulder. Like she couldn't help but look at me again. It's a look which makes me sit back down. Because it's not suspicion I see in her eyes. It's sympathy.

From that one unconscious glance, I can tell that since she last saw me a few weeks ago, I've begun to look visibly worse.

On the way home Max starts to fuss as we struggle across the leaf-smeared pavements. Our street feels miles away and my legs are leaden, so I walk at half-speed. I've pushed myself too hard today. I can hardly believe the mental spiral I've been down over the last few hours. Even if I could ever work out how the hell to find a heart on the dark web, I'd have no idea where it came from or if it would be a full match. There would be no way to know what suffering led to its sale. A kidney is one thing, but a heart would sentence another stranger to death. Someone I know nothing about. If I'm going to do this, then I owe it to my son and my conscience to do it myself.

It's got to be one of the people on my list.

Responsibly sourced. How ethical of you.

When I look up, I realise I've been lost in these thoughts and haven't taken the usual route home. Instead, I'm on Oakfield Road. As I trudge towards the crossing which leads back to our house, I realise I'm approaching number 88. Emily and Dan's house. I pause, staring at their sky-blue door with its fancy antique brass hare knocker. Wide bay windows peer out from behind a hedge of holly, its red berries offensively cheery. Then the door swings open. I hesitate, my knuckles tightening on the handle of the pram. Please don't be him.

A flick of hair, a classic camel trench coat. Emily dances out on the balls of her feet, like an off-duty ballerina. I throw a look up to the sky in thanks. As she closes the front door, I glimpse a tasteful panelled hallway with exposed floorboards, beyond it a kitchen island, bi-folding doors. A home office at the end of the garden. The image of the middle-class dream.

When she joins the street in front of me, we do an awkward pavement dance.

'Oh, wow… Emily? Hi!'

'Hi?' she falters. The note of a question tells me she hasn't placed me.

'You went to Bristol, right?' I prompt.

'Yes… Oh my gosh, yes! I thought you looked familiar.'

'Liv,' I say, pressing a hand to my chest. 'From the year above. I saw you at the blood drive.'

'Liv!' Emily rushes to finish my sentence as if my name had been at the tip of her tongue. 'That's right!'

'Thanks so much for coming. My husband's a GP locally so we organise one every year.'

'Oh, of course. My aunt is a haemophiliac so I donate whenever I can.'

I smile tightly, put to shame by her altruism. 'You were big into tennis at uni, right?'

She rolls her eyes. 'Well, "was" is the key word. I injured my ankle and I've hardly played since. To be honest, I think the reality of life as a professional was probably a far cry from the fantasy anyway.'

She has a warm, easy manner, with bright pale-green eyes above freckled cheeks flushed pink in the brisk winter wind. As she grins down at Max, all I can think is how healthy she looks. Vital. He gives her one of his most charming smiles as she asks all the usual questions.

'So, did you just move here?' I say, trying to sound casual.

'Yes, the end of last year. We were West before, but I wanted to be closer to my parents. They're in Hertfordshire,' she explains.

I let her continue for a few minutes, leaning on the pram as if I have all the time in the world, nodding and smiling. Eventually my legs start to tremble and my shoes feel tight, a sign I've been on my feet too long. I really need to get home. All I've achieved is finding a reason to complicate keeping Dan's name on my list; his lovely fiancée, brimming with life.

'Well, it's so nice to be neighbours,' I say quickly.

Then, as I'm turning the pram around, an idea strikes me. Maybe Justin's party is an opportunity. Rebecca will be there with Amir. I can knock on Irene's door, or post an invite in the letterbox. That just leaves Dan. The close call with Michael has shaken me. I can't just arbitrarily sentence someone to death, I *must* find out more about them. This is a chance to compare them alongside each other in one room. A twisted audition process for a role no one would want to win. Before I can think twice, I blurt out an invitation.

'We're having a birthday party for my husband, Justin, at ours on Saturday afternoon. There's a few old Bristolians coming. We'd love to have you both!'

Emily seems genuinely touched. 'Oh, how fun! It's always rough on the other side of Christmas, isn't it, when all the parties are done? We'll be there. I'd love to meet some more local people; it's a nightmare getting my lot to leave West London.'

She grins and rolls her eyes. We exchange numbers and, in a daze, I send her our address. When I turn away, the smile drops from my lips like melting ice.

22

The next morning, through the crack in our bedroom door, I see Justin sitting on my side of the bed, gazing at something in his hands. It's the framed photo of us bringing Max home from the hospital. Panic flares in my chest. If he opens it and finds the laboratory results hidden inside, I'll have a lot of explaining to do. In the hallway I cough. Justin startles, replacing the photo frame, as if he's been caught doing something he shouldn't. His expression sticks in my mind. He was staring so hard at the photo, it looked like he wanted to fall into the image, back to the time when our lives were easy and the future looked bright.

After Justin has left for work and before Dad arrives, I'm so distracted by the close call this morning that while I'm performing the tense task of clipping Max's tiny nails, I manage to nick his skin. The cut bleeds copiously, red and bright, like a vein has opened. Max wails in shock, betrayal. I feel faint. The sound of his inconsolable sobs seems to burn my soul. I try to stay calm. It's just a tiny cut that will heal by tomorrow; such is the miracle of babies' pearlescent, regenerative skin. I just need to find some antiseptic at the chemist's. I can manage that. It's only a short walk down to the high street. I'll go slowly. Part of me needs to do this. To prove I am still capable of looking after my baby.

As I'm pulling the front door shut, the bassinet fixture on the pram slopes unsteadily forwards. The weight of Max's head is pulling it down. He is too heavy for it. We need to switch to the stroller-seat fixture where he'll be sitting up, able to see the world. I've been putting this off. Every milestone seems to creep up overnight. One day it's on the horizon, the next we wake up to it. He is growing so fast it both delights and horrifies me.

There's no way I have the strength to go up into the attic for the other fixture. I'll have to wait till Dad arrives. But when I pat my pockets, I realise in my rush to get out of the house, I've forgotten my keys. I can picture them sitting on the side table in the hall. A wave of exhaustion rolls over me. I feel stretched so thin; overwhelmed and underslept. I can't push Max around the streets with the pram like this, blood covering his hand, but I can't carry him either. Drops of rain start to hit his face and I realise I've forgotten the rain cover too. I'm sitting on the wall by our front gate, tears brimming, when Irene and her dog stride up the road. Oh, no, please, not now. Not when I can barely think, with Max screaming inside the pram. I turn away, trying to hide my face.

'He's going to get wet like that.' Irene can't help herself.

'I know.' I half-turn, wiping my cheeks. 'I've forgotten my keys. Inside.' I point hopelessly at my front door. 'I was just going to the chemist's for some Savlon.'

Irene pales. She clucks at Florrie, pulling the dog closer as if my misery is infectious. She peers over the side of the bassinet and sees Max's red-tinged fingers. Her face betrays a disapproval I can't unsee. Judgement. She has no sympathy because I asked for all this; no one forced me to procreate. Perhaps my mother would have thought the same.

'I see. Right,' Irene says. 'Well, I suppose you'd better come with us.'

She turns around abruptly and marches back towards her own front door. I blink at her brusqueness, not totally sure I heard her right. With her key held to her door, Irene turns.

'Come on then. Before he catches his death.'

'Oh. Thank you,' I say.

My only other option is pushing Max around in the rainy streets, his head sloping dangerously towards the ground, until Dad arrives. So, before I can change my mind, I follow her in.

I walk past her house almost every day; it's right next door. Most days I don't even notice, but today I look at it in a new light. Inside, the baby falls quiet in this new, dank world, taking in the faded brown wallpaper, coffee-coloured carpets, the seventies gas fireplace. The walls are barren apart from two faded landscapes of an unremarkable rural view. I am surprised when the heater is *tick-tick-ticked* on, the red bars starting to glow, mesmerising Max. I was expecting a more miserly welcome. There's a single framed photograph on the mantelpiece of a dyspeptic-looking man in a navy overcoat, staring at the camera as if it has offended him. I'm wiping my cheeks as Irene returns, holding out a cup on a saucer. It's only half-full of weak tea.

'Thank you,' I say. 'I shouldn't stay long, I do need to get some antiseptic for his cut.'

I fall quiet because Irene has stood up. She leaves the room without a word, returning to thrust a tube of Savlon at me.

'Oh,' I say, struggling to conceal my surprise. 'Thank you... That's – that's very helpful.' Max whimpers as I tenderly wipe the antiseptic over his finger. 'He won't be any trouble. He's always happier in new places. Gets bored stuck at home with me.'

Now that Max has stopped crying, I'm calmer. He's looking with interest at the glowing fireplace. Finding myself here, inside her house, her life, I realise I have the chance to find out more about her. Irene isn't known for her conversation, but if I could just look around... Thinking like this with her standing right across the room makes me want to run right back outside.

Opportunity doesn't knock twice.

'Could I use your bathroom?'

'Upstairs on the left.'

I nod, but as I leave the room Max's mouth curves down and the tears return. I hurry back over to him.

'Sorry, his separation anxiety is starting,' I explain, taking him into my arms. I'm trying not to carry him as much as before, while I get more tired and he gets heavier, but he's noticing. He's reaching for me more and more. I bet Irene is thinking I'm a soft touch, that I need to keep to my boundaries with him or he'll turn into a nightmare toddler, but I don't care. He's so small that withholding my comfort feels sadistic. My pulse rate rises uncomfortably as I pad carefully up the stairs, so I slow down. One step at a time and deep breaths.

Though it's just next door, her house is narrower than ours, with lower ceilings and without the pitched roof. Trying to ignore how ugly it feels, I peek gingerly around the doors standing ajar along the landing. The spare bedroom is devoid of signs of life. Another anodyne print sits on the wall, a faded watercolour of a bridge over a river in a cobbled town. The bed is made, a faint trace of dust across the plaid blanket. The bathroom is just as minimal. No spare colourful toothbrushes or plastic steps to help someone small reach the sink. No mouldering bath toys stuffed in the cupboard. Clinks from the kitchen tell me I just have time to look inside her bedroom, steeling myself for this deeper invasion of privacy. Beige walls and white bedlinen hemmed with embroidered flowers, neatly made. The whole house is so quiet, I feel a prickle of sympathy for her. Then I see something that makes me put a hand over my mouth. On the floor at the foot of her bed there's a fraying wicker basket with a faded cushion dusted with fur. A patch of the carpet is worn where paws scratch during the night. Oh, no. The dog. Who would take the dog?

I descend the stairs, clutching Max tight to my hip. He's started to lurch around which Dad calls 'salmoning'. Now I endure daily imaginings of his little body flinging itself from my weak arms and over the banister. Soon the risk of me dropping him will be too high. I hold him closer. Not yet.

Irene is sitting in an armchair in the living room holding her teacup and saucer, back headmistress-straight. My pulse throbs as I sit down opposite her, my breathing heavy. I shouldn't have carried Max upstairs. He whines again as I try to put him down and lunges for my shoulder, mouth agape. One cheek is flushed red.

'Teething, is he?'

I nod, surprised. His cheek is a giveaway to other parents, but as far as I know Irene has no children in her life. 'The first two came through the other week. Just the first tiny rice grains, but it must hurt.'

'Have you tried offering him a frozen washcloth to chew?'

I look up at her as Florrie fusses around my ankles. 'Oh. No. I don't know that one. Thanks. How did you—'

'I was a midwife,' Irene mutters, as if I might not hear. 'A long time ago. Before I got married.'

My stomach drops. A midwife. I would never have guessed. However remote she may now seem, she's helped to bring life into the world. I swallow the revelation. Though I scan the room warily for any other clues which might derail me, the house gives nothing else away.

Irene shoots another glance at the baby.

'Do you want to hold him?' I say. It feels terrible to use Max as bait, but it might get her to open up.

'Oh, no, no.' She shakes her head vigorously. 'Had my fair share.' But the glances don't let up.

'Do you have any children in your family?' I venture, awkwardly. I'm not naturally outgoing like Nads and Billie. It's why I love their company so much; they fill the air with noise so I don't have to. I can just enjoy the atmosphere.

'My brother has a grandchild,' Irene says stiffly.

'Your great-niece or -nephew then?'

'I suppose.'

I pause at her unusual phrasing.

'They live in Australia,' she says, by way of justification. 'I've never met their children. We don't... get along.'

I nod, stumped for any way to respond. So there is a family, of sorts. But not one that will miss her. The baldness of the thought makes me wince. All of a sudden, this bland living room feels too claustrophobic and I start to get to my feet, about to make our excuses. Then something else occurs to me.

No one knows you're here.

My movements slow. No one saw us entering. Thoughts start to race in my head. There would be nothing to connect me to her, would there? Just my DNA on her teacup, my fingerprints in her bathroom. I could clean them off. Make an anonymous call from a neighbour who heard a crash. An accident.

My hands shake, sending a trill of alarm through the porcelain saucer. The dog's ears flick towards me, as if she can hear what I'm thinking. Inside my chest my heart hums, high on a growing tidal wave of adrenaline. But is this as good a chance as I may ever get? Here. Right now? I can hear the crunch of the fall. Wince at the sickening crack of skull on wood. Feel the utter horror at the slow wet trickle of thick blood flowing.

'Are you alright?' Irene is looking at me oddly. The colour must have drained from my cheeks.

'Fine, fine,' I stammer. 'I'll just put him in the pram... he's sleepy.'

Hold it together, I berate myself as I tuck Max in, my hands shaking. His eyelids droop in the toasty heat. I straighten up slowly, my mind still twisting in knots, playing for more time. Could I...?

'Good,' Irene says, briskly, brushing invisible dust from her skirt. 'I'm glad to get your full attention.'

The words make me freeze. It sounds like a criticism.

'Sit,' she gestures.

I wobble back to the armchair. She can't know what I'm considering, there's no way... We face one another in stilted silence and I wipe the sweat from my palms onto the faded fabric.

'So, I have something to say to you.' Irene's sharp eyes are fixed on me with a new focus. A proper scrutiny. 'Don't worry, I won't bite.' A sparkle of self-awareness. 'I wanted to ask something... of you and your husband.'

I start to blink, my eyes dry from staring. She takes my silence for assent.

'I am putting my affairs in order. A vital spring cleaning, if you will.' She clears her throat, and I can see her eyes jump to the man's photograph on the mantelpiece. It must be her late husband.

'I remember Dr Hargreaves...' she only calls Justin that, '... likes dogs. Had some when he was growing up, I believe.'

'That's right.'

Justin's father kept lurchers, tightly disciplined gun dogs that stood trembling at his heel, hungry for commands. The kind of dog that suited his temperament. Justin's childhood rebellion was to feed them scraps secreted from his dinner when his father wasn't looking. I think the dogs kept him company for much of his youth after his mother died.

'Well, I am looking for someone to take Florrie. In the event of...' Irene's voice tails off. She clicks her fingers and the dog jumps up and pads over, placing her muzzle on Irene's knee.

'Oh.' My mouth falls open in surprise.

'You do like dogs? Florrie seems fond of you.'

I've never noticed anything that suggests this might be true, but I sense a faint flame of vulnerability behind Irene's words. She's watching me intently, a fervent need to know that her last and only loved one will be taken care of after she's gone. A feeling I recognise all too well.

'Right. Of course... I'll... talk to Justin. But, yes, I'm sure we... we could.'

Irene nods, patting Florrie's head, as if she'd known I would agree. As if it was only right and proper that I should.

'Right. Good. I'm glad to clear that one up.'

The fact she has asked us, near strangers, to take on what means the most to her in life, hits me like a blow to the chest. Sympathy rises in a surge which forces me to my feet. Then my phone buzzes with a text. Dad's around the corner.

'I should go. You've been so kind, but my dad is nearly here.'

Irene barely waves as she shuts the door behind me. Walking down her front path, I realise I forgot to invite her to Justin's party, but I can't bear to turn around and knock again after what she's asked.

In the days before the party Max is more fretful than I've known him. It's as though he has picked up on my adrenaline, like the buzz is moving through his blood too. I've been distracted, leaving meals abandoned, sentences half-finished. Justin thinks it's because I am throwing my all into making the event a success.

He has no idea what's really going on in my head.

On the morning itself, I'm walking back from the bakery. Safely stowed on the pram shelf is the cake with Justin's name iced on it, an extravagance we can't really afford but I've impulsively bought anyway. People will start arriving in a few hours and I can't shake off a lingering feeling of apprehension. Doubts are rearing up in me.

Now that I've posted an invitation through Irene's door, they're all invited.

My special guests.

Can I really host them? It's so cold, so *calculated*. And can I even stand to have Dan in my house? Above all could I ever make such a cruel choice in my own home, surrounded by my family and friends?

It didn't stop you at Christmas.

There she is again, always ready to remind me of my flaws. I close my eyes, wishing it weren't true. Then Al's words from the café resound in my mind; *whatever you need*. I ache to tell him more, but I can't tell anyone this. Once those words come out of my mouth, I won't ever be able to take them back.

I'm so deep in my thoughts as I walk up the road towards our front door that it takes me a minute to notice the flashing blue lights strobing anxiously over our house.

23

A police car is parked on the street by our garden gate. The front seats are empty. I clutch the pram handle. Is it our house they're at? What's happened? Is Justin okay? Dad? I glance both ways down the road. Everything looks normal. No signs of trouble. It must be the neighbours. A stolen bike or... or a noise complaint. Do the police even come for noise complaints or is that just on TV?

Perhaps they're here for you.

My jaw tightens as I struggle up the front path with the pram. Has someone at work checked the CCTV? Was I wrong about Brian not replacing the memory drive? Or did someone see me following Mike Kendall and report strange behaviour? Follow me home too? Or can I have dropped my notebook with its incriminating list of names somewhere along the road, in my stressed, sleep-deprived state? Max isn't sleeping well and even though Justin insists on doing the night feeds, I wake up all the same. Has someone found the notebook and worked out what I'm considering?

Oh, God. What can they want?

I fumble urgently for the keys, my fingers clumsy, struggle with the lock, half mad with worry something terrible has happened, half furiously rehearsing excuses for my past behaviour. As I shove our door open and wrestle the pram into the hall, I can hear voices in the living room. I freeze. Through the crack in the door, I see two police officers sitting in the living room. Instinctively, I turn away, as if they might recognise me. As if they could read my thoughts from my face.

'Thanks for your time,' the taller officer is saying to Dad. 'It's nice to know Mrs Atkins has such good neighbours.'

I feel a jolt in my chest. The police officers look up as I appear at the doorway. Irene is sitting beside them, looking pale.

'Of course,' Dad replies.

'Is... is everything alright?' I ask quickly.

'I caught someone trying to break in last night,' Irene says brusquely.

I catch my breath. 'Oh my God. That's awful.'

'The police here were just knocking on the neighbours' doors to see if we heard anything, but I explained I wasn't here last night. Did you notice anything?' Dad asks.

'No, I don't think so... no, nothing.'

'Well, you've got the crime reference number if anything else comes up, Mrs Atkins,' says the taller officer as they both get to their feet. 'They'll be finished up dusting the door for prints shortly and out of your hair.'

Irene nods stiffly. The police smile reassuringly at me as they walk down our front path, and give Max a little wave, before heading back in through Irene's door. Conflicting emotions run through me; relief that it's nothing to do with my family, but dread that the police are standing in the house where I was just a few days ago contemplating murder.

'I'm so sorry, Irene, are you alright?'

'Perfectly. About time I got an alarm.' She rises to her feet, clicking her fingers to Florrie. 'I'll be out of your way.'

'Are you sure?' Dad says. 'You're welcome to stay on.'

'No, no, lots to sort out.'

'Well... if there's anything we can do,' I say as she opens the door. 'Will we see you—' The door shuts before I can finish asking if she's coming to the party.

I sit down on the sofa, breathing deeply, the adrenaline rush slowly abating as Dad puts Max down onto the playmat.

'Funny old fish, isn't she?' Dad says, watching through the window as Irene goes back inside her house. 'You okay, love?'

'Yeah.' I muster some conviction. 'Fine!'

'Burglars don't tend to come back,' he says softly.

'I know.' I try to smile as if that's what's going through my head.

It's not like I love the idea that people are casing the houses on our street, but the police could have been here for a much more serious reason. Or the break in could have been successful; Irene could have been hurt. The burglars could have attacked her. Killed her even.

But then your wait might have been over.

The darkness of that thought makes me grimace.

I hate thinking like this when Max is with me, even if he is the reason I do. For a brief moment I think I can see something accusatory in his gaze. You aren't really considering doing something bad, are you? he seems to say. I hesitate, pulling my top closer around my neck against an invisible breeze. I'd be doing it for you, I think. My tiny bright-eyed boy. Everything is for you.

Faint palpitations of alarm still echo through me. Stay calm. Nothing's happened. You haven't done anything.

Not yet.

Billie and Sinead arrive to set up in a whirlwind of cake boxes and paper cups. I can sense Justin stiffening at the sight of an armful of fairy lights Sinead is looping around the kitchen. He tries to distract Max so I can do the final touches to the snacks, but Max keeps twisting around to find me, screaming when I move out of sight. Amir and Rebecca are next to arrive. Rebecca loiters awkwardly, the age gap between her and my friends almost painfully apparent. Whenever I look at her, I'm reminded of the last time she was here. Christmas with Junie. I take Max back, grateful to feel my arms around him, holding his pudding-soft thighs against my hip to disguise the tremors in my hands. I can't lift a glass without liquid spilling out.

People start arriving and I crowbar a smile onto my face. Justin mans the door, greeting everyone with his standard steady handshake. When he opens it to Nadia and Oz brandishing a bottle of champagne, Oz looks a little underwhelmed at the domestic vibe. Nadia shoots him an anxious glance as she totters into the house shrugging off her coat. She drags Justin into a hug, which he endures stiffly, then waves down the hall at me.

It remains a source of sadness that my friends have never quite bonded with Justin. Nadia and he are cut from different cloth, and he doesn't understand our friendship; affection rolled up in barbs that both of us know are only spoken in jest. Sinead is polite and engaged, asking questions about his work. Billie always tries with him, but that's just the problem; the woman who likes everyone has to try.

Over Nadia's shoulder I see Al approaching behind Oz on the doorstep. My pulse quickens as I walk down the hall towards the awkward backslaps of men who don't know the right greeting. I've never worked out how Justin feels about Al. He knows we're close and respects that, but in his circle there are fewer friendships between the opposite sex. I've never told him about the weeks where Al and I were together all those years ago because there hardly seemed to be any reason. He's never been an 'ex' in my eyes, he's just Al.

'Hi.' Al stands there with his lopsided grin.

'Hi.' I'm glad he's here. That we can get back to normal.

Max coos up at him and within seconds Al is pulling silly faces and blowing raspberries on his cheek, provoking shrieks of laughter. Justin retreats to the kitchen with a restrained smile. He rarely plays so vigorously with his son and perhaps is rarely rewarded with such enthusiasm as a result. In that moment I'm struck by what it means to have had a loving father. Al's Dad, Phil, was a gregarious man with a smile that seemed to reach both ears. I can still remember the sounds of Al and Ben's laughter as he chased them around the house with his hands held out in monster claws. Justin, on the other hand, has been left with the residue of a cold-hearted father who felt children were best kept out of sight and earshot. I don't doubt Justin's adoration for Max, but it doesn't come naturally to him to be easy and open with his feelings.

We head into the living room where Dad sits talking to Sinead. He double takes when he sees Al.

'Alistair! I didn't know you were home!' He opens his arms wide as Al grins at him.

'Hi, Terry. Only just. A few weeks.'

'Well, good to have you back. I must look up your mother. It's been too long. You can blame this little mischief-maker.' He reaches over and tickles Max's neck.

The doorbell goes and Billie heads down the hall. I peer around the corner to see who it is, and, as the door swings wide, I flinch. Because on the doorstep, brandishing bags filled with bottles, is Steph.

My mouth dries. Her name was not on my list, but here she is. An uninvited guest. The last person I wanted to see today.

You believe in fate, don't you?

Billie smacks a kiss on Steph's cheek. 'You are a bloody life-saver.' She takes the bottles and spots me. 'I forgot the mixers!' she explains, rolling her eyes at herself. 'Stay for a drink, Stephy?'

Steph grins. 'Is that okay, Liv? Hi, sweetpea!' She waves at Max.

The smile feels frozen to my face. 'Of course! Yes. There's loads to eat, we need all the help we can get.'

Steph beams at me and starts to take off her coat.

Al pops his head into the hall. 'Livi, where do I find a bottle opener—' He smiles at Steph. 'Oh, sorry to interrupt. Hi!'

'Steph, Al, Al, Steph. My cousin!' Billie says over her shoulder as she heads for the kitchen.

'Nice to meet you.' Steph smiles at him. 'Better go help the taskmaster. Can I get a cuddle with the baby later, Liv?'

'Yes, totally. He's a little tired now, but when he's napped is a better bet.'

'Can't wait.'

I go over to close the door, still reeling from her arrival, but more people are turning into the gate. For a moment my mouth opens and closes, like the fish impression I do for Max. It's Emily with a bunch of flowers and a bottle of wine. Hovering behind her, looking desperate to be anywhere else, is Dan.

They actually came. I dart a look at Al, see him clock my odd expression. He'll remember Dan. Remember the bad place I was in back then, after it ended. I snap myself into action, welcoming them over the threshold.

'Emily, hi. So glad you could come.'

'Of course. So glad to be neighbours!' She thrusts the wine at me and Al swoops in and takes it. 'And hello again to this little one!'

Max gurgles merrily. Over Emily's shoulder I force myself to make eye contact with Dan. Horrified confusion mixed with suspicion is passing over his face. He must not have realised who Emily meant. Old Bristolian people, she'll have said, not knowing our shared history. Now it's too late to make an excuse. Far too late.

'Dan, hi,' I say as smoothly as I can. 'It's been a while.'

I can see thoughts racing behind his eyes. It was a million years ago, he'll be thinking. She won't bring it up. Though he's trying to look anywhere else, his gaze is drawn to Max. I catch a glimpse of his hand, the ripe veins pulsing with blood that matches mine. Pumped by a sportsman's heart. I remember that he rowed at university. From the look of his build, the local gym's ergometer still gets regular attention.

'Olivia,' he says. 'Blast from the past.'

Then he steps over the threshold into my home, as if nothing significant happened between us, and a bolt of nausea runs through me.

Al reaches out to shake Dan's hand. 'You were at Bristol, right? I was at school with Liv. Al. Used to come down to visit her a lot at uni.'

'Oh, nice,' Dan says, smiling.

I can see Al taking the measure of him: the All Saints shirt, the pointed leather shoes, the larger than necessary watch. As we squeeze past one another in the hall, Dan darts me a wary look, but I turn away. Let him worry.

'Of course I remember you!' Billie says enthusiastically, pulling Emily into a hug like a dear old friend. I'm more thankful than ever for her warmth. 'Come, kitchen, drinks!' she says herding us all down the hall.

Justin spots us and smiles at the new faces.

'This is Emily and Dan,' I say quickly. 'We were all at Bristol. You remember I said they've just moved in a few roads away?'

'That's right. Pleasure,' Justin says evenly, holding out his hand to them both. He's never succumbed to the air-kiss introduction which has caught on, as if we all wish we were as chic as the French. Dan gives him a firm handshake while Max watches on with fascination, kicking in the carrier on my chest. I'm starting to feel the weight of him.

'Good of you to have us,' Dan says with the easy megawatt smile I remember. 'And happy birthday, I believe.' He raises the beer bottle Billie has pressed into his hand in a toast to Justin.

'Thank you. So, were you on the same course?' Justin asks.

'No, I was in the year below,' Emily says. 'But you two?' She gestures at Dan and me.

Dan shakes his head, taking a swig of his beer. 'No. We just knew each other from around and about, I think. Right, Liv?' He throws me another wide grin and I nod.

'Great pad you've got here,' he says. 'Love the kitchen.' He knocks on the countertop. 'These marble? Look quite like ours, don't they, Em?'

'Um, granite, I think,' I say, looking at Justin. It suddenly feels horribly exposing to have Dan in my house, assessing my life.

'Oh, much more sensible,' Emily says brightly. 'Marble is a pig's ear to clean – so porous!'

'How are you finding North London?' Al asks conversationally as I stand awkwardly between my past and my present.

'I've been coming over this way for years,' Dan replies. 'I work in music; always got to be scouting at the small venues.'

'Like that one in Camden where Madness started?' Billie asks.

'The Dublin Castle – yeah. But more often the Shacklewell Arms. In Dalston? Further east.' He looks around, as if we ought to know it.

'I've… just got to go and speak to my dad,' I mumble. Hearing about Dan's thriving career is the last thing I want to be doing right now.

I head for the living room, trying to think of something to ask Dad, when Rebecca pushes past me along the hall.

'Excuse me,' she mutters, moving towards the door. I pause. Her leaving so soon ruins my plan. My fragile hope that, once I have them together, it will somehow become clear which of the three of them it should be.

'Not leaving already?' I ask hurriedly.

'No. Of course not,' she says, as if the very suggestion was an insult. 'I'm getting the door.'

I frown. The bell hasn't rung, but Rebecca pulls the front door open. She turns to see me watching, a smile spreading over her face. I don't understand its meaning. Until I look past her down our garden path to beyond the gate and see who is getting out of a car parked just outside.

Louise's curly blonde hair has grown longer since I last saw her. Elegant grey highlights intermingle with the gold. She is someone who doesn't feel the pressure to apply the layers of face paint that society demands of women. I may not be expecting my husband's ex-wife to turn up, but she's not the reason my heart is pounding out such a painful rhythm.

Beside her, unfurling his lanky frame from the passenger seat, is Nick.

24

Justin and I agreed it would be strange not to invite them both, so he sent Louise a message. After Nick's no show at our wedding it felt unlikely they'd pick this occasion for a reconciliation. When we didn't hear back I was relieved, Justin as well. His fiftieth birthday party wasn't the best occasion. Too public. But now here they are.

Rebecca sails onto the doorstop as if she owns the house. Holding out her arms, she embraces Louise, who looks slightly startled. Nick manages to duck the same treatment by thrusting forward his hand for her to shake.

I need to warn Justin. He isn't prepared for this. Onlookers witnessing such an uncomfortable scene is his worst nightmare. Rebecca's Cheshire Cat grin suggests she's well aware of that. Al appears down the hall and sees my expression.

'What is it?' he mutters at my side.

'That's Justin's son,' I manage to murmur back as Louise spots me. I hurriedly rearrange my face into a smile while she strides up to me. We've only met a few times over the years. If I didn't have bigger things to worry about, part of me might be intimidated by her. Wonder if Justin might want her back. She is always so calm, collected. Her presence has a levelling quality; you can tell she would never panic in an emergency. The sort of stability I wish I had.

'Olivia,' she says politely, pressing a cheek to mine. 'I'm sorry we're late. This must be the new arrival.'

I smile and adjust my grip so that Max is facing her. He gazes up at her, his little mouth hanging slightly open in that blank, disarming way he has. There is nothing like the raw, unfiltered stare of a baby.

'It's good of you to have us,' she says. 'We won't stay long.'

'I… of course… We didn't—'

She assesses my expression. 'Perhaps Rebecca forgot to pass the message on. I'm sorry not to respond formally, it's just been such a busy time. And I wasn't sure till today if…' She tails off, looking at Nick. There's an edge to her voice, a wariness about the situation.

I glance at Rebecca who is talking to Nick. Of course she 'forgot' to pass the message on. My teeth clench. Louise gestures to her son.

'Nicky, come and say hello.'

He shuffles over awkwardly, offers me a nod, his eyes drawn straight to Max. With pitch-perfect timing, Max gives him one of his deepest smiles, the kind that suggests the recipient has been approved of from on high. He chuckles as Nick offers him a finger to grab, and the tension evaporates. I forgot how useful babies are in fraught situations; one well-timed squeal can clear the air. Given that Max is Nick's half-brother, I'm relieved. I try not to stare at my stepson, to scrutinise his features searching for a fraternal resemblance. But Nick takes after Louise. Though he has the ghost of his dad's bone structure, all his strongest features are hers.

Al has disappeared from my side. I scan the crowded room. Down the hall I see him in the kitchen next to Justin, whispering in his ear. As Justin puts down his drink and makes his way through the people thronging the hallway, I thank Al silently for his quick thinking. At least Justin has a few moments to collect himself. My heart aches for him. Only I know the minutiae of his face well enough to see what he's doing as he closes the gap between us. He is pocketing his pain. Searching his mind for the right words to say to the son he hasn't seen in over three years. To her credit, Louise moves over as soon as she sees him, leans up for a chaste peck on the cheek, then brings him towards Nick. Time seems to slow down as father and son look at one another. I'm trying not to watch but my gaze is pulled to their faces like magnetic forces are at play. Louise seems nervous, the stakes as high for her as for Justin. Even Rebecca has withdrawn, finally showing an iota of tact.

The doorbell rings again. I hand Max to Billie and squeeze down the hallway, trying not to trip over the growing pile of shoes. Passing the living room, I overhear Al talking to Steph about hiking up a volcano in Indonesia. She looks captivated. As I pull the front door open, I let out a little 'Oh' of surprise. On the doorstep, clutching her handbag and Florrie's lead, is Irene.

'Irene! I'm so glad you could co—' I begin, but she cuts me off.

'It's a weekend. You could turn the music down.'

The welcome fades from my lips. 'There's not actually any music playing.'

She harrumphs and squints, as if that will make it easier for her to hear. I feel like a teenager being accused of an illicit house party.

'It's Justin's birthday,' I explain. 'I put an invite through your letterbox.'

She sniffs. 'Oh, I don't look at junk mail.'

I try to ignore her brusqueness. 'Would you like to come in?'

'No, I must get on.'

'There's plenty to eat. We can put Florrie in the garden. Justin would love to say hello. And I'm sure you could use a drink after last night?'

Billie appears at my elbow with Max who reaches out for me. 'Hello, who's this?'

'Our neighbour, Irene.'

'Lovely to meet you! Can I get you some cake?' Billie asks, and the strength of her sunbeam charm has Irene inching reluctantly forwards.

'I do have a lot to be getting on with today, but I suppose we'll stop in for a moment.' Billie guides Irene inside, prising her coat off and ushering the dog towards the garden.

I look around the guests in the living room. Emily is speaking to Rebecca and Amir. Nadia and Dan stand together, as Irene reaches for a plate at the food table. A few metres away Steph is talking to Nick which must be Billie's work, connecting the only two people in their twenties in the room.

They're here.

All four of the matches are in my house.

I'm aching to see Justin. To lean against the solidity of his body, like a tree with deep roots. He must be reeling too from seeing Nick after so long. Eventually, I spot him in the garden, staring into the gathering gloom like he does when there's too much on his mind. I slip outside, shutting the door on the chatter behind me.

'Are you okay?' I whisper, sliding my arm around his waist.

He turns, putting an arm around my shoulder. I can feel him inhale the top of my head, my hair, like we both do with the baby, his professional veneer dissolving for a moment. We get all the warmth of him, Max and I. The truth about him that no one else is trusted with. I love the deep tenderness with which he carefully feeds Max spoonfuls of puree. The soft voice he uses to hum him to sleep which no one else hears; a register exclusive to his baby. I hope today is a chance for him to repair his relationship with Nick. Because, in a way, my husband is walking around with a fractured heart, just as I am.

'Did you talk much to Nick?' I murmur.

'A little,' he says.

'It's good he came though, isn't it? A good sign.'

Justin nods. 'Perhaps.'

I want to ask him more, to understand this wound which never seems to heal, but before I can, the back door opens behind us. We both attempt to mask our surprise. Irene is stepping outside. She reaches down and pats Florrie who has rushed over to buffet her ankles. When I told Justin about Irene's unexpected request, he only smiled sadly and agreed that we would take the dog if the time came, saying nothing about it being another thing for him to worry about. Another dependant.

Irene stops in front of us. 'I'm glad I've caught you both together. I wanted to thank you for...' She nods down at Florrie who stares up at her with deep devotion.

'Of course, Irene. We're only too happy to help,' Justin says.

'Well, look,' she continues, uncomfortable in her vulnerability. 'There was something else too.' Her eyes are locked on the dog's, as though she wouldn't be able to say what she wants to if she looked up at us. 'The boy...'

'I'm sorry?' I prompt, confused.

'The baby,' she continues quickly. 'Your son.'

Justin and I blink. Where can this be going? She's barely looked at Max before now other than to criticise my parenting. Does she intend to expose me for locking myself out of the house the other day?

'In return for your kindness, I'd like to leave him some money.'

My racing thoughts grind to a halt. Irene is still staring at Florrie, as if we don't exist and she is having this conversation with the dog instead.

'W-what?' I stutter.

Could this be a trick? But she worships Justin, she wouldn't play any sort of joke on him. Irene huffs as if it doesn't need explaining.

'I have decided that I would like to leave my money to your baby. I have no family. You are the people I know the best, so I have decided that, when the time comes, the right thing to do is to give the little one a better start in life. I am aware that you are all… struggling. With the matter of your health. So, I have named him as a beneficiary in my will.'

We gape at her.

'That's… um. Irene, that's extremely generous,' Justin begins, his voice strangled by surprise.

'There's nothing for you to do,' she cuts him off. 'I don't expect anything in return. The paperwork is all underway. I'll just need his middle names and date of birth for accuracy. I thought you ought to know. Thank you for the hospitality.'

Before we can reply, she has turned back for the door, the dog trotting loyally behind her. I stare after them, stunned. I had no idea this belligerent woman spared any thought at all for us.

'I'll… I'll go and thank her,' Justin says quickly. He throws me a look of total bafflement as he heads inside.

As I stand there in the garden, in the fading light, I catch my reflection in the kitchen window. A lone, pale figure in the gathering dark. My friends and family on the other side of the glass, hands in bowls of crisps, laughing, swigging beers. They might as well be in another world. I wonder for a brief, dark moment if this is what it will look like if I don't make it. Will they all be here then, in Justin's house, dressed in black, raising a toast to me, the air thick with anguish for Max? My stomach knots.

And then it hits me.

If Irene has done what she's said, if Max's name is on her will, then, on paper, there would be a motive. A clear connection between us. A reason I might wish her dead. If for any reason her death were to be investigated as suspicious, I would be a suspect. My hands start to tremble as I watch Justin wave her off at the front door. For a second I remember being at her house, alone, considering my opportunity.

Imagine if I'd done it then. Imagine if I'd pushed her.

I cannot survive a transplant only to wind up serving a life sentence. Irene's name must come off my list.

25

Suddenly it's all too much. Steph's appearance had already thrown me, and now with Nick's arrival and Irene's bombshell, everything is in disarray. I can't collect my thoughts with all this playing out. Why the hell did I think this was a good idea? I make my excuses and take Max upstairs for a nap.

I zip him into his sleep sack, relishing the quiet of his bedroom, the gentle *shush* of the white-noise machine. I stroke the spun-sugar hairs at the back of his head, his doughball cheeks, his chubby, roly-poly legs that kick with satisfaction while he drinks milk, his tiny hands that he holds out in front of him to admire, like he's had a manicure. For a moment I wonder if my mother ever inhaled my icing sugar skin. Did she resist the pull of an elastic smile, a laugh that catches with delight at the back of the throat? Then I shake the thoughts away because they scald. Here in the soft gloom, with the sound of Max contentedly sucking his thumb, his nappies in stacks at my feet, my cold-blooded guest list seems ridiculous. I should have kept things separate, kept my home a sanctuary from all the darkness in my head.

I slip out of his room into ours and carefully extract the results letter from the photo frame on the bedside table. I look down at the list of names. Only two options remain now. Rebecca; Justin's best friend's wife, and Dan; someone I'd hoped I would never have to speak to again.

And...?

And Steph who has turned up at this party, as if the fates are speaking to me. My best friend's cousin, who I'm pretending is not on this list at all. I shudder and stuff the paper frantically back into the frame. I wish it didn't exist. I wish I didn't know about any of them. I wish my life was normal. That I was just here enjoying a carefree day, celebrating my husband's fiftieth birthday party.

You've come this far.

It's true. I've stolen medication. Stolen blood. Committed crimes to get the answers I needed. Now I have to do something with them. Don't I?

When I finally go back downstairs, I see Louise has her coat in her hand and seems to be giving Rebecca a hug. She must be leaving. I'm about to slalom through the guests to say a mature and pleasant farewell, feeling odd that we've hardly spoken, when I feel a hand on my arm.

It's Nick. His shoes and coat are already on.

'Hi… Oh, are you going too?' He nods stiffly. For a split second I see Justin at his age, hunched and awkward, only just shedding the mantle of teenagerhood. Nick has inherited both his father's height and his reserve. 'We just dropped in with a present. But I wanted to talk to you…'

He tails off, shooting a look over to where his mother is saying goodbye to Amir.

Hope swells in my chest as he leads me to the quiet of the living room where only a few guests remain. I've been longing for the chance to spend time with him, and with all the strangeness of the day, I thought I'd missed my opportunity. I have Max to thank for any brief bonding we've done. I've always secretly suspected Nick can't stand to be around us. After all, Max and I are the reason his family will never be whole again. Though he claims not to want his parents to reunite, not showing up at our wedding seemed to send a clear message to the contrary.

'Thank you for coming.' I'm fumbling my words in my eagerness to connect with him. 'It means so much to your dad. He thinks the world of you.'

Nick hesitates. He's studying my face, but I can't work out what he is looking for. Then he speaks.

'I don't really care what he thinks.' His words are abrupt. Unvarnished.

'Oh,' I say. Without any explanation from Justin about the rift between them, I'm at sea. Nick shifts his weight uncomfortably, then speaks again.

'I don't really care about anyone who hits women.'

The words pummel into me like a gunshot. There's an awful silence. I stare at him, searching his expression for some explanation to justify this lie.

'What... are you talking about?' I whisper.

Nick takes a step closer and lowers his voice. 'I didn't come here for him. I came here to see you,' he says quickly. 'Ask him about when I was eleven. Ask him about when he hit my mother.'

I gape at him.

He leans in closer. 'I'm not making it up, I saw it happen,' he continues, reading my face. 'I would have said something before your wedding, but Mum wouldn't let me. That's why I wouldn't come.'

He shoots an angry glance at his mother. She's spotted us talking and I swear I can see a glimmer of concern on her face.

'But I heard that you're not well...' Nick continues. 'And the baby... I thought you should know the truth. And no one else seems to want to tell you.'

'Nicky!' Louise is calling to him from the door. 'Have you said bye to your dad?'

Nick nods to her over my shoulder, though I know he hasn't.

'Just... take care,' he says meaningfully, eyes locked on mine.

Then he turns away and together they walk out of our house.

The rest of the evening passes in a haze. I can barely summon any more small talk, using Max time and again as an excuse to go upstairs. Nick's words reverberate on repeat in the quiet. It's nonsense. He's lying. There's no way it can be true. Mild-mannered, reliable Justin violent? No. Helping people is part of who he is. He may not talk about his previous marriage, but that's from a sense of chivalry. Besides, I may hardly know Louise but I'm sure she's not the kind of woman who would let something like that slide and just pretend it didn't happen.

Isn't she? Or have you got them both wrong?

My hands tighten on the rail of the crib. Should I tell Justin what Nick has said? How could I drop this bomb in the middle of his birthday party? And what would I even say? It sounds ridiculous enough in my head, let alone spoken aloud. I've got to ignore it. Treat it as the terrible, unforgivable lie it is.

But he sounded so certain. How can you be sure?

I try to imagine Justin hitting Louise, hitting *anyone*, but I can't even picture it. My mind rejects the image. I gaze down at Max in his crib, thumb in his mouth, sucking furiously, and a horrible new thought emerges.

What if he's not safe? What if your baby isn't safe with his father?

'No,' I whisper under my breath. 'No.'

Finally, two blurry hours later, only the loyal dregs of the party remain. Billie and her husband Tom are locked in the sloppy drunk embrace of tired parents in a corner, Rebecca stands stiffly by Amir as he chats to some of Justin's medical school friends, while Al chats to Emily and Dan. They come over to make their polite exit.

'We've got to head; it's Dan's colleague's birthday do and I forgot we double booked, but thanks so much for having us,' Emily says. 'Dan even got a number!' She laughs as he waves his phone.

'Your friend Al just wants to use me for my ticket connects,' he says with a grin. I cover my unease at him befriending Al.

'We'll have you and Justin over for dinner soon?' Emily says as she hugs me.

'Great, we'd love to,' I say instinctively, desperate for the house to empty so I can be alone with my thoughts. Though soon it will just be Justin and me left and I've got no idea what to do.

There's a gentle pressure on my shoulder.

'Liv, have I missed the chance for a cuddle with the baby?' It's Steph, her coat in her hands.

'Oh, he's asleep. Sorry.'

'No worries, of course. Next time! Thanks so much for letting me gate-crash.' I flinch as she leans in to kiss my cheek. 'It was really good to meet Al. We had a great conversation and I think I'm gonna do it!'

She beams at me. I gaze back, uncomprehending.

'Take a trip, too, like his! I've always wanted to see all of Europe, and then, you know, work my way south. Get to Cape Town and the base of the world. It sounds so… romantic, I guess?' She laughs at her own sentimentality. 'Just need to start saving up…'

'Right,' I stammer. 'I'm… I'm glad he could help.'

'He's a great guy.' There's a twinkle in her eye as she says this and her gaze flickers over my shoulder to where Al is standing. My insides shift.

As Steph shuts the door, her words register with me properly. She's planning to leave the country. Soon. I feel a flare of panic. I lean back against the wall, clutching my tight chest. My legs throb and my body feels heavy; today's been too much. It feels like everything is starting to unravel. My head knocks against a photo frame on the wall, sending it clattering to the floor. I pick it up; the shot of Justin and me with Max, in his tiny duck-print onesie, at the park on our first-ever walk out in the world as a family, taken by Dad. I still remember his proud smile as he held the camera aloft.

I close my eyes, as if it might transport me back there.

Later, when I'm in bed, Justin appears at the bedroom doorway, a question on his face. He is in the spare room most nights to deal with Max's night wakes.

'I'll do the feeds,' he says. 'I just wanted to—'

I can't think of a reason to send him away. He curls up around me, one arm across my chest. Protective. My fingers twitch as if ready to shove it away.

'Thank you for today,' he murmurs. 'It was… nice. I had fun. It was good to see him. Nick. I… I'm glad he came.' He is talking half to himself.

'Did you speak to him more in the end?' I manage to ask.

'Not much, you know how it is at parties. Two minutes with everyone. Did you?'

My pulse is speeding, strobing. 'Just… briefly.'

'Did you think he seemed well?'

I mumble something about him enjoying university. Justin nods and nestles further into my shoulder.

'Everything will be okay,' he whispers quietly. 'You know that, Liv? It will. We'll get through this together. It's all going to be okay.'

This new fervent note in his voice makes my insides clench but I don't say anything. I don't know what to say. How can I casually ask my husband as we lie in bed if he assaulted his ex-wife? Accuse him of lying to me throughout our entire relationship? What would it do to us if I did? If he thought I was genuinely entertaining the possibility that it could be true?

Soon Justin's breathing has softened into a regular contented rhythm.

'It's not,' I whisper to the darkness. Over the course of one day the list of names which could save my life has shrunk, and my husband has been accused of a violent crime by his own son.

Everything is so very far from okay.

26

I pretend to be asleep when Justin kisses my cheek and leaves for work. Spending the day with Dad and Max, I try to forget it, but Nick's accusation hijacks my every thought. There's no evidence. It's all just hearsay. It can't be real. I search through my memories, our shared history, flicking past arguments, tensions, the rare fights. I've prided myself on the strength of our easy bond. How well suited Justin and I are; this charmed, affectionate connection between us. Could it be that I've missed something?

So desperate to have a man to keep you safe. So hungry for love that you didn't see the whole picture.

Somehow, subconsciously, have I been drawn to someone just like my mother? There have been so few moments of discord. Nowhere in my husband can I detect the heat of violence. Nothing to suggest Max isn't safe. Justin has never once raised his voice to our baby, or even lost his patience.

But when you took the test...

I remember the pregnancy test, all that time ago. How I kept it from him, fearing his reaction. How we came closer then than we ever had to really arguing. Our future hanging in the balance. What if we'd kept fighting? What would have happened then?

No. Justin is a good man. Nick is still young. He hates his dad for leaving his mum. He must be making this up in some warped attempt to torpedo the family he thinks should be his. The smiles he gave Max a cover for the bruised heart of an abandoned little boy. I can understand it, the power of that deep-seated jealousy. I feel sorry for him.

No. The man I share my life with, my *family* with, does not have a violent past. It's not true. I won't ask him.

Because you're scared of the answer.

I find myself with my nose to my phone screen, scouring Mumsnet forums. Page after page of women tentatively wondering if their DH – Dear Husband – might be abusive and asking plaintively for help, advice. Verbal abuse in twenty-year marriages. Men who are loving and caring husbands ninety percent of the time, but when the switch flips and the mean streak is unleashed, their wives are scared for their own well-being. That of their children. Sympathy chokes me and I swipe the search window closed. None of those poor women's lives reflect mine. I can't recognise any of Justin's behaviour within these tragic anecdotes.

Yet Nick's warning at the party won't leave my head. I can't let the lie go unopposed, but I can't tell Justin. It would break his heart to know what his firstborn son was saying about him.

And if it's not a lie? What about your indiscretion? What if Justin found out about that?

I'm not proud of keeping that secret but I need to for Max's sake. He can't lose both parents. I need Justin to stay.

But when the boy grows up? Becomes spiteful and full of provocation, like all teenagers do. What would happen without you there to defuse things?

I clench my fists. I don't have the time to find out. I don't have enough time. I drop my head to my hands as a sob shudders through me.

Is seeing Max through to primary school 'enough' to ensure he won't bear the scars of childhood grief? Living to see him finish school? Get his first job? Get married? When is it 'enough' parenting? There is no retirement from it. No ceremony where you're patted on the back and given a token to mark a lifetime's achievement. No one to declare how long a mother is needed. I want to see Max take his first wobbly steps. To hear what his voice sounds like as he starts to talk. To know what his favourite toy will be, or his best subject at school. I want to know my son as a child and as a grown-up. I want him to know me, not spend his life wondering who his mother was, like I have. I was so young when she left, I never had time to find out why she became the person she was. I've struggled to make peace with the fact that I'll never know.

A memory flickers into my head. Spying through the staircase spindles as my mother came down the hallway. As she reached down and fumbled for her handbag. Found the piece of paper I had left there for her. The list I wrote her. The pause while she read it. Her stance, the way her weight shifted as she crumpled the paper and let it fall to the floor. The sound of the door slamming shut as she left, without even once looking back.

The last time I ever saw her.

On my left arm, above my elbow, there is a place which aches whenever I see a playground. There's no mark visible on the skin, no scar, but it burns still. As though my body has never forgotten.

When I was seven, my mother took me to the playground. My excitement was electric. She never usually had the patience. I walked through the gates, holding her hand; young enough still to feel proud that she was my mother. With Dad I would rush straight off to the swings, but I wouldn't let go of her. Al was there with his dad, tearing between the climbing frame and the see-saw. Eager to show my mother off, I raced over to them, but she stayed by the bench, allergic to Phil's effervescent ease. For a while she just watched as Al and I took turns trying to clamber up the rope netting to reach the slide. Once we managed to wriggle up onto the platform, I found my confidence wavering. Al threw himself gamely down the slide, but I called out for my mother's help. She appeared by the ledge and told me that it wasn't high and I was being melodramatic. Al hovered uncertainly at the bottom, his shouts of encouragement quietening. Phil had gone to retrieve a ball that a little girl had lost to some nettles. My hands clutched the sides of the slide as other children started to cluster behind me in a rag-tag queue.

'Just get down,' my mother muttered, in the voice that told me her patience was unravelling. 'You've got to learn to do things for yourself. You're not a baby.'

I felt her hand on my back and my heart swelled. Here was the support I'd been yearning for. Then I felt pressure.

A firm push.

Instinctively, I slammed my feet down on the mirrored steel of the slide. My body lurched forward and I flipped headfirst over the side. The fracture in my humerus was hairline, but it was my shame which hurt so much more. I vowed then that if I ever had children, I would be different. Better. No matter how far my limits were tested. I vowed that I would *never* again be around someone who could hurt their loved ones.

And yet here I am.

In the low light of Max's room, as I sing him to sleep, I study his face. How the heart-shaped curve of his jaw mirrors my own. How one ear sits a fraction higher, like mine, leaving my reading glasses crooked, like Dad's before me. There is so much of me in him. He reaches sleepily towards my mouth and I kiss his tiny fist. Increasingly he is fascinated by the inside of me, as if he wants to push open my jaws and climb back in. I wish he could. Because it is a bald, inescapable fact that bringing a new life into the world is to birth a death too. An unbearable thought. One day, one of us will face the world without the other. I have written his beginning, the world will write his end. How can I leave him to a life where the only echoes left of his mother are in his own skin? Where his father may not be who he says he is? Don't I have to fight for us to have all the years together that a mother and son should have? Whatever the cost.

As a child, obsessed with mythology, I read that the Ancient Greeks believed fate was manifested in three sisters. The Moirai. One sister spins the thread of human lives, the second lays it out and the third cuts it with shears, deciding when death comes to each person. How much time they have. Back then, I found the notion that everything is preordained to be beguiling. Now it feels ugly. Terrifying. Now it is clear that I must fight, tooth and nail, against my fate. Stop the hand of the sister who makes that fatal cut. In order to protect my son from whatever the world throws at him, I must seize control. I need another's thread to be cut and it is up to me to decide whose.

Then, I must wield the shears.

Part Four

27

Almost every day now I wake up from a sickening half-dream. More of a nightmare. I'm sitting in the middle of a strange white desert, a set of ornate black iron scales beside me. In each pan lies a raw, weeping, beating heart. The scales pitch up and down, weighing up their pounds of flesh. Trails of ruby blood trickle from them, staining the pure white sand beneath a violent red. I wake before the scales fall still. Before they settle on an answer.

As the icy grip of winter starts to retreat, the first brave flowers poke their heads over the battlements, but my fears will not thaw. While Max marvels at the scattering of purple and yellow crocuses in the garden, I creep around the house, trying not to cower at the sound of Justin's footsteps or flinch at the smallest of his movements. He can tell something is up but he hasn't broached it; a man with a lifetime's experience of burying inconvenient emotions. I know he'll be putting it down to the stress of my condition. The wait. We've been told to expect some extreme emotional ups and downs. Radical, fervent hope followed by crashes into despair.

I haven't gone back to another meeting. After a message from Cathy about their Spring Get Together, with a visit from another post-op member to buoy our spirits, I've silenced the WhatsApp group. I can't face any of them now. Not with what I am planning to do.

Instead of asking what's on my mind, Justin redoubles his efforts to make my days bright. Little touches like a flower in a water glass on a tray of breakfast or bringing my slippers upstairs so they're ready and waiting in the morning. Every gesture makes the idea of confronting him even harder, as if I hold a grenade in one palm, the tip of my finger poised at the pin ready to blow up my whole life. Instead, I'm burying it all deep where it can't hurt. Where I can't wonder what the fuck I'm meant to do if it's true.

Or what he would do if he heard from Al.

A prickle of fear sweeps over my skin. I'm running out of time. The remaining names on my list run on a loop around my head.

Rebecca. Dan.

And…

Steph, who isn't yet even twenty-five. Steph, who is planning her own adventure around the world. Steph, who is my best friend's flesh and blood.

No. Two. A deadlock.

Shouldn't Dan's name be at the top of the list? Karma?

He and Emily are hosting dinner at their house tomorrow. I said we'd go when she messaged after the party, but I've been thinking of excuses ever since. It was bad enough having him in my house.

Rebecca is ten years older than Dan, she's enjoyed more life, so isn't it fairer to choose her? Then again, her heart is older than his too. I wonder about their futures. Would some culture-shifting musical talents go undiscovered if Dan were to die? Rebecca's company helps support refugees who come to the UK in search of asylum. Isn't that a greater contribution to society? I shut my eyes and a scene plays out; a funeral, Amir standing in a crumpled suit looking hollowed out. Justin, supportive, stoic, at his side.

I drop my head into my hands. I don't know. I have no idea how to make this choice.

When Billie calls she knows something's up, though I don't tell her anything. I mean, where would I start? That my husband might be violent? That I am considering ending a life to save my own? That my list of options is shrinking?

'You're still coming to Emily and Dan's tomorrow, right?' she asks. 'Shall I come by yours on the way and pick you up? Tom's staying in with the girls.'

'I… not sure.'

When I agreed to Emily's invitation it was with some vision of getting into their home, painting a picture of their lives like I did with Irene. But in the cold light of day, the idea fills me with dread.

I look down at Max sat at his activity cube by my feet, spinning the cogs on one side with unfiltered glee. He looks back up at me with blind adoration, then flaps his hand at the cog. *Bah*, he declares. Even when he's asleep that invisible thread binds us close and it hurts to move too far away, like we are stretching our souls apart. I know many mothers feel like this, but my need to be near him is born of a much deeper fear. And now that fear is doubled. Before the party I would *never* have questioned if Max was safe with his father, but now there's a seed of doubt, no matter how hard I try to quash it.

'Are you feeling okay?' Billie says, her voice thick with concern. It makes me flush with guilt.

'Yeah. Just, you know, tired.'

'You should come, it'll do you good. You need a break. Some fun. You won't even need to move, I'll wait on you hand and foot. You've got to look after your mental health too, Liv. Max needs you to do that.'

She's right. There's so much weighing me down. I wish for one night I could forget it all. Pretend this horror is happening to someone else and I'm just like any other woman going for dinner with her mates after a rough week.

This is an opportunity. You can't afford to pass it up. Not now.

Emily and Dan have invited Justin too, so I call Dad to see if he can babysit. It's not really fair on him to call so last-minute. I can hear the angst in his voice when he says he's got plans.

'So sorry, love. I've been trying to get together with an old colleague for yonks, or I'd rearrange.'

'No, please don't,' I say quickly. 'It's on us for being disorganised. It's fine.'

'Is Justin not around?'

'He is… Yes. He can be in. It's all good. Thanks, Dad. Have fun.'

'Okay, love.'

I hang up and stand there, listening to Justin shuffling around the study. I can't suddenly stop letting him parent. Not just because he'll notice and demand an explanation, but because I physically can't. I'm reliant on him. I can't do it solo, even with all of Dad's help. I have to find some way to extinguish the doubt: I'm stretched too thin. And Max has started sleeping longer in the early evening. He probably won't even wake up before I'm back. He will be totally fine.

So, once he is down, I brush my hair up into a top bun in an attempt to look put-together and throw on some lipstick. I have to tug the laces on my trainers looser because my feet are swollen. Even bending down to do them up makes me uncomfortable, breathless. I have a brief flashback to the end of my third trimester; how these sensations provoked anticipation rather than dread. I swallow down the bubbling fear and leave Justin reading on the sofa. From his expression I can see he's hoping time with my friends will be a salve. Restorative.

If only it was that simple.

Nadia is outside Emily and Dan's house smoking when Billie and I arrive. She stubs her cigarette out immediately when she sees me.

'You don't have to stop,' I say, gesturing at it. '*That* won't kill me.'

She raises an eyebrow. 'Dark, even for you.' It's a compliment.

I grin and put my arm around her. 'I didn't know you were coming.'

'Sorry, I wasn't sure you'd...' She says. 'I just thought...'

'Don't just think, ask. I'm still here.'

She grips me tight. 'You aren't going anywhere.' It is a rare display of emotion that takes me by surprise. We hug tightly for a minute. Then she checks her phone.

'Oz's nearly here,' she says, tapping out a text. 'We all got talking at Justin's party. Turns out Dan works at this indie music label. Not sure if Oz's music is their bag but can't hurt for them to hang out more. Connections et cetera.'

'Come on.' Billie strides down the front path and reaches up to rap on their ornate brass hare knocker. On the doorstep I bite my nail, shift my weight, trying to think what to say, how to be with them. How long I need to tolerate being in their home. I managed to avoid Dan almost entirely at Justin's party, but now things are different. Now my list is shorter. My fidgeting doesn't escape Nadia.

'Hey, I forgot about your little dalliance at uni,' she says quietly. 'Not your finest hour. Is this going to be awkward for you?'

I try to roll my eyes. They all know about my fling with Dan, one of the university's more notorious womanisers, but not why it really ended.

'No, God, no, of course not. It's fine. It's… it's been years. Another lifetime.'

'Good.' She squeezes my arm. 'Not sure how much he's changed though.'

'What do you mean?'

'You know, just in that *once an arsehole, always an arsehole* kind of way—'

She tails off as Emily pulls open the door and we all flock inside, thrusting our wine bottles and enthusiasm at her.

In the kitchen, I try not to gawp at the high-spec white marble island and chic grey Poggenpohl cabinets, complete with tasteful gold handles and one of those taps that emits boiling water. Their extension has a huge floor-to-ceiling window and a bench seat looking out over a lush lawn. In the fading light I can just make out the spacious wooden home office at the far end. Back when Justin and I were deluding ourselves we might just be able to afford to redo the kitchen, I spent hours on interior design websites, salivating, but then we needed the money for the IVF and that dream was extinguished.

Dan is pulling a steaming rack of lamb from the oven as we come in. He places it carefully on the counter, throws his oven gloves over one shoulder and comes over to us.

'Great you could come, Liv.' He holds out one hand to me and turns on a full-beam smile. All his unease from the party has evaporated now he's prepared and we're on his turf. His grip on my fingers makes me flinch. 'Sorry to miss your husband.'

'Hi,' I stutter, thrown by his charm offensive. 'Yes, he's sorry not to be here.'

'Next time,' Dan replies, smoothly. 'So, let's do this. Drinks. I thought red to go with the lamb.'

He heads straight to one of the cupboards which I realise hides a huge wine fridge. In one swift motion he's uncorked a bottle with practised hands and racked up a row of glasses with a flourish. I remember this confidence from university; his tendency to dominate a room. He had an energy and enthusiasm which reminded me somehow of Al. It didn't hurt that his chiselled features and stature made a mockery of the boys back home. Anecdotes about Full Moon Parties and island hopping in Southeast Asia were tales of a big wide world I'd never seen. It sounded so grown-up, like I was now surrounded by men instead of boys. Of course that wasn't true. We were all still just teenagers.

'Oh, I'm good, thanks,' I say quietly as he slides a glass towards me.

'Right.' For a second his glossed veneer shifts as his eyes flicker down to my chest. He knows. He doesn't know how to broach it, but he knows.

'Or...' Nadia says with an impish look, pulling a bottle from her bag, 'tequila! Our US office sent it – apparently George Clooney makes it. So good you don't even need lemon supposedly. No excuses. Except Liv, I'll allow it.' She winks at me.

Billie claps her hands, off duty. 'Yes!'

'Done,' Dan says, recorking the wine bottle. 'Shots first.'

Emily has paled slightly. 'Not for me. Can't drink that shit since uni.'

I sense an undercurrent of something else in her face. She shoots a sideways glance at Dan, one I'd have missed if I weren't already scrutinising them. He doesn't react, but I think I've understood. Oh, God, I hope I'm wrong. I hope she's just an anxious host; warning him not to go too hard, too fast.

Emily hovers around us all throughout the meal, barely staying in her seat or touching her food. It's endearing, she clearly wants us to like her. She doesn't drink either; muttering about Pilates in the morning.

'Hey, does Justin play squash?' she asks me brightly as we're finishing our mains and dutifully praising Dan for his skills. I'm not even lying when I do; the lamb is delicious. It's one of the first meals since I joined the transplant list where meat hasn't stuck at the back of my throat. I find myself hungry for seconds, enjoying the brief surge of energy it brings.

'Um... not for a while, I think.'

'Dan's just joined this club in Crouch End,' Emily adds.

'Oh, the Coolhurst?' Billie says. 'Tom plays there sometimes.'

'Great!' Emily enthuses, beaming at Dan. I realise we're being courted; all of us. She said how recently they'd moved. How she'd left most of her friends back West. This isn't a one-off dinner, she wants to make us her local friends. Suddenly the delicious aftertaste of the lamb turns sour and all I can taste is guilt.

Another bottle of wine down and Dan's words are starting to slur but he's showing no signs of slowing down. At Bristol he prided himself on being the last man standing. Perhaps Emily's clean living is grating. The strength of his charm all night has confused me. Whatever misgivings he seemed to be feeling at Justin's party have dissipated and he's only been an attentive host. Has he changed? Has my memory demonised him, conjuring a version of him warped by the passing years?

I excuse myself to go to the bathroom, taking the chance to examine the rest of their home while the others are preoccupied. I hate this part, this ugly snooping I'm reduced to, searching people's home for scraps of who they are. As I come out of the downstairs bathroom, I stop to look at a piece of art on the wall. A calming abstract acrylic painting in dreamy blues, greens and gold. It's the kind of aesthetic I would choose, if we had the money to spare. I look around at the hall's tasteful panelled walls painted a rich woad blue. At their comfortable, beautiful life. A life which, if things had panned out differently, might have been mine, though not one that would have made me happy. A floorboard creaks and I turn to see Dan behind me in the hall, wine glass in hand. As if he's been waiting.

He comes closer. Over the course of the evening a new light seems to have come on in his eyes, growing slowly more noticeable, like a dimmer switch being turned up. It hasn't escaped me just how many times he and Oz have slipped off to another room and returned sniffing.

'Listen,' he says thickly, his voice low. 'At Bristol. When we—'

My stomach flips over. I don't want to talk about that here, now, with our friends, his fiancée, just next door.

'We don't have to talk about it,' I cut in quickly.

'Right.' Relief blooms over his flushed face. 'Yeah. Sure. Good. 'Cos, I haven't... Emily doesn't know...'

I clench my jaw. He wasn't about to apologise. Or ask how I've been since we last saw each other, or after my health. Of course, that's why I'm here. Dan agreed to invite me for dinner with an ulterior motive. He wanted to confirm that his reputation will remain intact. Beneath the sheen of public-school charm, he hasn't changed. Still as selfish as he was then.

'It's all good,' I say, forcing a smile onto my face that says it's water under the bridge.

'I mean, we were just teenagers. Right?' Dan shrugs, sinking the last of his drink.

He gives me what I can only assume is his best rakish look and I realise he thinks I'm here, in his house, because I'm still interested. I know people like him. I met plenty in my previous life as a lawyer. The overconfident types who get off on power play. Given the chance, he will reel me in until I'm virtually in his lap, a fish swinging on the line, but it would always fall to me to make the decisive move. No matter how drunk he gets, he wouldn't ever lean in. That way his defence will stand. *She kissed me. It was a misunderstanding.* It's not even about the sex. It's about control. I can't deny there is a frisson to being desired, just like there was back then, but I wouldn't ever go there again. Because I haven't forgotten what happened.

I remember. Of course I remember.

28

I'd only had a handful of fumbled sexual encounters before university. As seemingly everyone else recounted the escapades of their gap year or spoke from within the comfort of an ongoing relationship, I felt like a painfully embarrassing minority. During my first year I was too preoccupied with making friends, or making it to lectures with a hangover, to have much success with boys apart from a few sloppy drunken kisses. So, it took me by surprise when, one night in second year, across a smoke- and sweat-hazed dancefloor, Dan began to circle. He was on the rowing team and exuded raw, unchecked confidence. I'd assumed he would only have eyes for Billie's kind of classic beauty.

That night, I let myself be pulled into Dan's orbit, enjoying the envious looks of other girls at the edge of the dancefloor. He stumbled home with me afterwards via the chippy van. It was the first time I had really enjoyed sex. Which made what came after all the more painful. For a month or two, the air seemed to pulse with potential. I wasn't kidding myself that he was the sort who wanted a girlfriend, nor did I especially want a boyfriend, but I was flattered when he kept coming back. The implicit approval was like a drug hit.

Until the day I missed a period.

I still remember Dan's face when I told him. His look of pure panic.

'Oh... Christ.' He shot a glance around, as if someone might overhear. 'How do you... How do you know it's... mine?'

I stared at him, my expression his answer. I felt a curdling inside me. We'd never said we were exclusive and yet the romantic part of me had quietly wondered, hoped. I looked away, stung by my own naivety.

When he ignored my calls for days after, I began to realise what was happening. This was my mess and he wasn't going to let it mire his university adventures. His bright future. After a fortnight I confronted him at the faculty, but before I'd even started speaking, he virtually wrestled me out into a courtyard and told me to drop my voice.

'Look, I don't know what you want from me. We're students. I... I've got plans. I can't have a kid. I don't even want kids.' He was talking fast, impatiently. Still shooting looks around us as if there were paparazzi in the bushes. As if the world cared about our predicament.

When I said I needed to think about it, he was astounded. 'What the fuck is there to think about? It's *crazy*. You... you need to sort this out.'

It wasn't as if at nineteen I felt ready to be a mother, but the flippancy with which he was suggesting we simply erase what he clearly saw as a blip, felt so cold. Heartless. As if it wasn't extinguishing a life. As if it didn't need proper consideration.

Then it was Dan who was calling me constantly, and I who left his messages unanswered. I needed to get clear of his judgement, his declaration that there was only one possible option. I needed the space to imagine what my life might look like as a parent. I'd always seen it in my future; the chance to do things differently. To be the mother I never had. Although not like this, knocked up by some student who couldn't wait to put a full stop after my name. When it would mean dropping out, after all the work it took to get here. Starting over in unchartered waters. Alone.

Then, four weeks after I first took a test, Dan confronted me at our student house, pulling me along by the wheelie bins. Billie was watching *MasterChef* inside, none the wiser.

'Why don't you answer the phone, Olivia?' His eyes were alive with a frenzy I'd only seen in people on MDMA. 'You *cannot* do this to me,' he hissed. 'This is not how my life is going to go. You have to end it. If... if you don't make an appointment, I'll deny it all. The kid won't be mine. You're on your own.'

The callousness of his words sent a chill down my neck, though I was burning with anger.

'I'm not... I can't do that,' I said quietly. It wasn't until I actually said the words aloud that I realised I'd made my decision. My choice to keep the baby. Even though it would throw my life into chaos, it was what I wanted. 'I won't do it.'

Dan's face seemed to sharpen. I turned around and started up the steps to the front door when I felt his grip on my arm.

'Then fuck you,' he hissed.

He shoved me away, just as I was tugging myself free from his hand. Hard enough to unbalance me. I stumbled. My shoe caught on an uneven step. I went down fast and hard. On my front. No time to break my fall. Pain radiated through me. Blood oozed from a scrape over my hip bone. Grit on my palms. Guilt replaced fury on Dan's face as he helped me up, but I think I already knew the damage was done.

In the days after, as I sat on bathroom floors and in impersonal GP waiting rooms, life draining out of me, trying to pretend it was happening to someone else, I replayed the moment forensically, wondering if I could have changed things. Of course, I wasn't to know then that it was almost my only chance to have a child.

I barely spoke to Dan for the rest of university. Turned around on the street if I saw him. Left clubs where he was monopolising the dancefloor, eyes on some other potential conquest. I didn't want to breathe the same air as him. I never told anyone the full story, not even Billie. I was too ashamed. Instead, I explained it all away as a broken heart.

That was eighteen years ago. Things might now be so different. I'd have a teenager, perhaps off on their own university adventures. Ever since then I've lived with the question of whether the miscarriage could have caused the problems Justin and I faced; the doctors could only ever describe our issues as 'unexplained infertility'.

So, Dan's wolfish look makes my skin crawl. He is a reminder of a time when my choices, my body, my future, lost out to his. That can't happen again.

As I take my seat back at the black wooden dinner table, with their carefully chosen matching coasters and trendy stemless wine glasses, I think I might have made up my mind.

For the rest of the meal I avert my eyes from Emily. As she gets up to clear the dessert plates away, my body feels heavy, as if there are stones in my pockets. I've got what I need. Now I can't stand to be here a moment longer.

'You know, I'm feeling a little done-in,' I say. 'I think I need to call it a night.' For a moment I'm struck by a sense of déjà vu. The sound of Junie saying something similar on Christmas Day. The memory stings.

Emily puts the plates by the sink and comes around the table.

'Of course, you must be shattered. Dan can give you a lift home?'

Our eyes meet across the table. Dan looks like a deer in headlights. We're both scrambling for excuses.

'It's fine,' I say quickly.

'We'll share an Uber,' Billie says, though I'm not really on her way and she's probably not even ready for her night off to end. I throw her a grateful smile.

In the hallway, Emily helps me into my coat. 'Thanks so much for coming, Liv. Let's do it again soon? When you can bring Justin too.'

'Absolutely,' I say, already heading for the door. As Billie and Emily hug, Billie leans in a little closer and drops her voice.

'Don't forget the folic acid,' she whispers with a smile. 'Lots of sleep and no stress!'

My eyes widen as her words register. Inside me, a tightness constricts my chest.

Emily nods shyly. 'Thanks, Billie. Really appreciate all the advice.'

Seeing the question on my face, she glances back to the kitchen where Dan and Oz are getting the tequila back out, as if she's deciding whether to confide in me too.

'Dan and I just agreed to start trying,' she explains quietly.

I sway, clutching at the wall. That look they exchanged. Emily not drinking. I was right.

'You're not going to wait till after the wedding?' I blurt out.

'Oh, um, no.' Emily lowers her voice further. 'Dan wouldn't like me to admit it, but to be honest, who can afford a wedding these days? The renovation plus the mortgage means it's hard to justify. We'll do something at some point, but right now it's not a priority.'

A familiar bright-eyed excitement shines on her face. I remember that feeling, that beautiful hope, when the decision to start trying for a baby felt momentous. A threshold. So different from the years taking precautions, bearing the burden of contraceptive responsibility.

'It's so good to be back in touch with you both,' Emily says. 'I don't actually know many people with children so…'

'Of course,' Billie says, squeezing her hands. 'Here for any questions. And when the time comes, very much here for soft-play dates.'

With anyone else I would be happy for them. I'd be keeping my fingers crossed, hoping they don't have to go through what we went through to have Max. But then I think about the list. Dan's name. And, instead, I find myself praying that they fail.

As I climb into the Uber with Billie, my legs tremble with effort, anger raising goosebumps over my skin. At how Dan got to pick and choose the course his life took. At how he doesn't have to bear the scars. The clear-skied future ahead of him while I'm fighting each day to cling on to mine.

I feel a queasy lurch as I think about my list. The scales which weigh up Rebecca and Dan. His gym body, his ripe bulging veins. Then his bleary eyes, the constant refills of wine, the shots and the sniffs. How his healthy exterior might mislead. But most of all, how he has promised to share his life with Emily, who is so eager to have his baby.

That has to be it. My one boundary. My one brittle moral line. I cannot risk taking a parent from a child.

So, then there's only one name I can choose.

29

I park behind Rebecca and Amir's dusk blue Volvo XC60. A substantial, practical car, ready to absorb four pairs of wellies, four sets of beach towels, four heaving suitcases. A car wasted on them. My hands clutch the steering wheel. I can hardly believe I'm here. My thoughts are blurred, as though the only way I can contemplate this is to disconnect from reality. It's about two hours before I'll need to get Max from Dad's. I hope it's enough time to ensure my choice is the right one. I knock once, too quietly, like I don't really want to at all. Then again, harder.

It's Friday, late afternoon, so Amir should have finished work; my excuse for the visit. Rebecca is part-time and doesn't work Fridays. She answers the door, red-faced in a sweat-stained T-shirt. I've interrupted her exercising and it's like seeing a teacher outside of school. She frowns as she tugs at her top instinctively where it clings to her waist.

'I-I'm sorry to interrupt. I just needed... a word with Amir,' I stutter, not meeting her eyes. The name at the top of my list, live and in the flesh. No matter how much I dislike her, it's all too real.

'He's not home yet,' she says tersely.

'Oh... okay. Can I wait?'

'Alright,' she says. I can tell it's with reluctance but that she's assessing the optics of being overtly cruel to a dying person.

Sitting down on the sofa, I adjust my expression, my posture. It's the third time I've entered someone else's house and tried to understand all of who they are. Scouring their home for clues as to what would be left behind. Or any opportunities I might take advantage of. A wave of sickness hits me.

You're going to need a stronger stomach than that, my girl.

Rebecca disappears to the kitchen. I glance after her, trying to imagine what it would feel like to have her heart beating inside me. A wry thought creeps in: at least she exercises. She's been looking after it. I grimace. She returns, a jumper pulled over her T-shirt. 'He'll be home soon. I assume it's nothing I can help with?'

'No,' I say. 'A medical question.'

'Right.' She looks at me as if to say, couldn't I have just called him?

I'm only half-concentrating on what she's saying as I throw hurried glances around the house. The back garden is sparse, uniform, no plant permitted to stray outside its place in the bed. Nothing so homely as a bird feeder at the window. I glimpse the back door, the lock. The keys hanging on hooks in the hall. A botched burglary? Could that work? My breathing gets shallower. Oh my God. This is truly insane. I glance around the kitchen extension to where the sports kit and yoga mats are rolled up and stacked against one wall. No golf clubs or cricket bats on show. My hands feel sticky against my trousers. I don't dare lift them up in case she notices the shaking.

My gaze flicks to a wedding photograph, a snapshot taken outside the church. Amir's smile, his shining eyes. Poor, kind Amir. I see him alone in this house which reeks of her presence. How slovenly would he get without Rebecca to keep things ship-shape? Would the garden run to ruin? Would a smell gradually pervade the once-pristine interior, the scent of unwashed clothes, neglected washing up? What would it feel like for him to know the last of her was living inside me? That his wife had kept his best friend's wife alive? At least he's close to his family. He'd have people to support him, comfort him through the grief. That matters, doesn't it?

In the photo a younger Justin stands next to Amir, hands clasped in front of him, smiling broadly. His hair is thicker, darker without the speckles of grey. His face free from the weight of the problems he's faced after this point. He's still wearing his old wedding ring. Then something occurs to me; something which pulls my thoughts from their dark path. The way to answer the question hanging over our marriage like a guillotine. The one person who could corroborate what Nick is claiming is his mother. Louise.

'I wondered,' I start falteringly. 'Could you share Louise's details?' Rebecca arches her eyebrow as I fumble for a justification. 'I… she… we spoke at Justin's party and I wanted to thank her for coming.'

Rebecca rearranges her hands on her crossed knee. She's loving this. Me needing something from her.

'I keep forgetting to ask Justin,' I add quickly. 'And since you're here. It would be really helpful. One thing off my to-do list.'

Prostrating myself is humiliating but I don't have to be here much longer. Just long enough to be sure. Really, I'm making myself face Amir too. Face up to what I'd be doing to him.

'I suppose so,' Rebecca says eventually, rummaging in her bag for her phone.

As I save Louise's contact, I wonder if I'll have the guts to call her.

Rebecca eyes the clock. 'He ought to be back by now.' She clucks with irritation. 'We're picking his brother up from the station in twenty minutes.'

My mind snaps back to attention. This is my real task here, gathering information about them, their family.

'Oh, yes.' I scour my memory for Amir's brother's name. 'Faisal? Is he… the one with a child?'

'No, Khalid has the daughter, though she's grown up now. She's finished at university.'

'Do you see them much?'

Rebecca looks put out by my curiosity. 'No. They're up in Edinburgh. Very far to go.'

Not that far for someone you love, I think. For family.

'And your brother?'

'Darren is in Windsor.'

'With his wife?'

She narrows her eyes. 'He's not married.'

One niece by marriage, who she doesn't see. A tingle runs through me. She doesn't seem close to any family. No one except Amir.

'Right. I'm probably getting him mixed up with someone else,' I say. 'My brain's all over the place.'

'Yes, you must be... tired. How is the... search going?' She says it with an uncharacteristic tentativeness. I'm thrown.

'The search?'

'For the... heart.'

My pulse quickens and I curl my fingers against my palms. Stay calm. Her face betrays nothing more than a bland interest. She's just being polite, asking the question she feels she should. Or maybe disguising a morbid curiosity about just how close I am to death.

'Oh, well, it's more of a wait,' I mutter. 'There's not very many... available. A shortage.'

She nods at this. 'Yes. Right,' she says primly. 'Still. It's no excuse.'

'I'm sorry?'

'For what they've done. Really, it's no excuse.' My bafflement must show on my face because Rebecca keeps talking. 'Amir tried to explain it, but honestly I still think it's atrocious. People not being given a choice.'

'A choice?'

'To donate.'

I realise what she's suggesting. That having to Opt Out of being an organ donor equates to a lack of consent. I stare at her.

'You do have a choice.' I say it carefully, slowly realising that Rebecca has been waiting for this chance to say her piece.

'You do not,' she retorts. 'Not since the government changed the rules without even telling anyone.'

'It was publicised—'

She snorts, cutting me off. 'Not that I saw. I just heard about it through Amir. I might have a direct line to someone in the NHS but plenty of people don't. There weren't even any leaflets at the GP's. Nothing! Totally immoral.'

She says this as if it's my fault. Her slide into vehemence betrays her. She *asked*. She asked Amir when they heard about my diagnosis, my wait on the list. She bothered to ask just how hard it might be for me to survive. A spot of casual rubbernecking. Her questions for me are white lies; she knows *exactly* how long the wait for suitable organs is in our country. And she knows you now have to Opt Out of the donor program. So dire is the shortage that they have been forced to change the rules to save more lives. If you don't want to be an organ donor, you now have to actively say so.

'Of course, I see the need for...' She gestures at me as a representative of the needy. 'But really, it's shocking. People need a choice in something so important.'

She folds her hands on her lap. There's a loaded silence. She's trying to provoke me, I know that. I purse my lips and press my fingernails into my palms. All this is only making me hate her more and hating her is useful. I just need to leave without arguing with her, keep our relationship peaceful. Not leave any room for a query as to possible motive. I take another sip of water, trying to decide how to end this nettle-sting encounter, but then she speaks again.

'Honestly, it's why I've Opted Out myself. In protest more than anything.'

The water rises in my throat. I cough violently and slam the glass down. It clatters against the coaster, spilling onto the table. Rebecca tuts under her breath and gets up for a cloth, turning her back on the devastating blow she has dealt me.

She's Opted Out.

Just as I have chosen her. Just as I have begun to tolerate the thought of Rebecca's bitter body inside mine, her heart, her sour heart, is no longer an option.

30

The next day I'm sitting on the floor staring into space as Max pats at my toes. Justin has gone to the shops. I've barely spoken all morning, passing it off as exhaustion, I don't know how successfully. Since I hurried out of Rebecca's house muttering excuses, all I can think about are the red videogame hearts of my possible lifelines being extinguished one by one, until it's game over. My desperate scheme. Maybe it is all just a wild fantasy anyway. Maybe there's no way it could ever have become real.

I lie down on the rug next to Max, nose to nose, and he touches my hair reverently. I stroke a finger over the velvet of his cheek and wish this was it. That time would stop right here, on the floor in the living room on a grey afternoon. Everything else would go away and it would be just me and him forever. I barely hear the knock at the door.

Amir is standing on the doorstep, one hand in his pocket, looking awkward.

'H-hi?' I manage, my fingers bone-white around the door handle.

'Hi, Liv,' he says with a cheery smile which doesn't quite reach his eyes. 'Listen, Rebecca said you came to see me yesterday? I was sorry to miss you. I thought I'd just— Can I come in?'

I try to cover my alarm. 'Right, yes. Of course.' Pulling the door wide, I beckon him in and wave towards the sofa, wishing I hadn't been considering what his wife's heart might feel like inside me only yesterday.

'How are you?' His expression shows genuine concern.

'Yes, I'm... I'm okay. Pretty shattered sometimes, you know.' I'm trying to organise my thoughts.

It's rare I get to speak to Amir alone. Could he know the truth about what happened back then with Louise? He's stood by Justin, that's a good sign surely? A sign that it's all a lie. He's Nick's godfather, knows him extremely well. Maybe he can reassure me that Nick has made it up. Maybe I won't need to make the excruciating phone call to Louise.

Amir is about to speak when I interrupt.

'I was actually hoping to ask you something... about Nick.' He looks thrown but I press on. 'It was a bit of a shock to see him at the party. He seemed...' I falter, searching for the right words. 'Troubled, I think.'

'Really?' Amir looks perplexed. 'Well, he was on top form when we saw them at Christmas.'

'It was just that – he said something... about the past. When he was younger. About what happened between his parents.' I clear my throat. 'The... violence.'

Amir's smile fades away. 'Right,' he says tightly. 'Yes. It was... it was a difficult time.'

My stomach drops. 'What do you mean?'

He looks at me, frozen in this awkward moment, but I don't say anything to help him. I need to hear the words from his lips.

'Well, as you know, it was... Nick was on the verge of adolescence, playing up. Justin's hours were so full on. There were... problems. It was clear to anyone. They'd called time on the relationship anyway. It only ever happened that once.'

I go cold. Slump backwards onto the sofa.

Seeing my reaction, Amir tails off. 'Has Justin not... have you not...? Christ, Liv.'

He turns away from me, one hand rubbing the back of his neck in agitation as he realises the news he's just broken. He turns back.

'Look – he moved out the next day. Took himself *straight* to therapy. Worked it all through. It was... it was a huge mistake. Justin's never forgiven himself for...'

The sound of the front door unlocking interrupts us. Amir falls silent immediately, guilt etched in his features.

'Please, don't tell him I said anything,' Amir whispers as we listen to Justin in the hall taking off his coat.

The familiar rustling sound pulls me back through the decades. A rush of delighted relief fizzing up inside me at the sound of Dad getting home from work. How I would tug open the door to my bedroom and scramble down the stairs, to fling myself into his waiting arms, both of us ignoring the sounds of the TV in the living room. Pretending not to notice the conspicuous absence of my mother in the hallway.

As Justin appears in the living room doorway, laden down with bags of formula and nappies, my insides twist. This image of the perfect husband, doing everything he can to make my load a little lighter. Is that who he is? Who he *really* is?

'Hello, pal, to what do we owe this pleasure?' Justin exclaims, striding over to Amir. Their hug is brief, Amir's posture stiff. Justin looks over at me. 'Everything alright?'

'Yes,' I say quickly. 'Yes.'

'I won't stay,' Amir says. 'Got Faisal at home and we promised him a tour of the Emirates.' He smiles with effort at Justin who is a fair-weather Arsenal fan to his Spurs devotion.

'Oh-ho, stepping onto enemy territory?' Justin teases.

Amir stretches his grin wider. 'I was only popping in to apologise actually.'

Justin looks puzzled. 'For what?'

Amir glances at me. 'Well. Frankly, it's a little awkward. I... Rebecca told me what she said to you, Liv. She was unforgivably rude,' he continues, looking pained. 'When she told you about having opted out of being an organ donor.'

'She's done that?' Justin looks shocked.

'I'm afraid so.' Amir looks at his feet. 'She has it in her head it's some sort of human rights breach. I've tried to talk her out of it, but you know what she can be like. We... well, we had quite the barnstormer about it.'

Justin clenches his jaw as he digests this. I can see him vibrating with a righteous indignation, but he's got no idea just how much of a loss it is to me.

'Please, it's okay,' I say, after a pause where none of us quite knows how to rescue the situation. 'Really. We're all... entitled to our opinions. But I appreciate you coming.'

Justin shows Amir out while I sit down, pull Max up onto my lap and wrap my arms around him to still the shakes. I press my lips to his crinkled palms as what I thought I knew about my marriage goes up in smoke around us.

Max wakes earlier than usual the next morning, as if he is picking up on my mood even through the walls of our room. He won't be put down these last few days. The minute he is left in the crib, his bottom lip protrudes and his face crumples. I hurry to him, gathering him close, soothing, cooing, folding him safe to my chest. His cries subside as soon as the comforting sound of my heartbeat is against his ear. The first sound he ever heard.

There's movement in the spare room, Justin is stirring. It all comes rushing back to me, everything I've been avoiding. Amir's words, confirming my worst fears. I can't bear to see Justin this morning. To have to look at his face while I try and decide what on earth to do next.

What I want is to see Al. To steep myself in the warm, familiar company of my oldest friend and forget about all this for a while. I send him a rushed message asking to meet up. I don't say why, just that I'm struggling. He replies straight away, ever the early riser. I've got an appointment at the hospital in a few hours, so we agree to meet in the park nearby. Dad usually takes Max when I have appointments and Justin's at work, but today he's got a long-planned catch up with his old university friends. They only get together once a year, so I refused to let him cancel when he does so much for us. Besides, the trip to the park will be a welcome change of scene for Max and me both.

Over the last months my world has started to shrink. I'm grateful that the medications mean I can still manage slow-paced walks, but I can't stray far from home. The guilt of it weighs heavier each day. I should be taking Max out, showing him all the things there are to wonder at. The way ice forms over the canal when it's biting cold. Or how warm breath puffs from the mouths of the deer in Richmond Park and hangs in the air. The bustle of crowds in the Tate Modern, the boats passing beneath the

Millennium Bridge, or how you can see the tigers in the zoo if you stand in the right spot at Regents Park.

I settle Max into the pram, his little head covered by a hat with teddy-bear ears, big eyes peering out from above the foot muff. The kinetic energy of the outside world – people passing by, car horns honking, cyclists' jaunty bells – a new and fascinating drama for him. He's getting heavier with each passing week. I try not to think about the point when he'll be too heavy for me to venture out alone with him because it can't be far off.

On the bus I pivot the wheels safely into the pram and wheelchair spot, securing the brake with my foot, then hurry to the front to pay. As I do, an announcement plays out on the Tannoy.

'Please stay with your pram for your child's safety.'

I spin back towards Max, torn, then thrust my card against the reader before dashing back to him, my hand clutching the pram so hard my wedding ring digs in to the bone. All I'm trying to do is ensure the safety of my child.

A little girl of about seven stands up so I can sit by the pram. Her mother looks down at Max as he surveys the other passengers.

'You can really see their personalities start to come through at that age, can't you?' she says. 'Your little one looks like a curious chap.'

I return her smile gratefully. 'He is.' I lurch forward as Max chucks his Lamaze rattle from the pram, but not fast enough. The girl quickly picks it up and brushes it off. Her mother smiles indulgently, charmed by her daughter's empathy as she hands it back. Emotion swells within me. I hope Max will be considerate like that when he's older. The thought makes me ache. Another reminder that I may not get to shape what kind of person he becomes, to pass on all the things I think are important. To be a proper parent.

At the park, a few brave souls smack a tennis ball back and forth on the empty courts. Moments after we arrive, Al appears at the park gate, parka zipped up over a thick fleece, a beanie pulled down over his head. He's on the phone as I approach.

'Alright, Mum, got to go, Liv's here,' I hear him saying. He's talking to Annette. I don't expect an affectionate message. No 'Give her my love!' for me.

Al gives me a hug and Max's hand a gentle squeeze. 'How are we all?' His tone is light, as if he knows it needs to be, but I can feel his scrutiny.

'I've been better,' I say with a wry smile, trying not to let my voice wobble. I have a sudden, intense urge to tell him about Justin, but I don't know how. Or what he'd do if I did. He'd probably tell me to leave. That it's never once with someone who can snap. I can see his concerned face. Telling him would make it all real when I haven't even begun to process it myself.

We walk slowly around the park, past new parents pushing their bassinets carefully over bumps where tree roots have breached the tarmac in yawning cracks. For a while we just chat about his work, his family. Dreamy thoughts he's having about his next holiday, a train trip around Northern Italy via the lakes, because like all those with nomadic urges he's already got the itch again. I nod along but I can't relax. All I can think about is my violent husband, and my list of names.

About Dan alone in his home studio, headphones on, listening to a work mix, his back to me, oblivious. My hand trembling on the door handle. A golf club held behind my back. But even in my imagination, I can't do it. I don't have the strength to lift it over my head. Dan turns and sees me, his eyes widen. He gets up and I stumble away.

'Liv?' I blink back into the present. Al is watching me with concern.

'I know there's something up,' he says quietly.

I keep my eyes trained on the path in front of us. Could I involve him? Ask him for help with my list? Maybe, subconsciously, that's why I've summoned him here, now that I'm down to one name. Even after what I did to Junie, he hasn't abandoned me.

Not yet, but everyone has their limits.

Shivers run through me, not just because of the cold.

'I'm serious,' Al continues. 'There's something going on that you're not telling me.'

I let myself imagine what it would feel like if I had an ally. Someone to share the weight of this burden. The temptation is so painfully strong, but it would make him an accessory. I've hurt him enough. I can't tell him.

'It's just... been a full-on few weeks,' I say slowly. 'Max is teething and not sleeping well so I'm really shattered.'

'Well, if you think of anything... whatever it is... I'm here. When's your appointment? Got time for a coffee before?'

I glance at my phone. My appointment is in twenty minutes and the hospital's a short walk away. I'll have to take it really slowly. I've pushed myself in the park and my legs are aching and puffy but I just needed to get out, see the sky and breathe the air, away from the strained atmosphere of home.

'I don't think so. But we've got movie night at Billie's on Sunday. Come?'

'Done.' He smiles. 'Shall I walk you to the hospital?'

I nod gratefully. 'Thanks for coming all this way today, Ally. I appreciate it.' I squeeze his arm.

Sensing I'm tiring, Al takes charge of the pram as the path follows an incline towards the exit and the main road beyond. A young family passes us. The father holds a girl of about two, while an older boy slaloms uncertainly on his shiny new bike up ahead. The mother has a tiny baby strapped to her chest who can't be more than a few weeks old. My eyes flicker over her, remembering that raw, sleepless time, and I give her the instinctive smile all new mothers give to each other. *Oh, the things we've seen. The things we know.*

The father grins at us. 'It starts with one, guys,' he says with a cheeky nod at Max and then a glance back over his brood.

There's no time to correct his mistake as we go by them. I can feel Al stiffen. We fall quiet as he pushes the pram back out of the park towards the main road leading up to the hospital. My arm is linked through his, letting him help bear my weight. For a moment the strength of his love for me is so apparent that I feel ashamed. His mother's right. He's used up all his love on me and that's why he's not found anyone else. Part of me wonders again if he thought that night before his trip might be the rekindling of something between us, but I disappointed him again. I was never going to leave Justin.

We walk up the road and for a while I'm lost in the effort of moving through the everyday hubbub. Retirees picking up their morning papers and twenty-somethings their flat whites and pastries. Cyclists whipping past. On the pavement the corpse of an unlucky mouse, legs bent unnaturally, fodder for some smug fox. I look away from it to the looming rectangular red-brick building, the flashes of the bright blue signs pointing out different departments. Hospitals used to be alien places I'd only ever seen in TV soaps, but now they're almost as familiar as home.

As we wait at the zebra crossing, the jingle of a pharmacy doorbell rings out across the road. An older woman comes out. Her hair is lank and dishevelled, amber highlights grown out leaving a wiry grey chunk of roots. She stumbles, missing the step, almost falling to the pavement. A passer-by stops to help but the woman rights herself with the stick in her other hand. Her eyes are red-rimmed and she coughs wetly into her sleeve, the rattling sound carrying across the road. She walks on carefully, painfully, scanning the ground for uneven paving. I feel a flush of sympathy.

I've turned back to the pram and am starting to cross the road when I glance over my shoulder at the woman. Some force compels me to study her face again. She's moving along the pavement towards us at a snail's pace. The pace of someone decades older than she seems to be. Like someone who hasn't got long left.

When she looks up, I stop still in the middle of the road.

Traffic slows. Car horns blare.

'Livi—' Al is trying to hustle me towards the other side, but I can't move, can't tear my eyes away. He's saying something, but I can't hear it. Everything is swimming as the woman's face comes into full focus. A broken woman. A woman I have broken.

Junie.

Her bone-weary gaze shifts as she takes in the person standing in the road in front of her. Her face folds into a frown and she squints over at us. Like there is something familiar about me, but she can't grasp it.

I turn and stumble towards Al.

'What's wrong?' he asks. 'Hey! Liv…'

I shove the pram desperately at him as the world around us blurs.

31

Panic envelops me when I open my eyes. '*Max?*' I cry, my voice weak as I strain to look around. 'Please. Where's my baby?!'

'Ma'am, you need to stay calm,' a professional-sounding voice says from above my head. A paramedic is peering down at me. I'm strapped into a stretcher, my arms straitjacketed to my sides by straps. Somewhere nearby I can hear crying.

'Max!' I call hoarsely.

Then Al is at my side, Max screaming in his arms. His little face is flushed a blotchy red. His cries have reached the fever pitch that I alone can console. I try to disentangle my hands from the straps, reach out for him.

'You can't hold him right now, ma'am, I'm sorry,' says the paramedic firmly as she wrestles an oxygen mask over my face.

'Let me have him, please,' I beg, sucking in breaths through the mask.

'He's okay, he's fine, Livi,' Al reassures me, but it's not enough. I can't bear it. I need to feel the soft, sturdy weight of my son against me, the grip of his little hand on my skin. To whisper in his ear that I'll never leave him.

The paramedic turns to Al. 'There isn't room in the ambulance. Can you bring him to the hospital? It's just up there.'

'Of course, of course,' Al replies, pale-faced. 'Livi, I've got him. We'll follow on. I'll call your dad. Just try to stay calm.'

His voice rises as they start to push me away and sobs wrack my chest. My eyes are locked on Max who lunges for me. Al jiggles him, bopping him up and down to soothe him, when what he needs is to be held close and calm. I try to stem my tears as the paramedics speak calmly around me. Max's howling intensifies and he writhes as he sees me wheeled away from him. As I'm loaded into the ambulance, I have to close my eyes.

I barely hear the doctors as they come back and forth to my cubicle, taking more tests, delivering results that mean more to them than to me. The wait until Al arrives with Max is hell. The cardiology ward is full of walking ghosts shuffling by with IV bags mounted on wheels. Lost souls searching for salvation. I sit staring at the ceiling, trying to drown out the chorus of chesty coughs and beeping machinery. I passed out in the street, Al breaking my fall so I'm not seriously injured, but the doctors are worried. They ask if anything happened. I can't bring myself to tell them the truth; that what my heart couldn't handle was the weight of my own guilt.

Finally, the doors to the ward open and I see them. Al and Max. My beautiful Max. As soon as he sees me, his gaze locks onto mine.

'Oh, lovely, this must be Dad and baby.' One of the nurses bustles over. 'She needs calm and rest, okay? Just an hour then we'll need to sleep.'

Al doesn't bother to correct her and I have eyes only for Max. Al helps me move the bed further upright so I can support Max's weight. A calm swells through me as his cold hands explore my face; my chin, my nose, as if he's checking all of me is still there. Still in one piece. I whisper soft comforting nothings. Tell him it's all going to be alright. The worst of parental lies.

'Your dad's on his way,' Al murmurs as he sits beside us in the plastic chair. 'Jesus, Livi, you gave me such a fucking fright.'

He looks utterly shaken. Eyes wide, wired. Clothes crumpled and hair sticking up in all directions.

'Thank you,' I say as I press Max's soft cheek to mine. 'Thank you for being there. I can't even imagine if—' I break off, emotion closing my throat.

'Of course,' Al breathes, his hands tight around mine.

Soon after that Dad comes hurrying in, a bag of our things clutched in his arms. He places it on the wheelie tray table by my bed and gives us a tight, careful hug. His face is stricken with worry. He looks years older and I can hardly stand it. Because now I know how it feels. I know just what has formed those worry lines, the crepe-paper skin; how love has worn him thin.

'I didn't know how long you'd be in for,' he says, catching his breath. 'Have they said anything?'

I shake my head. 'More tests.'

He nods, resignedly. 'I called Justin. He's on his way.'

My pulse quickens. I don't know how to pretend that my husband's presence will be a comfort. 'I... I think visiting hours will be over before he makes it,' I blurt out.

'I'm sure they'll let him pop in for a bit,' Dad says.

I pretend to consider this. 'I'm... so tired. They'll ask you all to go soon anyway. And Max is going to need dinner.' I try to sound like I just don't want to make a fuss.

'Of course, poppet, I'll go and call him off. Tell him to start whipping something up for Maxy.'

I nod slowly as if it's for the best and Dad hurries off to find some signal. Max is drooping in my arms, exhausted by his traumatic day. He makes muted attempts to press himself higher on my chest, but I hold him close until he falls asleep, cheek against my breastbone. He rarely does this anymore, there's too much to see. Too many exciting new things to crane around for. His little body rises and falls in time with my breathing, just like it did in the hours after he was born. I don't ever want to let him go.

'He's coped,' Al says softly. 'He's fine.'

'Only because you were there,' I whisper. 'I just... What if... What if I'd been alone?'

It's a thought I've been holding at bay, avoiding the sheer horror of playing out that scenario. My baby alone in the world, his mum out cold at his feet, at the mercy of strangers. His helplessness, his pure, terrible vulnerability. Of me coming around to find an empty pram. Just the thought makes me gag. Even the imaginary version is intolerable.

'I've got to do something,' I say to myself, forgetting for a minute that Al can hear.

Something in me has shifted in the last few hours since the fall. This is it now. I know from the doctors' faces that I've deteriorated further. I'm lucky they aren't admitting me permanently.

'What do you mean?'

'Nothing,' I mutter. 'Just... something I have to do.'

Al gives me a strange look. 'Do what?' He frowns. 'You're freaking me out.'

I stare at him, at the face I've known for most of my life, wishing I could confess, but he would never let me go through with it. 'You can't understand. Not unless you're a parent.' I know it's condescending, but it is true.

Al is quiet for a few moments. Then he shifts in his seat. 'Well, I could have been, right?'

I blink. 'What?'

'Couldn't I?' He flickers a glance at me, then Max. 'The night we... It was just before you got pregnant. You must have done the maths too. The timing of it. So, I guess in another life...'

My throat tightens. It's not clear if this is a statement or a question. Al studies my face as if he's searching for clues. For answers.

'I mean, you got a test done, right?' His tone is light, as though this is everyday chitchat.

Involuntarily, my arms tighten around Max. 'A test?'

'To check he's... check whose he is.' From Al's expression I slowly start to realise that every strained conversation we've had since he's been back has been building up to this moment.

'There's nothing to check. He's Justin's.' I drop my voice as Max's head shifts on my chest. 'You and I, we used a... we used protection.'

Al's knuckles whiten on the arm of the hospital chair.

'No, we didn't,' he says quietly.

I stare at him. 'Yes, we *did*. I wouldn't have... we...'

Then I tail off because I've realised something. A truth I have turned my back on, hoping if I ignore it for long enough it might vanish into the past.

I realise that I can't actually remember.

I assumed we used protection; I have convinced myself that I wouldn't have been so reckless. But the whole thing was reckless.

The whole thing was throwing caution, my marriage, my family, to the wind.

'Tell me that you got a DNA test.' Al is speaking evenly, but he isn't looking at me now. His eyes are locked on Max's sleeping form. 'Just tell me that you know for sure.'

My thoughts race. Ever since that positive pregnancy test, I haven't looked back. I just took the conception as a blessed gift at the end of a long and painful journey. Our problems conceiving weren't ever explained, there was nothing to suggest we couldn't, so it was far from impossible.

'I didn't... We don't need one. He's Justin's. He is—'

Dad reappears through the curtains, sweat glistening on his forehead. 'Message received and understood by Justin,' he says, catching his breath, before clasping his hand over his mouth on spotting Max is asleep.

'How are you feeling?' He rubs my shoulder.

'I'm fine, Dad. Honestly.'

Al is still staring at Max. The nurse appears at the curtain.

'I'm afraid visiting hours are over now,' she says gently.

Dad kisses my head and carefully gathers Max up. 'See you in the morning, my love. Back as soon as we can.'

As they turn for the doors I glance at Al. He is staring at me like he is aching to stay. To say more. Even as he walks away, I wonder. I wonder if what I said is true. And I wonder if I want it to be.

That night, in the ward's dingy bathroom, I listen to the sounds outside. The slapping footsteps of passing nurses, registrars. Medical students in the first tentative years, weighed down by the responsibility in their hands. Greying consultants, fatigue in their faces; lives devoted to the saving of other lives. I think about the oath they have taken. Do no harm.

I stare at my reflection. In this wraithlike version of me, dark half-circles under my eyes, for a split second I see my mother. My memory of her is a tangle of recollections and inventions from my ten-year-old mind. Dad didn't keep many photographs, but I found an old passport photo of her in a drawer once. Her expression is remote, revealing no secrets. Over the years I have come back to it, scrutinising her features for my own, as if over time I might somehow unlock something, but I never have.

The conversation with Al lodges under my skin, a splinter I can't retrieve. When those pregnancy tests were positive, my only thoughts were for Justin and myself, any faint alarm bells drowned out by the chaos of other emotions: pure joy, aching relief, cheek-chewing anxiety. Everything all at once. But… could it be true? Where would that leave us? Then I realise what matters.

The *only* thing that matters is that Max is mine. And I am his.

That truth crystallises in me. This is the vow I made when I became a mother, the vow every good parent makes. An oath, sworn with our flesh and blood, that we will do whatever we need to for our children, with all the strength we have. Some don't have it in them to make this promise. Most who do aren't challenged to examine the depths of it. But a few of us are truly tested; the potency of our love, our devotion, weighed and measured. A strange calm begins to settle over me. There's no more time. Now that I'm not sure I can even trust my husband. This decision has tortured me, but the wavering has finally ceased, leaving only a simple fact.

If I'm to survive, someone has to die. My last and only choice.

So that my son will not have to endure a lifetime of grief that will damage him irreparably. Of an absence never to be understood or filled. So that he isn't left in the care of a man who may turn out to be cut from the same cloth as my mother. Everything else must wait.

Emily's words echo in my ears. They've only just agreed to start trying for a family, so it has to be now. No more hesitations, deliberations. It's no longer 'if', it's 'when'. No longer 'who', but 'how'.

So, say his name. Don't be a coward.

I stare at my reflection, not letting myself look away.

'Dan.' A whisper, as if I'm scared it might summon him, like some mythical demon.

Louder.

'Dan. It has to be Dan.'

A life for a life.

32

A week later, as I'm wheeled out of the hospital entrance with stronger prescriptions and many cautions, I emerge into a new world. The doctors have further optimised my medication which should buy me some time; a grace period where I'll be feeling a little better. I just don't know how long for. Until now I have been prone to dither, to overthink. I don't have that luxury anymore.

Justin and I don't speak on the drive home. After my conversation with Al, there's more than one reason I can't look at my husband. He may struggle to emote, but he's not insensitive to the calibrations in the atmosphere. The pressure drop between us which has continued since the party. I stare out of the window. After a while he clears his throat and reaches for the car's touchscreen. He taps in a few numbers and then a dial tone rings out on the loudspeaker. When he starts talking it takes me a moment to understand he's phoning up to order more visitor parking permits for Dad. Ever the pragmatist. Cool and collected. Nick's accusation echoes in my mind but I push it away, lie back on the headrest and shut my eyes. Not now. Now I need to rest. Conserve my strength for Max.

And for what's to come.

Once Max is fed and down for his nap, Justin looks at his watch. 'Do you need me to stay home from work?'

I shake my head. 'No, you should go back. I'm feeling okay. And Dad will be here after lunch.'

He nods. A strange expression rests on his face, like he wants to say something but can't. 'Please take it easy,' he mutters. 'I'll be home as soon as I can.'

'Of course.'

The front door slams and the emotions of the last few days surge over me. Nick's revelation. Al's question. My choice. What I have to do. It feels like I'm watching a ten-foot wave rolling in fast across a bay, but I can't let it break, I've got to keep going before I have second thoughts. So, I shove it all aside, all the questions, all the doubts, and I focus.

Grabbing my notebook, I start to list all the information I have. I know that Dan works from home in his new garden office most of the week. I know he's more likely to be at home in the day; night-times are for gigs and schmoozing the talent. I know that Emily has started going to a yoga class on Tuesday mornings with Billie. So, I know when Dan will be alone in their house. My instructions from the hospital are strict, bed rest as much as possible. No unnecessary effort. But I can make it over there, can't I? Get myself invited in somehow…

I start some intensive research, poring through medical papers. Exactly what kind of accident I will have to pull off. For a surreal moment it's like I'm back at my desk at the law firm, sifting through company filings for an angle. For once I'm grateful for those years, that logical, systematic way of thinking coming into its own. It needs to happen in such a way that his heart won't be damaged. Most people whose organs are donated are in comas after car crashes. It's well beyond me to engineer something so complex, so that leaves only a few other options. He needs to fall from a height. Or take an accurate blow to the head. I swallow down bile, there's no room for queasiness now.

Could I stage a break-in? Or take one of Justin's golf clubs, make it look like a random attack? My pen twitches between my fingers as I think about it. I can't take something of Justin's, that could implicate him if anything went wrong. I'll have to buy a new one from a shop. Use cash and throw away the receipt. No paper trail.

Before the idea has even finished forming, I am getting to my feet. I've got to do it. Now. While I still have the energy. I zip Max into a pramsuit and grab the car keys. I struggle to get him into the car seat, swivel it into position, then brace myself against the door, panting. Dad's coming soon; I won't have long. I don't like driving with Max on my own, there are too many 'what ifs', but this desperate determination has come from somewhere and I need to ride it. I'll go to the business park with the big sports shop. It's close; only a ten-minute drive, just beyond our warren of residential streets.

My hands are clammy as I pull out into the road. Stay calm. Take it slow. Within a few minutes Max is drifting off in the back. It's not his nap time so Dad will pay for this later, I think, wincing. I catch sight of myself in the rear-view mirror and wonder if I should have brought sunglasses. A hat. I'm rushing, not thinking this through. The shop will have CCTV, surely I need some sort of disguise? I rummage hurriedly in the glove compartment, find an old beanie hat of Justin's and tug it on. Glancing over at the sat nav, I notice with a lurch that the route is taking me along Oakfield Road. I'm almost outside Dan and Emily's house. I try to turn around and find another way but there's another car behind me. It honks impatiently. I pull into a space. As it speeds past, I sit, shaking, staring towards their house.

You don't have time for this.

I indicate, checking the road behind me and start to pull out. That's when I see their door open.

Dan emerges, a gym bag slung over his shoulder. Instinctively, I duck beneath the dashboard, smacking my cheek on the steering wheel, but he's glued to his phone. He makes to cross the road, heading towards the bus stop opposite. I start to pull out as Dan steps down from the kerb. He's not even *looking*, exuding an inbuilt confidence that cars will stop for him. My foot hovers over the accelerator. There's no one around. No passers-by.

No one would see.

Then Max murmurs sleepily behind me. He's stirring already, sensing the stillness in the car. It breaks my fugue state. I must really be losing it.

This situation requires a little more subtlety. Don't get sloppy.

Max's grizzling escalates.

'It's alright, my love,' I murmur to him. 'It's okay. Mummy's going to keep driving.'

Once Dan has crossed the road I drive on, but Max is fully awake now. He begins to snuffle and struggle in the back. I realise why from the smell; he needs changing. He's overdue a bottle too. I press down on the accelerator.

In the shop car park, I pull over hurriedly. Max is wailing now, that pitch where it seems to penetrate through skin and bone, right into me. I lay him on the back seat and wrestle on a fresh nappy. It's a cold day and the sight of his bare little frog legs makes me weak with shame. He should be at home in the warm, not half-dressed in a shopping-centre car park. Am I making him an accessory by having him here? I dart looks around to make sure my haphazard parenting isn't being witnessed.

When I get to the sports shop, I'm panting as if I've run a 5K. I catch sight of my reflection in the window and almost double take. Who is this hollowed-out stranger staring back at me? Day by day I seem to grow more pale, a pencil sketch being rubbed out. As though my own blood has started to abandon me.

Max's cries bring me round and I push the pram into the warmth as I dig a bottle and some formula from the bag. A group of teenagers studying the latest Nikes look up at the noise as we approach. My chest tightens. This isn't blending into the background. I quickly assemble the bottle and hold it to Max's lips. He's so worked up he hardly notices.

'Shhh, Maxy. Shhh... Look! Here's some tasty milk,' I mutter urgently. My nerves jangle. When he's this upset I can never think straight. Finally, he accepts the teat and his shouts subside into aggressive gulps. The shop suddenly seems so quiet, as if every person in there is watching me. Listening.

I move slowly around the aisles, taking deep breaths, forcing myself to stroll. I'm just there looking for a gift for my husband. That's all. I stop at the golf section, by the stand of gleaming silver clubs with their heavy, bulbous heads. Or the iron ones with narrower, sharper edges.

'Hi, can I help you find anything?' A shop assistant beams at me. 'Were you looking for a driver or an iron?'

'Oh… I don't know.' I should have thought this through. I really don't want to be dragged into a conversation so I grab the nearest one. 'Just a club, like this.'

'We do the Cobra irons in graphite too if you'd like to—'

'No, it's okay, this is the one he has already. It's just a replacement.'

'A great choice. Handles nice and light.'

'Thanks! Thanks so much for your help,' I say, pushing the pram towards the checkout.

As the woman behind the till scans the club, I keep my head down. She grins at Max who babbles up at her, back to his chirpy self now his stomach is full.

'I had the same one,' she says.

'Sorry?'

'The pram. The Bugaboo. We had that one with my two.'

I try to smile though inside I'm reeling. For once I wish having a baby didn't invite conversation between strangers because now she will be able to place me. They'll match me to CCTV footage. The shop assistant will confirm it. If this becomes a murder weapon and it's ever found, they could trace me back here. Me and Max. I thrust the club beneath the pram, turn so abruptly that I almost clip a stand of box-fresh footballs.

'Sorry,' I mutter stupidly as I hurry for the exit.

You're all over the place. Get it together.

I can't be this erratic. Impulsive. It'll end in disaster.

Later that night, I stare out of the window as the moon disappears and reappears from behind the clouds, like one of Max's Peekaboo books. He took an hour to settle tonight. His sleep is disturbed; he fights naps, refuses to calm or be put down. His little arms reach for me from his crib. He wants to be up and about in the world, practising his new skills. He has almost worked out how to pull himself up on the baby bath and stands there, wobbly and naked, ruddy-skinned and proud. More than anything, he doesn't want me to leave his sight. As if he has sensed there is a risk that if I walk out of the room, I may not be coming back.

Justin has gone to bed early. He came home frazzled. One of his regulars, an old man, just died. His wife came in to let them know. Justin may not be a surgeon on the front line of the battle between life and death, but his job has its fair share of tragedy. Instinctively, I reached out to rub his arm before pulling away. I don't think he or Dad noticed. I asked Dad to stay on through dinner and to help with Max's bath, blaming it on how tired Justin looked. Really, I just hate the silence widening between my husband and I. The question I cannot bring myself to ask him.

After Dad has gone home, I pace across the living room having this silent argument with myself.

You need to hear the truth from him.

How can I pull on the thread that might unravel everything I hold dear? Max adores him. I've never felt unsafe.

But why wouldn't Justin have told me? It makes no sense. If I'd heard it from him, maybe it wouldn't feel so sinister. So scary. Maybe it's not as bad as it sounds?

Or there's more to it. His friend doesn't know the whole story.

I look up at the mantelpiece. At the photo of the sonogram scan. Max bouncing around inside me, before we even knew that would be his name. Then the photo of Justin and me from our wedding, me clutching the bunch of dried flowers which still sits in a vase next to the frame, thinking I was so clever to have a bouquet that would last forever. My arm is tucked under his so tightly and I can see in my face the faint trace of disbelief that the day was real. That, finally, I'd made a success of something. Dad is looking on proudly. I reach out and stroke a finger down the side of one of the dried roses. It comes away thick with dust.

Our anniversary is coming up in May. It strikes me that we've made no plans for it, no mention of it even. I turn back to the sofa underneath which the box with the golf club is stashed. As though I'm the perfect wife, always ahead of the game, and have bought a gift well in advance. What would he think if he knew what it's really for? I'm standing here tying myself up in knots over whether he was violent in the past when I'm considering something so much worse. I remember the piece of paper hidden away in the photo frame by my bed. The test results from the blood samples. Evidence that can't ever be found if I am really going through with this. Especially not by Justin.

Creeping slowly up the stairs, I slip into my bedroom and pick up the photo frame; the first image of our fresh, exhausted, stunned little family. From the back I withdraw the paper. It trembles in my fingers. My heart pounds, percussive, arrhythmic, as I stare at the list of people who could save my life, now dwindled.

In the kitchen I wrench open a drawer, fumbling for the lighter we keep to relight the stove. I spark it. The flame flickers, unsteady. I hold it up until the paper ignites, wishing I could burn everything it signifies too. Fire licks greedily at the names, consuming them one by one. Soon only ash remains, as if the list was never there.

I am rinsing the sink, my mind whirling with ideas, methods, when there's a noise.

Bang, bang.

A thumping at the door.

It's almost ten. I'm not expecting anyone this late. Billie or the others would have told me they were coming. I hurry to the Ring monitor in the hall. Through the camera's lens I see a figure in a black parka.

33

The figure comes into view under the porch light. His face is flushed, eyes wired. I hardly recognise him. He looks like he hasn't slept in days. I pad quickly to the door, hoping the noise hasn't woken Justin. Static flares in front of my eyes and I have to pause for a minute. When my sight clears, I yank open the front door.

'Al, what are you—'

'I n-need t'come in.' His words are garbled; he's drunk.

'No, you don't.'

I push him back onto the doorstep, pulling the door closed behind me. I glance up, hoping Justin's light is out. The window of the spare room is dark. He's slept in it for so long, I'm starting to think of it as his bedroom.

We stand in the amber glow of the streetlights. I tug my sleeves down over my hands, wishing I'd grabbed my coat. The evening is cold, quiet, like the street is listening in, but there's no way we can have a serious conversation with Al in this state. Not one he'll remember. I need to get rid of him before he wakes Justin.

'Were you ever going to tell me?'

'Hey, this isn't the time or the place,' I say. 'We can talk tomorrow. When you've… had some sleep.'

He takes a step back, steadying himself on the wall bordering Irene's garden. 'Does he know you're not sure?'

'Al, please be quiet. I'm serious. We'll talk. We will. But tomorrow. It's too late. I'm super tired. Okay?' I'm trying to sound calm, but tension is vibrating through me. I glance up at Justin's room again.

'I'll get you an Uber.' I dig out my phone. Justin thinks it's a waste of money when public transport is so good in London, but sometimes a quick, quiet exit is what's needed.

'Liv,' Al whispers, pantomime quiet. 'I need to hear you say it.'

There is torture behind his eyes. I know I need to face this but just not now. Not when I need to spend the evening planning how I am going to kill a man. I need to hold it together and this conversation could break me.

'Please, Ally—'

'Just say it! Say that... he might be mine.'

His expression melts me. Shame flushes my cheeks. For the question I have left in his life, in both our lives. When I don't deny it, Al lets out a sound, like a little gasp. He bends over, hands on his thighs.

'I'm sorry,' I murmur. 'I'm so sorry. Let's... let's talk tomorrow. When you're sober. We'll talk about it all then, okay?'

When he straightens up there are tears in his eyes. 'I need you to find out. You have to get a test done,' he mutters. 'I need to know if *he's* got my life.'

I only just catch the last words because he is half-talking to himself, looking down at his shoes. That's what has broken him. Not my papering over the unknown, but that Justin might have stolen something from him. That Max and I might have, could have, should have, been his.

For a split second I wonder what it would be like if Al were inside the house now instead of Justin, waiting for me in the bedroom. I shake it away. Thoughts like that are of no use now.

'If you don't, I'll tell him.' Al looks up at me. 'I'll tell Justin.'

I freeze. He's in control enough to know what he's saying. To know what threat he's making. He raises his voice.

'He deserves to know as much as I do.' He almost shouts it.

He's right. Of course he's right. These two men deserve better than the misery I've wrought on their lives.

'Okay. Okay. But please, just go home.' My voice wavers. 'I can't – can't deal with this right now.'

I press my hand over my mouth, trying to trap the emotion inside me, but it's bubbling up. The weight of all the secrets and lies, the constant weighing up, the choosing, all of it hangs over me every hour of every day, threatening to fall and flatten me. I clutch at my chest. The doctor's words ring in my ears. No stress or exertion. I force myself to take deep breaths.

'Please. I can't...' I gasp. My arms feel numb, tingling.

Suddenly I am on one knee. When Al sees my distress, a switch flicks inside him.

'I'm sorry.' He's at my side instantly. Sympathy floods his face. 'I'm sorry. Breathe with me,' he slurs. 'In an' out.' He repeats it like a mantra while he holds my arm. 'I'm being such a dick. I've... I don't know what I'm doing... an' you've got so much going on.'

'You-you don't understand,' I pant as I struggle to breathe.

My chest is so tight, like my ribs might crack under the force of all my lies. This, on top of everything else. On top of my husband's secret past. On top of my body failing. On top of planning a murder I wish desperately I didn't need to commit. It's all too much. The strain of it is destroying me.

'Then tell me, just tell me,' Al mutters. 'I know you, Liv. I know there's something else.'

So, I do. In a hushed whisper so quiet he has to lean closer to hear me, I tell him everything.

'At the blood drive, I... on the list, I saw some names. People's blood types. That... match mine. People I know.' I hardly recognise the words as I say them. Like someone else has taken control of me. 'I... I don't have much time now. I can feel it—' My voice catches.

Al's watery eyes are locked on my face. He's drunk; I am convincing myself even as the words leave my mouth. He won't remember this. Even if he does, he'll pass my confession off as a drunken dream.

'I can feel that I won't last the wait. They as good as told me that at the hospital this time. I... I have to do something. I have to...' I step forward until we're almost nose to nose. 'I'm so scared, Ally,' I admit in a sudden frenzy. 'I don't want to die. I... I've only just had him. I... I can't leave him, I can't do it. Max. He's my baby. My *son*. I have to be here. I-I can't bear the thought—' My voice cracks again and the words dissolve as I press my fingers to my temples. 'It's like it's all just this deranged bad dream but it's not, it's real. I…'

I make myself look at him.

'If a heart doesn't come up soon, I need to find one for myself,' I whisper. 'So, I've got to… I need to… choose someone.' Those words cling to my tongue, like barnacles to a rock. Words still in the future tense. 'No, I've chosen.'

Al stands very still. He hasn't spoken.

I'm leaning on him, heaving in deep, slow breaths as I wait for my heart rate to settle. The static in front of my eyes is clearing. The panic that comes with it is abating too, but I feel weak. Wrung out, like my skin is hanging off me.

Once I'm steady, Al releases me and steps back. He rakes a hand through his hair and turns away. I'm glad I don't have to see the expression on his face as his oldest friend becomes someone else to him. Finally, I have pushed his affection for me past its limits. The person who knows my whole history of secrets and shame. All the worst things I've done, until now.

He walks to the end of the path. For a minute I think he's going to leave. Just walk away, saying nothing. Maybe this time he will call the police. I shrink back into my clothes, folding my arms across my chest, feeling the cold metal grip of handcuffs on them. Then Al turns back around.

'Who?'

I swallow. 'Dan.'

The name drifts off into the quiet of the evening.

Al is silent for a few long minutes. Then he walks towards me and I see his eyes gleam in the light of the streetlight. Glistening with unshed tears.

'I can do it,' he says softly.

My mouth falls open and I stare at him. His eyes never leave mine.

'I'll do it,' he repeats.

Shock reverberates through me. He's not considering reporting the crime, he's offering to commit it for me.

I wish that I could nod. Go back inside into the warmth of my home as he disappears into the night to do my dirty work.

Sit beside Max's crib and murmur to him about the magic of the world, ignoring the fact that some things are hideous beyond description.

'No,' I say. 'No, you can't. I could never let you. It has to be me. He's... I need to do it. It's my mess. My life. I've got to look him in the eye. He might be a selfish prick, but he deserves that at least.'

'What d'you mean?' Al doesn't know what happened back at university, but he's picked up on the venom in my words.

'Nothing, it doesn't matter.'

'Liv. What do you mean? What has he done?'

I squeeze my lip between my fingers till it hurts. Do I tell him?

'Did Dan do something to you?' He steps forward.

'The Uber's nearly here. Go home. Call me when you wake up.'

'I'm not leaving until you tell me.' His voice is rising. Anger billowing out like ink into water. 'For once, just tell me the whole truth!'

'Shhh, Ally, please,' I say urgently.

In a whisper, I tell him an abridged version of what happened back then. Dan's ultimatum, how he wanted the baby gone. Then the accident. The miscarriage. The choice I was robbed of by his flaring temper. How I wish I could go back and do things differently.

Al's face is thunder before a storm.

'He's the one who should have done things differently,' he growls.

'It was a long time ago. We were barely more than children. But *I* have to do this. I *need* to. I'll figure it out somehow. Just... forget what I've said. Please. Forget it all. Go home. Have a shower. Sleep it off. Please, Ally.'

Brushing the hair from his forehead, I hold out my arms for a hug. He looks away. He's still digesting everything.

'Promise me you'll get a test,' he says fervently, sounding clearer than he has since he turned up, as if our conversation has cut through the alcohol. 'Justin and I both deserve to know.'

'I will. I promise you, I will.' There's a crunch of tarmac and the Uber finally pulls in at the kerb. 'We'll speak tomorrow.'

Al slides into the back of the car. I watch from the doorway as the Prius glides noiselessly away.

Gooseflesh has risen on my skin by the time I close the front door. Confessing has brought a rush of endorphins, like I've just run a marathon or given birth. When I turn around, my eyes take a minute to adjust to the dark hallway. The coats hanging on their hooks; mine, Justin's, then Max's. Navy, with a tiny hood and wooden toggles that make him look like Paddington Bear. The pram folded up against the wall, the rain cover stashed over the radiator drying. The hallmarks of a normal family's life.

It's only when I'm at the foot of the stairs that I realise I'm not alone. At the top, someone is sitting in the dark, watching me.

My heart jolts. I gasp involuntarily.

'Justin.'

34

My pulse ricochets. I can hear it in my temples, feel it in my palms, my wrists, my neck. Unsteady on my feet, I have to brace myself against the wall. It's the first time Justin hasn't jumped up at the sight of my fragility.

'What do I deserve to know?' He speaks quietly, calm and controlled.

I dig my nails into my palms. I don't know how much he's heard. What do I say? Make something up? Conjure up some lesser, more palatable secret?

'It's... can you come down here? So we can talk.'

'I'm fine here.'

His voice is terse. Hard. Emotions as ever on a tight leash. Nick's words flash through my mind. Is Justin's steadiness a carefully constructed cover? The ultimate act of repression? Not my husband. Please.

'Justin, I can't even see your face, can you just come—'

I stop, blinking up against an unexpected glare. He's flicked on the hallway lights.

'Better?' The sour note in his voice is so unfamiliar.

I can feel a lump in the back of my throat. A lurking sense that what I'm about to say will be a turning point for us.

'Please, can I... I'd like to explain,' I say, treading carefully.

'I'm all ears. Explain.'

My heart thuds hard. It sends a prickle of fear through me. I press a hand against my chest. Not now. Calm. Slow down. I don't have the strength to track the threads of another lie. This one needs exorcising. There's no other option.

So, standing at the bottom of the stairs, I confess.

I tell him about the pub, the many drinks. He thought I'd stopped drinking for the fertility treatment so this is another betrayal. Then about the dancing. About needing to forget my life. Escape into unreality. Going back to Al's. Every word feels repulsive in my mouth. Apologies and justifications falling over themselves. After I'm finished a cold silence falls over the hall. Justin hasn't moved. Hasn't shifted, hasn't reacted.

'When?' One word. Sharp.

'Last year. Before... before he left.'

I'm too far away to read his face so I go up the stairs, carefully, one at a time. Hovering just at the top, like a child up past bedtime, I look at him to find out if this is it for us.

Ask him. Ask him now. You're not the only one with secrets. You're not the only one who should seek forgiveness.

I reach out with a tentative hand. To this man I married. This mystery, who might have his own secrets.

'Justin—'

Smack. With a jerking movement he slaps my arm away. I pull back, startled. The skin on my hand stings. My mouth falls open. He gets up and I recoil, stumbling down a step. For a long moment he stands there, looming over me. I've stopped breathing. The world seems to slow.

Run.

My hand trembles on the banister rail.

'So,' he says slowly. 'It turns out that you're exactly like your mother.'

He stares at me long enough to let me know that he wants me to hurt as badly as he is. Then he turns around. The door to the spare room snaps shut. He hasn't slammed it. Though I'm vibrating with adrenaline I hold on to this. Even in the depth of his pain, he is thinking of the baby.

Stumbling up the last steps, I limp into Max's room. He snuffles in his crib as I slide down against the door until my forehead rests on my knees. I'm still shaking. Because in Justin's reaction, the viciousness of his tone, the violence of his motion, I can see a possibility that I've done everything in my power not to see.

The next day I wake to find him gone. Any other Saturday he would bring me tea, we would have a quiet morning, perhaps with a slow walk around the park, then I would rest while he played with the baby. But this morning he's left me alone with Max, something we've agreed to avoid as my energy wanes. I check the spare room. He always makes the bed, a hangover from his strict upbringing. Today the sheets are ruffled, like he doesn't care. That detail sends a shard of guilt through me.

I call Billie. My tears convey the gravity of the situation. She comes straight over to pick us up.

Against the familiar background chaos of the twins flinging themselves around on the sofa cushions, in a whisper I tell Billie what's happened. About Al, about that night, that stupid, reckless night. Then about what Al asked me at the hospital. About Justin's face when he heard; doing the mental maths. Her jaw drops, her face flushing with shock, but she's silent until I finish, rocking Max in well-practised arms.

I make myself look up. She's studying me, working out what she can say.

'Bloody hell, Liv, that's… a hell of a lot to be dealing with,' she says carefully. Shame washes over me. She would never have made this mistake. She would never have jeopardised her family. The fact that she is sidestepping any judgement makes me squirm both from gratitude and a deeper humiliation.

'Look,' she starts, casting about for the right words. 'He'll… Justin's a grown up. He knows people aren't perfect. You were under huge amounts of stress. And you don't know that Max isn't…'

That he isn't Justin's. That I haven't stolen a son from Justin, a family. His second chance. Her attempts to justify my behaviour ring hollow. There's no defending it. I broke my vows to Justin, and I did it with the person he's never quite clicked with. As if his primal brain sensed a threat in Al, hackles always raised.

Al and I have walked side by side all our lives. Our friendship will find a way to weather this. As for my marriage? Who knows.

Justin's not innocent either.

'There's more.' I tell her about Nick's claim. Amir's confirmation. Billie's forehead knots in shock.

'My God. Liv, I'm so sorry… that's… awful.' A tear snakes down my cheek and she instinctively shifts closer to wipe it away. 'Oh, my love, it's okay. We'll work this out. We will. Somehow. I promise.'

Though I appreciate her arm around my shoulders, it sounds a lot like she's trying to convince herself too.

The afternoon drags on and I still haven't heard from Justin, so I suck it up and call Amir.

'Hi, sorry to interrupt your weekend,' I try for a tone that suggests a breezy lack of concern. 'I was just wondering… is Justin with you?'

Amir clears his throat. 'Yup. He's with us.'

'Ah, okay, well… great. Just let him know I called. I'm heading home.'

'Right-ho,' Amir says, awkwardly. 'Suspect he'll be staying… a while longer. Maybe overnight.'

I pale. If Justin isn't coming home it will be because he's been drinking. He doesn't like Max seeing him drunk, even the hazy state after just a few. It reminds him of his father, I think.

Or makes him feel less in control. Less able to control himself.

Though I hate that her voice has put it into words, the thought resonates in me. Does it go deeper than that? Does Justin not trust himself around our baby? Now I wish I'd had the courage to face it all before. To ask Justin the truth and hear it for myself.

'Will you be alright?' Amir asks.

'Yes… yes. I'm with Billie now and my dad is coming tomorrow.'

Stammering my thanks, I hang up. Billie throws me a sympathetic look. I'm wilting, a cut flower out of water. She suggests I lie down in their spare room. I accept, so grateful to have a friend I can trust with Max. A friend who loves me like family.

Curling up under one of the girls' blankets, propped up on Peppa Pig pillows, I try to sleep but I'm wound dynamo-tight, playing through all the scenarios of what happens now. I see our marriage dissolving. Papers arriving in a brown envelope. Max shunted back and forth between homes. Our family split.

Shattered. Billie will say that we can make the best of it; many people manage to coparent civilly, happily even. But I struggle to see that happening here. And Al, what about him?

I open my eyes to a gentle knock at the door. Blearily, I get to my feet. It's getting dark outside. I wonder how long I've been asleep. When I open the door for a minute I just stare because it's not Billie holding Max, it's some strange clone version. Similar but different. Uncanny. In the gloomy hallway stands Steph. Beautiful, buoyant Steph, holding my baby.

'I'm so sorry to wake you, Billie thought he might be hungry. We don't know where the stuff is—'

Max is awake and looking comfortable, if bemused. I hold out my hands, desperate to get him out of her arms. 'It's fine. I've got him.' I realise I'm being oddly brusque. 'Thank you for looking after him.'

Steph smiles widely. 'For sure. He's such a sweet little boy.'

Downstairs, I settle down in an armchair in the living room with the bottle and Max guzzles contentedly. Steph and Billie chat in the kitchen and I prolong the feed faff to avoid joining them. Eventually they head back through and relief floods me as I see Steph pulling on her coat.

'I've gotta head. Sorry not to chat more! Another time?'

I nod. 'Definitely.'

'Oh, and thanks for the intro to Al. I'm having such a blast route-planning. He's been so helpful.' Her smile has a kink in it. Something crooked. Cheeky. I wish I hadn't seen it.

'Of course. Not at all.'

When the twins hit their early-evening manic phase, Tom takes over so that Billie can drive us home. I've put off going back to the empty house as long as I can. As I slip Max into his coat his protests sound plaintive. He's picking up on the change to our routine. I'm packing up the last of our things when Billie's phone rings.

She shoots me a glance and shakes her head. It's not Justin. I don't know what I was expecting, I'm not sure he's ever called Billie.

'Emily, hi!'

My ears prick up.

'No. I'm sorry, I haven't.' Billie's voice drops in volume. She turns into the hall to get some quiet. I find myself creeping after her, my throat dry. 'Oh, gosh. Um... No, I've not spoken to him since we came to yours. I'm sorry.'

As I'm wishing that I could hear the other side of the conversation, Billie turns and catches me lurking.

'Hold on, Em.' She puts the speakerphone on. 'Liv's here too. Liv, have you heard from Dan? Emily can't get hold of him.'

I shake my head, forgetting I need to speak to be heard. Billie gives me an odd look. 'She hasn't, Emily. Really sorry. We're no help.'

'Oh, please don't worry. I'm sorry to have bothered you.' Emily's voice sounds tinny, but unmistakably worried. 'I'm probably being... He's usually passed out on someone's sofa! Classic.' She forces a laugh. 'It's just becoming rather a late lie-in!'

In the car on the way home, Max's eyelids are already drooping. I examine his features, searching for Justin in the curve of his chin. The shape of his eyes, the width of his brow. But Max is too small, his features still too round and diminutive. It's impossible to tell who is in there, looking back at me. I stare out of the window, Emily's voice in my head. Hearing Dan is on a bender makes me feel anxious. I need him. He is my last chance. I need to find him.

Once we're home Billie helps me feed and bathe Max, knowing better than to ask when I expect Justin home. Once the baby is asleep, she hugs me tightly.

'Do you want me to stay?' she says into my hair.

'No, don't worry. You've done so much already.'

'Are you sure?'

I nod. 'Yeah. Dad'll be here in the morning.' I can see she doesn't feel good leaving me. That my revelation is playing on her mind.

'Talk to Justin,' she says gently. 'And call me, night or day. I can be back anytime.'

Once she's gone, I grab my phone and scroll through for Dan's number. It might have changed but I've got to try and locate him. He can't go missing now. Not when I've chosen. My excuse is ready; Emily calling to ask after him. The phone rings out to his voicemail. I wonder how many times she's listened to this message, concern slowly crescendoing.

With a jolt, I realise with everything that has gone on today I haven't called Al to check how he is. He'll have had an almighty hangover. It's not a conversation I'm looking forward to but I need to stop running away from everything I've done. I pull up his number and dial. His phone is off. Sighing, I unpack our things, stoop carefully to pick up a few stray toys, but I am too tired to do anything else. It's only 8 p.m. but I'm longing for sleep's oblivion. I'm too shattered to even make it upstairs so I slump down on the sofa, staring at the ceiling. Questions are swarming in my head. What will I say to Al? Or to Justin when he comes home? Will he come home? All this when I should be thinking about the list, my choice. Dan who's out on some bender.

Then a soft buzzing. My phone is ringing.

My stomach clenches. Justin? Al? Dan?

I barely have the energy to roll over and answer it, let alone to deal with whoever is on the other end, but I push myself up onto my elbows and stretch out for it.

The Caller ID reads Transplant Centre.

I sit up in a rush. Too fast. My head spins. I have to force my trembling thumb to swipe.

'Ms Hargreaves? I'm sorry it's late, but we've got good news.' The coordinator is friendly and buoyant.

'W…what?'

'A suitable organ has just become available. We need you in as soon as possible.'

I breathe slowly as my brain catches up. 'Are you… You're… sure?'

'It's a lot to take in, but all being well with the checks and consents, we have a heart here waiting for you.'

35

Shaking, I ring Dad. I can hear him opening the car door before we've even finished speaking. I dial Justin's number too, but it rings out. I try again, a third time, but it goes to voicemail so I hang up before his message ends. I can't tell him this in a voicemail. I sit alone in the echoing quiet, vibrating with the news. Some poor soul, one of the millions of people who live in this city, has died in a quotidian twist of fate, just in time to save me. This is it. My ordeal is over. No more list. No more horrible choice.

Relief cascades over me and I briefly close my eyes.

Dad drives me to the hospital where I'm rushed through admissions and into the pre-op ward. The tests are time-consuming and time is of the essence now.

'Let's get you settled and get those bloods,' the nurse says as she wheels me to my cubicle. 'Make sure that heart's a good fit, eh?'

She plugs in the various machines that will keep an eye on my vital signs. As my heart rate is monitored, my blood pressure checked, I pull up my call log to try Justin again. I catch sight of my last call. Dan. Emily's voice resounds in my ears. The anxiety in her words: 'He's usually passed out on someone's sofa.' Dan never called me back.

I think of Al's expression when I told him about Dan. About Al's offer, the warped chivalry of it. How I haven't heard back from him either. How someone matching my blood type has died just as I told Al my plan. Just as he offered to do it for me.

Oh Al, what have you done?

With shaking hands, I send him a text. *I'm at the hospital. Please... call me.* Enough for him to guess that I know. That I've worked out what he's done for me. When the results of the tests come back in the morning there will be a match. Because the donor must be Dan.

A rush of self-loathing washes over me, so strongly that it catches my breath. For betraying Justin. For what I did to Junie. For all the other terrible things I've done and had planned still to do. The needles in my veins, the operating theatre waiting to crack me open and restart me, all this effort to save my life when, if it weren't for Max, I don't think I would consider it worth saving.

'Dad…What if… What if I deserve everything that's happened to me?' I whisper over the beeping of the heart rate monitor.

Dad's forehead creases. 'What do you mean?'

Max's eyelids are drooping so I keep my voice low. 'My illness. What if… what if I don't deserve to live?'

Dad looks scandalised. 'Stuff and nonsense, Olive. How can you say that? You have no reason to think that. None *at all*.'

'I do,' I whisper, barely audible.

'No, you don't,' Dad says quickly. 'I won't hear it.'

'I do, Dad,' I say slowly. I wasn't planning on telling him, but here at the cusp of either the end or a beginning, I suddenly need to. 'Because of Mum. Because I'm… I'm the reason she left.'

I stare up at his careworn face and then I am a child again. A little girl writing a list.

I've always loved lists. Intentions made real. Thoughts organised and controlled in a world of disorder. So, I wrote one for her. Scrawled in barely legible print on a page of my pink Polly Pocket notebook. My 'best' notebook, saved for special occasions. A list of reasons why she was a terrible mum, why I hated her. And why I wanted her to die.

I left it in her handbag, tucked inside her reading glasses case, where I knew she would find it. Then I watched her read it and walk away.

Dad stares at me, confusion written over his face.

'I told her,' I continue. 'I told her I hated her. I wrote her this list, all these awful things. Reasons why I wanted her to leave. Why I…' My breath catches but I keep going, pushing the words out. 'Why I wanted her to die... She read it and then she left. She left us because of me.'

Dad sits back in his chair, arms gripped tight around Max, muscles starting to tremble with the effort.

'No,' he says quietly. 'No, Olivia. You did nothing wrong. *Nothing* to deserve this.' His voice is thick with emotion.

I look over at him and he meets my gaze. Steady as ever.

'It wasn't you,' he says, giving a sigh heavy with emotion years deep. '*I* told her that you would be better off without her. That I... that we... never wanted to see her again.' He's blinking hard. 'Al... Alistair came to see me. He told me. About what happened in the playground. The slide. How you really broke your arm. I was so angry.'

He reaches out and gingerly strokes my arm, the exact spot. The invisible scar beneath his fingertips, as though he's never forgotten its location. I never told Dad what she did because I didn't know how to explain it and because, though I was a child, I knew instinctively that if he found out he hadn't been able to protect me, some part of him wouldn't ever recover. But Al did it for me.

'She was... I think she was never meant to be a mother,' Dad continues quietly. 'I thought that even though you were a surprise, she could learn to love our family. Learn to love being a mother. Her own was a piece of work, but I thought that wouldn't matter. More fool me. So... after I found out, I told her if it weren't for the fact we had created you, I would wish I'd never set eyes on her. I told her she didn't deserve you. And then, in the morning, she was gone. You see, my darling girl, it was me – not you.'

He pauses and gazes down at Max's peaceful face, then corrects himself.

'No. It was *her*,' he says, fervently. 'She was a disease and I couldn't have you infected any longer. Sometimes... Sometimes you have to do terrible things to protect the ones you love.'

I look up into his face and I see the eyes of someone who has contorted themself for years to be everything I need. A man who has tried with everything he has to build a safety net around me, his precious family. I reach for him and press my face into his shoulder, like I have countless times over the years. As my tears stain the woollen jumper, he strokes my hair over and over, his nose pressed to the crown of my head.

'You're not her and you'll never be her,' he whispers.

Deep down within me the snarled knot that has lived there for so many years, tangling my insides since she left, seems finally to work its way free.

The nurse appears at the curtain. 'So sorry to interrupt but it's time you had a rest, my lovely,' she says softly. 'Big day tomorrow.'

Dad gets reluctantly to his feet.

'Will you keep trying Justin?'

Dad nods. 'I'll track him down. Get him to you as soon as I can.'

'Thank you.' I've told him that we've argued, but not why. I can't bear to admit that to Dad.

'You'll be okay, Olive. My Olive.' We hug each other again, like it's the last time. Max wakes and clutches a fold of my gown in his fist. As I hand him over, I kiss his soft forehead, blinking furiously against the tears. Dad is blinking just as much.

'Look after him,' I manage to gasp as I detach Max's fingers. If I say anything more, I may not be able to let them leave.

'See you on the other side,' Dad says. 'You stay strong, alright? Chin up. That's my girl.'

I nod, squeeze his hand as they turn to go. Max looks longingly back at me as they walk away down the corridor. Dad's muttered distractions, pointing out the doctors in their colourful scrubs, echoes after them. I shift onto my side so I can't see them go through the double doors towards the exit.

Throughout the night, my phone pings with good luck messages from my friends. I realise in the rush to pack my things I forgot to put in the earrings Billie got me and superstition flares. Dad sends videos of Max playing with the wooden activity cube we got him for Christmas, looking perfectly happy in the indulgent company of his grandad. I simultaneously want to watch it on repeat, holding the phone right up to my nose so I might tumble through the screen back into their world, and to turn it off because even the briefest glimpse of Max's face scalds me like sunburn.

Eventually I turn my phone on silent and curl onto my side, as much as the narrow bed will allow. I lie there in the foetal position, with Dad's words echoing in my mind.

The terrible things I have done to protect the one I love.

36

The ward lights flicker on as the morning shift begins and sunlight creeps in. My cubicle doesn't have a window so is still gloomy. The nurse from the day before pops her head through the curtains.

'Manage to get any sleep, poppet?'

'A little.'

Her maternal manner is so unfamiliar it makes me want to climb up into her arms and be soothed. I wish Dad was here to tuck me into bed, read me a story, put a beaker of Ribena by my bedside, instead of looking after my child while he prays for my life.

'You're in the very best hands,' the nurse says gently, one eye on the machine tracking my heart rate. 'Try to relax if you can. The surgeons here are top of the transplant field.'

I smile gratefully. Then I pluck up the courage to ask the question which has kept me up all night.

'The donor... do... do you know what happened?'

She doesn't look at me, focused on the machine in front of her. 'I don't know much. A car accident, I think. A man. Otherwise healthy.'

My hands clench the bed rails. Oh, God. I'm right. It is Dan. The horror seems to be written on my face. I feel the gentle pressure of her hand on my shoulder as she smiles down.

'It's tough to think about. Bittersweet, eh? But try not to tie yourself in knots, love.'

I swallow with difficulty, nod.

'The cardiologist is on the way up.'

If the doctor is coming then there's news. The nurse's face betrays nothing. She doesn't know which way the dice have fallen for me. All she knows is the fine art of emotional support for people waiting to hear their fate. God bless the NHS.

'Hubby and Dad coming to join you this morning?' she asks, plumping my pillow and straightening the sheets.

Justin. I have been so lost in my own personal darkness, I've forgotten about our fight. The moment on the stairs. Even if we are currently vessels drifting apart, we have been through all this together so far. He wouldn't abandon me now.

'I think so.' I fumble for my phone. It's run out of battery overnight. I plug it into the charger and wait as a barrage of new messages arrives. None from Justin.

'Here,' she says, offering me a magazine after eyeing my empty bedside table. No distraction from the slow ticking of the clock. The sand swooshing down through the hourglass. I struggle to focus on the articles; it's like reading news from another planet. Other patients receive their visitors. There are intakes of breath, hushed embraces behind curtains, faint sobs. I have never been anywhere that feels as much like purgatory. Dad messages to ask if I want them to come back but, though it hurts to, I say no. I can't face saying goodbye to Max again.

When my curtain twitches, I glance up. Someone's outside. A curl of hair. Justin? Al? I shift to try and see who it is, then Dr Mirza appears through the curtains.

'Ms Hargreaves.' She is brusque but bright. 'May I?'

I beckon her in. Her energy is different this time.

'We've done all the necessary checks and I'm pleased to say we have a match, so we are able to proceed with this donor organ.'

My stomach twists.

'You just rest up here. I'd hope we'll have you under later on today. You'll be prepped as soon as the family—' She hesitates. 'As soon as we're ready to proceed.'

By 'ready' she means once the family have had the chance to say goodbye. It can take time for people to be notified, to get to the hospital. The teams wait as long as possible. The dying person is afforded all the respect they deserve.

I see a flash of Emily, head bent over a hospital bed. An intubated body, skin black and blue and red. A hand gripped in hers.

No response. My lip trembles. I never wanted it to be this way. This has all happened because of me.

Once I'm alone I check my phone again, but Al hasn't replied. I scrape my fingers through my hair. What have we done? It's only now, here, that I must face the full-blooded reality. This heart will beat inside me for the rest of my life. For however much time I am graced with, I will have to carry the weight of this theft within me. Before that, I need to get through the surgery. Hours under anaesthesia, a bypass machine breathing for me. And once it's complete, there is still a risk of my body rejecting the heart. I can only hope that fate is on my side.

Without warning, I'm hit by a mounting sense of claustrophobia. A feeling that if I don't go outside right now I may never see the sky again. My breathing growing shallow, I scrabble for the remote attached to my bed and press the call button.

The nurse appears.

'Please can we… can I just… I need to go outside. Get some air.' My hands are clawing at the rumpled blue blanket, the plastic mattress squeaking beneath me.

'Easy, love,' she murmurs, coming around the bed. 'Take a breath.'

'P-please,' I stammer, the fear threatening to overwhelm me. 'Just for a bit.'

The nurse glances at her watch and then over her shoulder around the ward. It's quiet. They've just discharged the person in the bed opposite. She disappears behind the royal blue curtains and comes back with a wheelchair. My chest loosens a fraction as I look up into her kind face, this generous stranger.

'Let's get you up then.'

As we wheel through the corridors, past ward after ward, I avoid meeting the eyes of the people all around. Doctors and nurses in coloured scrubs striding purposefully towards the next emergency. Patients and relatives with tear-streaked cheeks. The wan faces of those on seats lining the corridors, waiting. So much waiting.

Up ahead I see a sign for the Intensive Care Unit. I glance up at the nurse and she gives a slight nod. That's where he is.

Dan. His family. Somewhere in the bowels of this place, Emily is going through the worst day of her life. I imagine her face, pale, red-threaded eyes, vacant expression, the first vestiges of grief. Disbelief.

'Can I... can we... I'd like to see him. For a minute.'

The nurse kneels at my side, like I'm a child at nursery and she is coming down to my eye level to explain.

'It's not a good idea, love. He's...'

'Please,' I say. 'Just to look through the window. I need... I need to see it's real—'

A sob chokes me. Something compels me to see Emily. I don't know if it's a dark fascination, or a faint hope that if she learns I'm getting Dan's heart, it might go some small way to helping manage the pain.

The nurse is staring at me, weighing up the request. 'None of this is your fault,' she says gently. Then she presses her card onto the reader and wheels me in through the ICU doors.

'There's only a couple of beds occupied,' she murmurs, eyes flickering past each door. The blinds are drawn over the windows of some, but I can see through the slats.

The nurse puts the brakes on the chair outside a room. She reads the chart on the door then she nods. I steel myself and glance through the window. Inside, the room is flanked by two blue leather chairs, elongated versions of the waiting-room chairs, just as uncomfortable. Just as impersonal. On the wall are a series of prints, watercolours of some forget-me-nots in a vase, and a meandering river. Though the hospital has clearly done its best with the resources available, the only thing about this space that provides any comfort is the closed door.

There's a screen shielding the bed from the window so I can't see him, just the bottom of the bed, his legs beneath the blanket, and the edge of the machines keeping his heart beating for me. I force my gaze to the sofa. To her.

Emily is sitting with her head down over her knees, hands tangled through her hair which is tied up in a lank ponytail. It seems to have lost all its lustre, grief has sapped it of colour. Her hand is missing the engagement ring. Was it too difficult to wear it to the last hours of her fiancé's life?

I open my mouth to say something when it strikes me that Emily's clothes don't look like the kind of thing I've seen her wear before. She seems thinner too. Smaller. I squint through my restricted view between the blinds. Her hands have the skin of someone much older. Her hair... her hair isn't just lank and unwashed. Lacklustre. It's grey.

I blink. It's not Emily.

Oh, God. It must be Dan's mother. As her hunched form pulses with sobs, my chest tightens. A mother who has lost her son. Just then she moves and I recoil from the window.

'I think... I think I want to go back to the ward,' I whisper.

The nurse nods and reaches to release the brake on the wheelchair. Then the door to the room opens. Someone is coming out. The woman stands in the doorway and looks down at me. When our eyes meet, I lurch forward in the chair, bracing my hands on both armrests.

Because it's not Dan's mum standing in front of me.

It's someone I haven't seen for years but who is so familiar. Someone I can't comprehend seeing here, now.

Annette.

'W-what...? I don't understand...'

It takes me a moment to put it all together. Then I am fighting tooth and nail to reject the truth. It's Al's mum standing here in front of me.

Which means that in the room behind her is Al.

37

Annette stares at me. Unblinking. Unseeing. Her expression is stricken. My head spins. My throat is closing up. I am shutting down, trying to uncouple from reality. This is wrong. It's not real.

'Why are you here?' she rasps.

'I-I...' I flounder.

She narrows her eyes. The nurse glances between the two of us, trying to read the situation.

'I'm waiting for...' I glance at the room behind her and my vision swims with tears.

No.

It can't be.

Words fail me. Disbelief takes over. At where I am. What I am saying. Who I am saying it to. Denial built up its walls so fast that it is only dawning on me now, with a slow agony, what has happened.

Al. My Ally.

Annette's eyes widen. 'You? It's for you?'

Suddenly I'm nine again and she is examining my mother for her flaws. My breathing gets shallow. I can't fill my lungs. My fingers grip the wheelchair.

'I... I have to... I...' I'm barely making sense. I need to get out of here. I can't bear it.

'Let's just stay calm, alright?' The nurse crouches down swiftly at my side. 'You're just panicked, poppet. Breathe with me.'

I follow her coaching: in, out. In, out. For a moment I can hear Al's voice when he stood beside me on the doorstep saying the same thing. Feel his grip around me instead. The last time I saw him.

Annette's eyes haven't left me. Her expression hasn't changed.

'No,' she whispers, barely audible, shaking her head. Her gaze is still on me. I feel it like fire on my skin.

'No,' she repeats louder, looking at the nurse. 'No. I… She… she can't have it.'

The nurse's eyes widen in disbelief.

'Now, hold on a minute, madam, let's just take a moment.' She throws a glance at me as if she might be able to work out what is going on from my reaction. Hot, volcanic shame erupts in me. All I can do is concentrate on breathing, in and out.

'You need me to agree, don't you?' Annette's eyes are alive, flaring with a wild fervour. 'I can object. I…' Her voice breaks but she forces herself on. 'He called me,' she whispers. 'Left a voice-mail. He was drunk, barely making sense. But I heard him – he told me to look after you.'

For one horrible moment I think Al's told her. That in his drunken state he confessed all my ugly secrets to his mother, searching for some absolution for what he was about to do.

'He's not been the same since he got back and saw you again. He went quiet. So quiet. Just like before.' Her voice drops to a low hiss. 'You have *always* been a blight on him.' Her eyes don't leave mine. She is vibrating with the effort of saying all this; a mother possessed by suffering. ' This is your doing. You've done this to him.'

She looks up at the nurse. 'Tell them I've decided. I don't want to go ahead. I don't consent.' There's a choking sound as a sob escapes her. 'He's my… he's my baby!'

Then she dissolves, sinks to the floor, collapsing under the weight of her grief. A passing orderly hurries to her side, shooting baffled glances at us. As the nurse wheels me rapidly away and out of the ICU, I'm half-afraid Annette will follow us. The echoes of her whispered loathing won't leave my ears.

Back on the ward, someone is waiting by my bed, head in their hands. A man, clothes rumpled, like he's slept in them. He looks up as we approach. Justin. His face is etched with concern.

'Liv,' he murmurs, getting to his feet, but his voice fades away when he sees the state I'm in.

'She just needs to breathe,' the nurse says calmly, helping me onto the bed.

My mind is in freefall. I am melting under the force of Annette's anguish; it has carried with me like heat from a burn. I cannot breathe for the smoke.

'Can you get a paper bag?' Justin asks quickly. 'For her to breathe into.'

The nurse nods and hurries off.

'Just keep going,' he murmurs, taking my hand. I clutch at it. 'Your body will calm down when it has some oxygen. Big breath in… and out.'

This time I'm grateful for his expertise. The nurse rushes over to her station and makes a hushed phone call, eyes flickering anxiously our way. I struggle off the bed, wheezing. Grab my bag and lurch around stuffing my things inside.

'Slow down, Liv,' Justin starts, but I whirl around and scream at him. I scream and I scream and I scream until my lungs are empty and I'm gagging on air.

Al, my best friend, has died while trying to save me.

His mother has refused her consent. I won't be having an operation today. He has died for nothing.

Part of me wants to go back and tell Annette that it would break him if he knew, but she would never listen. Even if she would, I don't deserve his heart. I couldn't bear it. I just want to go home and shut the door and never again see the sun. Because she's right. I don't deserve another chance.

Al is dead because of me.

PART FIVE

38

Al didn't go home after visiting me. He didn't have a shower. He didn't go to sleep. Instead he called Dan. Dan, who is always out, and never one to turn down a drink. Al joined him at the Shacklewell Arms. Then, in his faithful old Nissan Micra with its knackered gearbox, Al drove them both to a different pub. Then another. After the two of them had sunk a small brewery's worth, they got in the car to drive back. But they didn't make it.

Al's Nissan was found entangled with a lamppost, glass littering the road like a broken chandelier. Weaving tyre tracks tattooed on the tarmac told the story. Another car caused Al to swerve but fled the scene. The driver's side took the impact. Dan was injured, but Al was worst hit. He wasn't wearing a seatbelt. The paramedics did what they could. The ventilator kept him alive until his family could get to his side. To say goodbye.

I don't learn this until later. Until I have left the hospital, driven in silence by Dad who cannot fathom what to say to welcome his daughter home from what ought to have been the operation that saved her life. When we get back Justin has to carry me up the stairs to the bedroom. I am stiff in his stiff arms. As he helps me crawl into bed, he tells me he's sorry for my loss, but I barely hear it.

The world fades to a hazy black and white. Guilt strips the colour from it. Grief turns down the contrast. Every time I close my eyes, images dance behind them of Al's final moments. Re-enacting his death is torture, like pressing the edges of an open wound, but I do it over and over; Sisyphus pushing the rock up the hill. What he was thinking, what he was feeling in those last blurry moments. What was he planning to do? What grisly scheme had his drunken mind desperately conjured up? Get Dan wasted enough to stage an accident? Go somewhere remote and run him over?

Did he know it had gone wrong when he had to swerve to avoid the other car? Did he know it was the end when the car crumpled around him and his seatbelt wasn't on? When he was flung through the windscreen? When he was lying on the wet tarmac, fragments of glass scattered around him, did he know then he would never get up again? When did he have his last thought? What was it?

Billie calls every day. She tells me Dan is stable. He's still in the hospital but he's out of the woods. His seatbelt bore the brunt of the force. It was luck that offered up Al's heart rather than his. Luck that Al's blood type matched mine. A strange whim of fortune. Luck too that Al wasn't at the blood-donation drive. If he'd donated, he would have been on my list. How different would things have been then?

Al's funeral is held at a church in New Southgate, near where we grew up. Billie gets a group email from Ben, his brother, saying it will be an intimate affair. Just family. That Al will be buried in the plot next to his father's. On the day, Billie comes over, her face stained with the marks of her own grief. We sit curled up on the sofa. She holds my hand very tight and we don't say much. She knows about Annette changing her mind. Dad told her what the hospital told him: that it was all too much. In the end, Annette couldn't bear the idea of donation. I've denied someone else on the waiting list a chance at life too. Billie tries to make sense of it, starts to say how much Al would have wanted to donate, but she falls silent when she sees my face. I shake my head and she knows the subject is closed. Only I know the truth, and the nurse who couldn't look me in the eye as she discharged me.

After Billie leaves, I drag myself up to bed and lie there, listening to the distant wail of sirens heading to some other emergency. Later, sounds from downstairs rouse me. A key in the lock, the door opening, then a high-pitched squeal. Max. My sweet boy. I recognise his excited heavy breathing, the swish of him kicking his waterproof puddle suit against Justin's coat as they disentangle themselves from the carrier. Justin took him out for the day to give us some space. I'm aching to see him after so long apart.

Justin brings him up to the bedroom and wordlessly props him against the pillow next to me. I turn over and that sunshine smile breaks over the baby's face. A smile that brings the world blinking back into technicolour. His need lights me up. His being keeps my heart pumping. Holding him is the only thing that brings anything close to respite, but my arms shake in spasms of effort. Static clouds my vision and I have to put him down on the bed.

'He rolled over this morning,' Justin murmurs.

'What?' I look up. 'When?'

'At breakfast. I put him down on the mat and he just wriggled and flipped over.'

He was due to learn it months ago. I feel a stab of dismay that I've missed a milestone.

'Freaked him out a bit,' Justin says with a slight smile. Then it drops and he watches us together in silence. 'At some point you'll have to get up. You can't just stay in bed forever. It's been two weeks.' He sounds faintly irritated.

I flinch. He's making it seem like I'm a moody teenager staging a rebellion. Can it really have been two weeks since Al died? How have I survived that long under the weight of this intolerable guilt?

'It will be good for you to move around a bit. I can help.'

'Not now,' I mutter.

Max starts to fuss, picking up on our tone, so I stroke his wisps of hair, shush him. Justin retreats, with the muttered instruction to call if I need him. I wish I didn't. I wish I could move freely around the house, my baby slung over my hip like any other mother. Hurl him into the air above me and catch the cascade of gleeful giggles. This week he has learned to deploy raspberries with verve, and discovered the simple joy of labels which he studies with an academic's concentration. I wonder what the next thing he'll learn will be.

I don't think about the list anymore. It was a fantasy. A nightmare made real. It's over now. I think back to the question I had when I was first added to the transplant list. How many people need to die for me to survive? All that time ago when I could never have imagined the number would be so high.

A few days later I am lying in bed, in sheets I haven't washed in who knows how long, when I hear a sound that makes me sit up. A shout from the living room. Justin is at work, but Dad is downstairs with Max. I scramble from the covers, my heart thrumming.

'Dad?' I call urgently as I take the stairs as fast my weakening legs will allow.

'I'm alright,' comes his strangled reply which says exactly the opposite. I find him in the living room, lying awkwardly on the sofa, Max peering up curiously from the floor.

'What's happened?' I kneel next to him, trying to read his face.

'Just... my back,' he croaks, wincing. 'Tried to pick the little one up. And it sort of... went.'

'Oh, Dad...' I stuff some cushions behind him. We're both acutely aware of the role reversal. I've been so reliant on his help that I've forgotten his age. He's seventy-one. His body is deteriorating too, I just haven't wanted to see it.

'Do you need to go to the hospital?'

'No, no. I'll just lie here a bit. I'll be fine.' He forces a smile. 'So sorry about this, love.'

'It's okay. Shall I get you some ibuprofen?'

'Thanks, yes, good idea. Have you got some handy down here?' His eyes dart towards the bathroom in the hall and I realise that, despite his agony, he's considering going upstairs to get them if necessary so that I don't have to.

'Yes,' I assure him, doing a mental inventory. I know there's none in the bathroom down here, but I keep some in my bag which is by the door. I scour through it until I realise I used the last pack. We don't have any in. I'll have to go to the chemist's. But I can't leave Dad like this.

I slip into the hall and call Billie. It's one of her half-days and she's only too happy to pop over. When she arrives, we get Dad comfortable then go to the kitchen to make him some tea. In hushed voices, while Max crushes steamed carrots between his palms with burbling fascination, I tell her just how worried I am. As my energy wanes, I've been relying on Dad so much more and now it's taken its toll.

'I don't know what to do,' I say quietly. 'I don't think he's admitting how much it hurts. Or how tired he is.'

Billie nods with concern.

'The cost of a nanny is more than my salary, even part-time, and I've checked all the local nurseries – their waiting lists are months long.'

We didn't sign Max up to anything when I was pregnant, my superstition forbidding it. I put my head in my hands and Billie rubs my shoulder.

'What about a childminder?' she suggests. 'They're a bit cheaper?'

I give her a look that says it's still money we don't have, not when I'm too ill to work. I've had to give up my few shifts and NHS sick pay is only a few months – one for each year of service. We're already in the final weeks. She knows we spent every spare penny on the IVF, and that Justin's salary only just covers the mortgage, Nick's university fees and his father's care home. Billie is quiet for a moment, even her fathomless optimism challenged to find a sliver of positivity. Then she makes a clicking noise with her tongue.

'Hold on, what about Steph?' she says brightly. 'She's been looking for somewhere to rent because we're getting a bit on top of each other at home, but she needs to save for her trip.' Billie is speeding up as her idea gathers momentum, her excitement mounting as my stomach drops. 'She's bloody brilliant with the twins. She can come back to us at weekends when Justin's home. Shall I ask her?'

'No,' I say quickly. 'No. There's no need to bother her—' I'm flailing around for a reason to reject this idea. This sensible, obvious suggestion which would solve all my problems. Almost all of them.

'Don't be silly, I'm sure she'd be very happy to help. I think it could be perfect, don't you? A great solution for everyone. And Stephy loves you. She's so fab with babies too, I don't really get why she doesn't want any. She's a proper natural.'

Her words strike me like a gong. Steph doesn't want children. I didn't know. Somewhere deep inside me something shifts.

No collateral damage.

My mother's voice has fallen quiet since I learned it was Dad who made her leave, not me, and my mind disentangled itself from the burden of guilt I needn't have carried all these years. Yet here she is again. Unvanquished. I shift uncomfortably. No. Stop it. Billie's sitting right in front of me, for Christ's sake. It might not be breaking up a future family, but it would destroy her. Break me. It can't be worth that.

'Let me…' The words stick in my throat. 'Let me… let me think about it.'

Billie seems to think my reluctance is pride.

'No one is going to think less of you, Liv. You've got more on your plate than most people have in a lifetime. I'm serious. Give yourself a break. You're grieving your best friend, parenting a new baby, and taking a cocktail of drugs while you wait for life-saving surgery.' Her voice catches over the last words. She's never said them out loud before. 'Anyone would be struggling. I wish I could bloody move in! Like uni all over again.'

But having Steph in my house, lively, vivid Steph with her glowing Californian complexion and her sunshine smile, knowing all the time that she could save me? It would be too much to bear.

'Ask her. Seriously, Liv,' Billie presses. 'Just ask.'

As she leaves, I promise her I'll think about it. And I do. For the rest of the afternoon I think about the brutal, acid-burn contradiction of living with Steph. Then I picture Justin's face from the top of the stairs. How cold things are between us. How the people who love each other seem to have got lost somewhere along the way and I don't know if they'll come back. With everything that's happened, I've blocked it out. I think about the sting on my wrist from his slap, and, for the first time, I have to admit that part of me is actually scared. As the days go by, I am starting to fear my own husband.

After I've helped Dad into a taxi home, his face stricken with pain, I pull out my phone. Billie's Instagram account leads me to Steph's. They are tagged together in a photo at the blood drive, matching sample tubes and matching Elcott smiles. I flick through Steph's profile, trying to ignore the wash of envy I feel at her grid and its life of sun-bleached ease. Hikes in Californian national parks, bibbed selfies from half-marathons across various states, then cobbled streets at the Edinburgh Fringe and cocktail nights at trendy bars in Camberwell now she's in London. Nights like I used to have once upon a time. Brushstrokes painting a life that looks out upon a bright future stretching on to the horizon.

I click my phone off, staring at my pallid reflection in the blank screen, feeling sick, deep in my gut. But as I turn it all over in my mind, I realise that I may not have any other choice. I have no money, no other options and very little time. If it wasn't for the match, it would be the perfect solution.

So, before I can hesitate, I pick up my phone.

39

Steph is more than willing. Grateful to be saved from London's brutal rental market. She'll stay with us for room and board during the week, then go back to Billie's at weekends. No extra costs for us, a chance for her to save, and space for Billie, Tom and the twins. It works for everyone.

Billie sends a jaunty text. *Thrilled Stephy can help you out. She's a fab cook too ;)*

Bile collects in my throat as I delete the message.

'You should have asked me.' Justin's voice is taut – a trip wire. 'I don't want a stranger living in my house.'

I stare at him. When did it become *his* house, not our home?

'I can't cope on my own. Dad can't be here now and you're at work. What else are we supposed to do?'

This is the most we've spoken in days. I am treading lightly on the frozen lake of our relationship.

This isn't all on your shoulders. What about his past? Are you just going to ignore it? Leave your son in the company of a dangerous man?

Justin strides into the hall and starts to wrestle his jacket from a hook.

'We can't keep pretending we're okay,' I call after him. 'I need help. I can barely get down the stairs on my own. Open your eyes.'

His jacket is stuck, tangled. He tugs at it roughly and it tears, leaving a gaping hole in the lining. Infuriated, he hurls it to the floor and stalks towards the front door. I feel my own anger swelling up inside me. I may have betrayed him, but he has left out a huge chapter in his story too. Edited who he is. And now he's running away from it all when I need him the most.

'Why didn't you tell me?' I cry as he pulls the door open.

He turns, a frown etched deep into his forehead.

'Tell you what?'

'About Louise. What happened back then...'

His eyes widen a fraction. He's staring at me, searching my face for meaning. Then he slowly closes the door. Something is flickering across his face. It looks for a moment like fear. I press myself against the wall for support. This is it, the conversation I've been avoiding for so long, Pandora's box creaking open.

'Nick told me,' I mumble, my conviction deserting me.

Justin stands stock still in the hallway. Then he takes two steps towards me, as if he can't quite hear what I'm saying. I flinch.

'What do you mean?' The heat is clear in his voice, a low flame.

'He told me about...' I drop my voice to a whisper as if the words are profane. 'About you *hitting* his mother.'

Justin doesn't reply. His torn jacket is still at his feet as I continue. Not one part of him shifts as he listens.

'He said there was a physical altercation. That you... that you...'

Justin is running a hand through his hair. My throat constricts. He's not denying it. He has started to pace along the hall, fighting some internal battle with himself. I slide back a few steps along the wall – out of reach. Then, without warning, he explodes.

'It's not true!'

I jerk away from him, my heart racing, one arm raised instinctively in self-defence. Holding out the other hand to placate him. 'Please—'

'It didn't happen like that.' Justin's voice is erratic. Panicked. There's a wildness in his eyes. 'It's not true. I didn't...'

'I don't understand,' I whisper. 'Why would Nick lie about something like that?'

'Because he doesn't know the truth!' Justin shouts. He looks at me as if he knows how that sounds. As if he doesn't know how to convince me it's not mad. 'We agreed, Louise and I, to lie about it. To... him. To Nick.'

My face twists in incomprehension.

'For his own good. And for hers. She... it was *her*,' he says hoarsely. 'It was Louise who was hitting me.'

I stare at him.

'I was holding her down. Restraining her. Until she calmed down. *That's* what Nick saw. If he'd come downstairs a few moments earlier, he'd have seen the reality. Seen his mother attack me.'

Louise? Composed, even-tempered Louise? A psychotherapist who helps others manage their emotions. Her? Rewinding my mental version of the scene, I try to picture this new dynamic. Try to believe what he's saying.

'She was drunk, furious. Trying to provoke me. We'd already agreed to separate; we were only bringing out the worst in each other. It was... it just happened once. She snapped. Came at me. She'd lost her temper in the past, even thrown a book at me before, but not lost it completely. I had to hold her down... and then I saw Nick in the doorway.'

His words are choked with emotion. I've never seen him this worked up.

Of course he'd say that. Don't be naive. What abuser admits to abuse? 'She provoked me.' 'It wasn't my fault.' 'Look what you made me do.'

'He... Nick... came in and threw himself between us. Put himself in front of his mum.' Justin's voice quivers. 'He was yelling at me to stop. Said he'd never forgive me. He was only eleven. Just a child.'

He blinks back tears, lost in the memory.

'Nick... He adores his mum. Always has. Lou was *terrified* that if anyone ever found out he would be taken from her. Domestic abuse includes a child witnessing violence in the home, even if they aren't involved; she knew the rules through work. It wasn't the first time she'd got that angry. She knew I had a case if I wanted to make it. That life was still black and white to Nick, good or bad.'

He pauses to draw a ragged breath. He's babbling now, a river undammed, the truth emerging in torrents.

'Nick already hated me; thought I was the reason we were separating. I'd destroyed the family in his eyes. There was no chance he'd want to live with me on my own. So, Louise made him promise not to tell anyone what he saw, on the condition that I left. He thought he was protecting his mother. I thought... I felt so awful for letting him down, I couldn't take his mum from him too. So, I agreed to shoulder the blame with Nick, if she never told anyone else about it.'

He fixes me with a look so fierce I feel like I might ignite.

'But Amir... he said it too,' I stutter.

Justin blinks at the revelation that his best friend and his wife have been talking behind his back. He closes his eyes, swallowing the betrayal.

'Nick told Amir I did it,' he says. 'He thought he was doing right by his mum, but Lou wouldn't risk *anyone* knowing. I swore to her I wouldn't reveal what really happened. Not even to Amir. I promised him it was a terrible mistake, told him I'd signed up for therapy. The works. He stood by me. But he doesn't know it's a lie.'

I try to focus on what Justin's saying. I look away. I want to believe it. Of course I do. My husband absolved of imaginary sins.

It sounds convoluted. Like a lie with too many layers.

That deep survival instinct within me is telling me not to fan the flames. Let all this settle, face it in the morning with fresh eyes and cooled tempers. Even after what he's said, I'm not sure.

Justin grunts like he's in pain. He snatches his jacket from the floor and wrestles it on, stuffing his hands in his pockets. Turning for the door, he wrenches it open. Instinctively I shush him, glancing up the stairs towards Max's room. Justin turns to me. His eyes are cold. I don't recognise him.

'It's not true,' he repeats. 'Nick didn't know the truth.'

He's looking at me like he's a stranger. Then he comes back towards me along the hallway, pulling his hand out of his pocket. In it he clutches an envelope, torn open. He throws it at my feet.

'Just like me.'

It's a letter on paper headed with a logo.

'Read it,' he says.

Now we're close, I catch a note of something chemical on his breath. Strong. Alcoholic. I notice the unsteadiness in his movements. His emotional volatility. It's the middle of the day but he's been drinking. It's shocking; so unlike the man I know.

Bending down, I unfold the letter slowly and start to scan the typed contents. Numbers, letters. My eyes slide towards the end of it, drawn to the parts in bold typeface.

Test results. So many tests.

There is a table with markers. Two sets of data. DNA profiles. Then, underneath the table, 0%.

Zero. Next to it just one sentence.

'The alleged father can be excluded as the biological father.'

My stomach drops. I can hardly swallow. The test I never wanted to take; the result I never wanted to know. Justin's done it. Taken a sample of DNA from Max and tested it alongside his own. My fingers tighten around the letter. The truth is here in front of me, unequivocal.

Max isn't Justin's son.

He is Al's.

My eyes fix on the stairs. I study the grain of the wooden treads in hyper-detail as my emotions climb over one another, clamouring to get out. I think some part of me always knew. Some part buried deep under shame and confusion. Questions flood through me, scraping at my insides as they pass, like hooks catching on flesh.

How will I *ever* explain this to Max? How will I tell him that his real father is dead, and it's because of me?

Justin is still standing there, his gaze wretched. Then he turns and strides out into the street, leaving me in the embers of our marriage.

40

Steph is due to move her things into the spare room today. Justin must have got home after I went to bed and I only know he's back because I heard him shifting around earlier, moving his bits downstairs. He'll be sleeping in the study during the week while she's here. We've not told her that explicitly; perhaps we both hope there's a chance he might make it back into our room eventually.

When I come out of the bedroom, Justin's emerging from Max's room having got him dressed for the day. All my fevered imaginings demonising him as a man harbouring dangerous secrets seem ridiculous in the morning light when he stands there on the landing, the baby in his arms. For a moment, I want to reverse everything. Rewind to my terrible mistake that night with Al. Do things differently.

But, if I did, I wouldn't have Max. This baby who is the reason I'm still here, still fighting. My miracle Max, who sparks ecstasy with the curve of his smile, the wave of his hand. This baby who has my eyes and my dad's forehead. This baby who, now I see it, has his father's fingers. His ears. The shape of his skull. His hairline. I can see it starting to emerge. The shadow of Al. I cannot regret it. I cannot wish it away. That mistake may be about to drive away my husband, but it has given me my son.

As soon as Max sees me, his face lights up and he lunges in my direction. Justin and I make the careful exchange, but he won't look at me.

'Justin, I'm so sorry—'

'Don't!' he cuts me off sharply.

I fall silent as Max babbles in my arms, oblivious to the atmosphere. A horrible heavy silence hangs between us. We are at a stalemate.

And now he has every reason to wish you harm.

The doorbell buzzes, interrupting the stand-off. Justin turns away and walks downstairs where I hear him greet Steph in his formal work voice, emotion back on its leash. As she moves her things into the spare room, I rearrange my expression, realising that while she's in our home, we'll have to perform the roles of happily married couple. Or at least not betray just how bad things have got. I wonder if there's any coming back for us now.

The next day Justin leaves for work before the rest of the household is up. Max squawks for my attention and as I leave my room, I see Steph poised ready at her door already dressed in yoga pants and hoodie. The presence of a stranger makes me jump. My pulse ramps up painfully and I press a hand to my chest.

'Sorry. I didn't know if you needed me to…'

'I'll get him up.' I say, forcing a smile. 'Just taking him downstairs for me would be useful if you're okay to carry him.'

'Of course,' she says. 'For sure.'

Her energy says 'first day at work' and I'm suddenly aware of our new dynamic. Though the payment structure is non-traditional, she's effectively my employee now. I'll have to lay out exactly what I need from her. Declare formally what I can and can't manage anymore with my own baby. Though her help is so welcome, her presence is also a harbinger of sorts.

Once we're downstairs and she's helped whip up some scrambled eggs for us all, she turns to me.

'Oh, Liv, one thing I forgot. Billie mentioned that you have those parking permit things? She's lending me her car to bring some things over. I'll do that later today if that works?'

'Of course. Let me find them.'

I pause at the door to the study. It's closed as if Justin is in there working away, finalising the paperwork he does almost every evening to keep on top of his workload. His desk is clear, organised. I picture him sitting here in the chair opening that fateful envelope. The letter falling to the desk as he absorbed the results. What they meant. Did he cry? I can almost feel his heartbreak, as if he's here in the room and I'm witnessing the moment at first hand.

As the sound of Steph packing the dishwasher clangs down the hall, I pull open the drawers, searching through Justin's many organised folders. I find the permit pack, but there's none left inside; we burn through so many for Dad. There might be some in the car.

Outside my breath steams in the cold interior as I rummage through the glove compartment. It hits me that I haven't driven the car since I saw Dan in the road. That brief fugue state where for a split second I thought I could go through with it right there, my foot on the accelerator. I shiver and keep searching. There aren't any permits here either; I'll have to phone the council up to request some more, but I haven't got the number.

Then I remember Justin making a Bluetooth call from the car to sort more permits for Dad as we drove back from the hospital. The number will be in the touchpad call log. Justin only really calls me, Dad, Amir or work so it won't be hard to spot. I switch on the engine and the screen blinks into life. Tapping clumsily at the menu, I eventually find his call history and scroll through until I find the right date. Spotting the 0208 number, I'm starting to type it into my phone, when something else catches my eye.

Another number on the call log. Just three digits.

999

I frown. When did Justin call the emergency services? He hasn't mentioned anything like that to me and surely he would. Am I forgetting a time I had a scare when he might have called for an ambulance? I click into the entry until the details come up. The call was over two minutes long. Not an error then. The date blinks up at me and my stomach flips violently. When my eyes dart to the time of the call, the hair on my arms stands on end.

Because the date is one I'll never forget – the day of Al's car accident – and the time is the early hours of the morning when Justin wasn't home.

41

Everything dissolves into slow motion as I shut the front door behind me. I remember what Billie said. The other car spotted driving away from the scene that they never tracked down. The swerving tyre tracks on the road. A slow, dark horror is dawning inside me and I sink to the floor in the hall.

Then Steph is there in front of me and I'm staring up at her.

'Oh, jeez, Liv. Are you alright?'

I nod. 'Water – just some water, please.'

Steph rushes into the kitchen and comes back, pressing a glass of water into my hands. She props me up in the hallway. Max has started to wail from his highchair, straining for me.

'I'm so sorry,' I murmur, sipping at the water. 'I just... got a bit light-headed and...'

'Please,' Steph says, waving my apology away. 'Do you need me to call the hospital?' She's on her haunches, like a sprinter waiting for the start gun.

I shake my head. 'It's fine. Just need to rest a minute. It's not serious.'

I have to force the words out of my mouth because the opposite is true.

I ask her to take Max out for a walk in the afternoon. It physically hurts seeing him strapped to her chest and not mine, but I can't bear to keep up the facade of normality. Over and over, I try to conjure up some other reason to explain that 999 call, but I can't. The truth strobes inside me, fluorescent, undeniable.

He was there. Justin was there the night Al died. The night we argued. The night I admitted my betrayal. The night he disappeared, stayed away.

Later, Steph has to help me upstairs to lie down while Max is napping. Usually I want to try the stairs alone, but today I've felt more faint with every passing hour. With each step I climb, my legs shake harder. I feel a hundred years old. As my hand trembles on the banister rail I hear a soft rattling sound. *Tap tap tap*. My wedding ring against the wood. Near the top I pause to catch my breath, to swallow the flicker of humiliation. Steph stands there patiently, bracing herself against the wall, taking half my weight. I glance over my shoulder and down the stairs. The houses on our terrace have high ceilings, staircases almost a metre higher than in the house where Billie lives. The stairs here are bare wood; Justin can't stand carpets, despite the dust that gathers at the corners of every tread.

Vivid images come surging out, clamouring to be remembered. Dreams I had as a child. Nightmares that recurred for weeks when I was ten, around the time my mother left. In them I would be standing at the top of the stairs in my childhood home, looking down at the bottom from exactly this vantage point. I would hear a voice. It would tell me I could do it. I just needed to jump. To trust. Because when I did, then it would happen.

I would fly. Like Peter Pan.

Panic would flare through me, in chorus with a thrum of excitement. To fly! Wouldn't everyone at school be so madly jealous if I'd worked out the secret, while they were all asleep, that you just had to jump. To believe. So, at the top of the stairs, I would gather myself, fists clenched.

Then jump.

An immediate, cloying pull. Gravity tugging me down. The sickening swerve of freefall. One moment of pure exhilaration, then, in those few seconds where the cluttered shoe rack shot closer, the realisation would dawn. It hadn't worked. I wasn't flying. I was falling.

Then, each night, the same impact. A savage *crunch*. My teeth bursting out to scatter over the hallway, splintered and spattered

red with blood and gum. My mother watching on, her arms folded. Shaking her head, then walking away just before I woke up.

As I stand there, leaning on Steph at the top of the stairs, an idea begins to flicker dimly in my mind, like a pilot light. Goosebumps prickle over my skin. The skirting has a sharp, protruding overhang. The balusters and spindles are square, thick. Solid wood. They bend around at the bottom, the final few leading down to the floor of the hallway which is covered in stone flooring. Hard enough to shatter bone.

One push. That's all it would take.

Blunt-force trauma to the head. One fall and all my prayers answered. A new heart, a new life, and time. Time to work out how to protect myself and my son from the monster that the evidence on Justin's phone log suggests he might actually be.

'Are you okay?' Steph swims back into my vision.

She is waiting, calmly, her left leg still on the last step but one. Still there, steady by my side. The concern on her face makes my insides ache. Theory is one thing, but the reality churns my stomach. Steph. Beautiful, sunny, innocent, gregarious Steph. All the best bits of Billie. I am confronted daily with her vitality, her presence. Who she is. Her turns of phrase. Her food preferences. What time she wakes up and goes to bed. How she makes the baby laugh by spinning him around, glancing over to check I'm okay with what she's doing. All these things make her painfully real. She is a godsend. A lifeline.

And yet.

And yet.

My hand moves to her shoulder, as if of its own accord. I turn away so I don't have to see her face. I am frozen. Undecided. After what I've discovered today, when it comes down to a choice between who is left holding my baby, don't I have to choose myself?

Just a bit of pressure. Just a little push.

Something occurs to me as we stand there at the top of the stairs. Maybe it's because I am her daughter that I'm able to consider this. Maybe, in the end, it's my mother who will save me.

Then there's a *click* from downstairs. The key in the lock; the front door opening. Justin letting himself in after work. I exhale unsteadily as the moment passes. A rush of relief tainted with bitterness cascades over me.

He looks up to see us at the top of the stairs. We lock eyes. For a moment his are full of a primal fear, as if to see me needing so much help is more than he can bear. His childhood rearing up, the past repeating itself.

'Hey, just helping Liv then I'll be out your hair,' Steph calls down. She's aiming to have left for Billie's before he gets home on Friday evenings, aware Justin is a reluctant landlord.

My hand shakes like I have a fever as she helps me up the last steps towards my room. All I can think about is closing the bedroom door and sinking into my bed, but a loud knock on the front door makes us stop on the landing. With a frown, Justin goes to answer it.

'Oh,' he says.

I turn to see someone else coming into the house and my breath seizes in my chest.

Billie.

My hands tighten on Steph's arm as Billie waves up at me and I feel my throat constrict. What the hell is she doing here? Then I spot the balloon in her hand. Dad comes into the house behind her, a cake box in his arms and a sheepish expression on his face. I'm struck dumb as more people enter through the front door. Sinead. Nadia. My head spins. Steph fights a smile.

'Sorry, she just told me to keep you at home this evening. I had no idea…'

She can tell something's off but probably thinks I'm not feeling great, thrown by my dizzy spell earlier on.

Dad comes back into the hall with Max in his arms blinking sleepily. A jaunty party hat is perched on his head, and I can see a badge pinned to his Babygro. It reads *Happy Unbirthday*.

'It's high time we had an Unbirthday celebration. Billie told me about the nine months in, nine months out trend and we thought three-quarters would do,' Dad says, gesturing at the balloon.

I realise what he means. Max turns nine months old today. As long as he was inside me. Unbirthdays are a joke Dad and I have after reading *Through the Looking-Glass, and What Alice Found There*. Every year we text each other on random days. Some years one of us decides to make more of a fuss and buys a cake, or a hat, a little surprise. Nothing outlandish, just a gesture to show our love.

'Surprise!' says Billie brightly, winking at Steph. By her side, Nadia is pulling out a pack of sparklers and lighting one.

'Wrong season, but you get the idea,' she says as it illuminates the gloomy hall, throwing jagged shadows across the walls. 'To nine months in, nine months out!'

'We wanted to do something nice for you,' Dad explains quietly, seeing the thunderstruck expression on my face. 'I know he should be sleeping, but only for a bit?'

Justin hasn't even taken off his coat. His briefcase is still in his hand as if he's considering turning around and walking right out again. His eyes find mine. I pull my gaze away; looking at him burns like salt on an open wound.

We sit in the living room, Justin perched awkwardly on the edge of the sofa, a gaping void between us. Max bounces enthusiastically on my knee, thrilled by the new arrivals, but I shiver like I've got a fever. The jaunty conversations go on around me, drifting over my head. I can only stammer thanks and hide behind the veil of my surprise. When Dad stands up and pulls out his phone to take some family snaps for 'posterity', I almost throw up. Forcing a smile onto my face, I hold Max between us.

'Shuffle closer!' Dad scolds us. 'Arm around them, Justin, come on!'

Billie darts over and adjusts my hair, pulling stray wisps away from my face, like she did as my maid of honour for our wedding photos.

'Gorgeous,' she whispers, and plants a quick peck on my cheek.

My mouth pulls back into a rictus smile as the members of my family, my nearest and dearest, unwittingly immortalise the worst day of my life.

42

I lie in bed, tears streaking to my ears. It's the next morning and Max is still sleeping. The house already feels empty without Steph. She left with Billie last night, after we'd finished forcing down the cake and mistimed good cheer. I can't contemplate getting up. My hands scrunch the duvet at the thought of having to talk to Justin, to pretend I don't know what I know.

What do I do now? What the fuck do I do? Do I go to the police? Report my own husband? Do I call Dad, Billie, bring them into this nightmare so I don't have to face it alone?

I roll over to look at the monitor, use the sight of Max's sleeping form to ground myself. Since he's learned to roll, night-time has become a horizontal acrobatic act. Every morning he wakes in a different orientation. I gaze at the screen like it's a film, still transfixed by the minute rise and fall of his chest, the uninhibited fanning of his arms.

Buzz. The sharp trill of the doorbell cuts through my fugue state. Blearily, I wait to see if Justin will get it. There are no sounds from downstairs. He must have gone to do the weekend shop. I crawl from my bed to the intercom we had installed at the top of the stairs. The Ring screen shows a deliveryman outside with two large flat cardboard boxes. It's the cot-bed we ordered a few weeks ago, knowing Max was on the brink of outgrowing his newborn's crib. A lump rises in my throat.

I want him to stay a baby, to stay the size of the crib, rather than accept that he will eventually grow to fit the vast expanse of a toddler's bed. I can't fathom that he will ever be that big. Back when Justin and I were still a unit, we spent an evening comparing cot brands online. We opted for the larger size which converts into a bed, to last Max until he's four. I found a fleeting comfort in making a decision that would have an impact so far into the future. Knowing where he will rest his head for the next few years. As if a cot chosen by his mum might go some way to replacing her when she's gone. The solid oak frame was more expensive than the others, but I wanted it. It looked so sturdy, heavy, like it could be trusted to keep him safe and secure for the hundreds of nights between now and then.

I stare dizzily down the stairs, then clutch the rail tight, descending as slowly as I can. The doorbell buzzes impatiently again. When I reach the door, I'm panting and everything is swimming. I open the door, leaning heavily on it.

'Could you… just bring them inside?' I ask shakily.

He eyes me. ''S really a two-man job. They're very heavy.'

'I'm sorry, I'm… um… not well.' I don't have the energy to point out his casual sexism. My pallor must prove my point because he swiftly crosses himself.

'Enough bloody flu around to halt the economy,' he grumbles as he drags the boxes inside.

He leaves and I sit down on the hall floor, imagining what it would be like if flu was the worst of my worries. The world keeps on turning. The days keep on dawning. Millions of other Tuesdays continue untouched by this ordeal.

Then I hear a cry. The noise has woken Max. I haul myself to my feet and look up the stairs, knowing I'm too weak to climb them but unable to ignore his cries. I crawl unsteadily up them on my hands and knees, and into his room. He strains for me from the crib. I reach down, but my arms are shaking more than usual. My legs and ankles are puffy and tight, with a ruddy flush. Fluid build-up. The medication losing ground yet again. As I stand there, my son reaching out for me, my vision swimming, breathless, I realise I don't have the strength to pick him up.

It's happened. The moment I've been dreading.

I sit and press my face to the gauze material on the side panel of the crib, fighting to hold my smile, talk calmly through shallow breaths as my lungs refuse to fill properly. Max's face puckers in incomprehension and then distress. He waves his hands more frantically, straining to get up from the crib.

'I'm sorry, my love. I'm so sorry. Just wait,' I whisper, trying to soothe him. 'Dada won't be long. He'll be back soon and then we can get you out.'

For the first time, when I say the word 'Dada' my chest tightens. Because Justin is not his dad. He's not even the person I thought was my husband.

When Justin gets back from the shop, I call to him from upstairs. In Max's room he finds me sitting on the floor pressed against the crib.

'My God,' he breathes as he strides across the room and scoops Max up.

'Take him to the bed for me. Please,' I manage to say as I crawl the few metres back to my room.

My bed is piled with pillows to prop me up. I can't lie flat at all anymore without losing my breath or feeling sick. Steph has rolled towels and placed them under the fitted sheets to form a ledge around the mattress. Max isn't yet crawling so this system works for now, but who knows for how much longer. I'm so excited to see him starting to move but it's tempered by a lurking fear of how on earth I'll manage when he does.

'Do you need anything?' Justin is standing at the doorway watching us. I can't read his expression. 'Should I call them? The hospital?'

I shake my head quickly, my eyes not leaving Max. 'No.'

Justin hesitates for a moment then heads downstairs without another word. My stomach feels so horribly twisted. We can't go on like this.

You need to do something.

Dad arrives. He was planning to drive us out to the countryside for some fresh air. 'A shower for the lungs,' he joked. I hate to disappoint him again after how shellshocked I was by his thoughtful surprise last night, but I'm so tired. Bone-deep, jetlagged weary under the weight of it all.

'Let me take Max for the afternoon instead,' Dad says quietly. 'Give you two some time.' He nods at the kitchen where Justin is sitting at the dining table staring into the garden. Dad knows. He's no fool. He recognises a fractured marriage all too well.

After they've left, laden down with bottles and nappies and hats and spare clothes, I notice the cot-bed parts are still leaning against the wall by the front door and curse under my breath. There's no way I can get them upstairs myself, but I was really hoping to set it up today. Now Max is rolling he's not safe in the crib; he could roll over and smother himself if the space is too small. Justin's footsteps approach.

'I'll do it.' His tone is clipped and I step instinctively away from him. My eyes stay on the floor.

'It's too heavy,' I mutter.

'I said, I'll do it.' The repetition stings.

As I haul myself up the stairs ahead of him, each footstep leaden, back to the relative sanctuary of my room, I'm suddenly angry. Wretchedly, hopelessly angry. At Justin's increasing distance from me since Al's death, which now seems so horribly suspicious. At his inability to have difficult conversations. But most of all at the growing fear that he's done something truly awful.

You know what he's capable of now. You've seen the core of him and it's rotten.

At the top of the stairs, I watch Justin lugging the unwieldy box up behind me. I remember the deliveryman's words, but I don't move to help. I couldn't even if I wanted to. Instead, I'm rerunning the events of Al's death. Thinking back to when I was at Billie's house, seeking refuge after the argument with Justin the night before. How he was at Amir and Rebecca's. He'd been drinking. Then how the next day he appeared at the hospital, his face drawn, still in the clothes he wore when I saw him last. Hours and hours in which his movements are unexplained.

'Where were you? The night Al crashed.'

The question leaps from my lips before I have time to consider the consequences of hearing the response. Justin glances at me. Something shifts in his eyes and when I see it, I think I have my answer. Under the layers of exhaustion and pain and betrayal there's a new emotion on his face. Unmistakable. One I recognise only too well.

Guilt.

I sit down hard on a step.

'What are you talking about?' he snaps, struggling with the package.

A sudden, strange calm is descending over me. 'That night. There... there was another car. People saw the tyre tracks.'

A few steps below me, Justin has slowed.

'You weren't here. Your car wasn't here... I saw... I found... You called 999 that night,' I whisper.

Justin looks up at me, sweat glistening on his forehead, his cheeks flushed from the effort of the climb. As we stare at one another the world seems to go into slow motion. I cling to the banister rail because just then I know that this is the moment; the severing of the cord that binds us together. This is the moment my family finally collapses, a house of cards in a storm.

'Were you... were you there?'

The air around us feels sharp as broken glass. Then he finally speaks.

'Yes.'

He says it calmly. My mouth opens and then closes. My arms hang limp at my sides.

'W-what?'

'You heard me.' Justin's eyes are hard. They seem to bore into me.

I stare at my husband in disbelief. Thoughts crash into my head like a dawn raid, desperate excuses to explain what he's just said.

He... happened to be in the area. At the same pub as Al and Dan? No. Too unlikely.

He wanted to... speak to Al. Tell him the truth about Max? Impossible. The news is still raw. He hadn't even told me.

He...

Here my reasoning dries up and all that's left is the answer I cannot bear to accept.

Justin stays silent, as if he's daring me to accuse him outright. To say the words aloud. A new feeling floods over me. The same agony which blazed in Annette's eyes in the hospital. The fury of the wronged.

Because I'm not the reason Al died. *He* is.

I remember Justin's face in the gloom on these stairs that night. Feel the sting from his hand on my arm. Hear the rage in his voice at Nick's accusation; his vehement defence which is unravelling in real time. Because if this is what he's capable of then I do not know the man standing in front of me.

Justin stares at me, thrusting his chin out, challenging me. My lungs hitch. In that moment I hate him.

I *hate* him.

There is a whisper from somewhere. *Do it*. Two little words. So quiet I barely hear them.

Then I stand up.

Then Justin is no longer in front of me.

Then he is in freefall.

43

Garish light probes the cracks under my eyelids, painting the world skin-red, like the glow of a womb. Liquid is crusted around my eyelashes. I peel my eyes open. I'm in a blue-curtained cubicle. There is a familiar symphony of beeps from the machines monitoring me. The ward. Everything is indistinct, spectral. Like I'm in the underworld, faced by the undead. A figure comes slowly into focus. One form, but two heads. I squint.

It's Dad, wearing Max in the sling – something he's never worked out how to do before. The sight makes me smile faintly, but then worry wriggles in. His back: it's still recovering. At his side is a nurse. I recognise her. She leans down and whispers in my ear.

'You're going to be okay, love. You'll wake up feeling much better. Just rest now.'

For a moment it isn't the nurse speaking. It's my mother, in her voice a tender, warm tone that is completely new to me. Then I drift off into the darkness.

When I open my eyes again, Dad and the baby are at my bedside wearing different clothes. I pull my lips apart, wincing as the dry skin splits and stings.

'W-water,' I manage, and Dad lunges for the cup with a straw.

'There you are, my love,' he murmurs. The liquid is cool over my parched throat.

'How long was I out?' My voice is slow, soporific. Like I haven't used it before.

'Um. Well, the surgery lasted five hours – straightforward they said. Then you've been sleeping for a day or two, on and off,' Dad says softly.

My forehead crinkles slowly into a frown. 'S-surg-ry.'

'Yes.' He pauses. 'They said... it went really well.' He clears his throat. 'You just need to rest now. Alright, my love?'

I nod, close my eyes again. Content that he's watching over me. I hope whatever they have done in surgery has helped. Hope that it will let my heart cling on a little longer.

The next time I rise to the surface, I'm alone. The cubicle is different, it has a window. I can see the clouds outside racing each other across the sky. A windy day. I try to guess from its colour what time it is, but the bleached white won't give up its secrets. After a while a different nurse appears. A new shift.

'Oh, good, how are we feeling? How's your pain?'

'Okay...' I croak.

'Try to keep your torso still. You'll feel pressure for a while. Tingling or itching is good, it means the wound is healing. If you feel any heat or like you have a temperature, you press this button, alright? Or if you need more pain relief. We're just outside and I'll be back to check on you soon.'

She presses the remote control with the large, squishy buttons into my hands. I grip it like it's driftwood in the open sea.

Darkness claims me again.

Then voices. A muffled squeal.

I prise my eyes open. Everything seems indistinct, hazy. The white shades of the hospital walls. The deep royal blue of the cubicle curtain casting its indigo shadow. Then my insides flood with warmth. Max is sitting at the foot of the bed, chattering to Dad. He is whispering, the baby is not. Max cranes his head unsteadily in my direction, grunts at me and pats at the covers where my leg rests.

'Sorry, love, we didn't mean to wake you. I think someone is getting impatient for a cuddle.'

Dad shifts closer and sits Max at my shoulder. The baby's eyes crease as his mouth curves into a wet grin. His little starfish hand reaches out and, very carefully, grabs my nose. I smile but when I lift an arm all my muscles revolt. I lie still, let Max's hands explore my face, as if he's reminding himself what I look like. As if we're reuniting after years apart. Dad watches us, his eyes damp. He reaches down and clutches my hand, squeezes. I squeeze back.

Crooked, jumbled thoughts swarm inside me. Snippets of lucidity. Snatched words. Fractured memories. I try to put the pieces together. Make up the image, the story of what's happened to me.

Blue lights flashing, refracting through the stained glass of the front door.

A rip in a cardboard package.

Flagstones with a smattering of blood on them.

An emotion then, like my heart is caught in razor-wire. Immense sadness, its roots entangled deep within me. Impossible to dig up. To tear out.

Al. I remember Al. A piece falls into place. The sadness.

But no. That's not all of it. This feeling is more than that grief. Fresher.

I have to excavate further.

'W-what happ-n-d?' I murmur to Dad. The words stick to my lips like glue. I have to repeat myself for him to understand.

He holds my gaze for a minute, then looks away. Rubs his face. Tugs at his beard. I recognise the gesture. He did it right before he told me my mother had gone. Right after I told him about my diagnosis. When he picked me up from the hospital after Al died.

'Love...'

'W-wh-re's J-stin?'

A strangled sound catches in Dad's throat. 'He's... Olive love, he...' Dad pauses, searching for the words. 'My love, after he fell they... they couldn't wake him up.'

Cold spreads over my skin. My teeth start to chatter in my mouth. Dad cups his hand tentatively around my shoulder, as if I'm porcelain and any pressure will shatter me.

'They tried everything. Justin... he had the best care, but... my love, he didn't make it.' Dad's voice is choked with emotion. 'I'm so very sorry, Olive. I wasn't sure if I should tell you yet – if you'd remember...'

My face is slowly crumpling.

'It's nobody's fault. A terrible accident. He was carrying something too heavy.'

An accident. A fall. I'm trying to force the memories into full technicolour but there are gaps. Cut scenes in the edit.

'Wh-at happen-d to me?'

'You were... barely conscious.' He swallows. 'They brought you in too. Then they... when they found out about the match. Well, you were here. You were still top of the list. I can't—'

He pauses, takes a wavering breath. 'The surgery needed to happen in a certain window of time. I was... I'm down as your next-of-kin. Justin... there wasn't anyone else to ask. I didn't know what to do. I tried to think what you would say.' His shoulders heave with the effort of holding back emotion.

Then the tears are winning, flooding his eyes.

'I-I thought you... would say yes.'

Max holds his hand out to Dad's face, reaching for the tears with fascination. Oblivious to their cause.

The words are slowly working their way through me. My thoughts are slow, dense with confusion. Comprehension lurks just outside my grasp, but I am forcing myself towards it. I squint my eyes with the effort of it. A dull ache pulses in my chest.

Then their faces distort and I'm drifting down again.

When I wake next, something within me has clicked. Pain sits just under my skin, like a hundred fishhooks are caught there and the lines have been pulled taut. While I've been lost to the world, my consciousness has been processing what Dad told me. I can hardly move. There is more pain deeper down too, like a burn penetrating through the layers which make me up. I can't tell one from the other. Physical and psychological agony heaped on top of one another.

When I close my eyes, Justin's face appears.

Nodding to Dad as we process to the desk in the panelled room at the register office, as though thanking him for his life's work. The tentative, shell-shocked care with which Justin hands Max to me, moments after his birth. His eyes sweeping the room at his fiftieth birthday party, realising how many people think him worthy of their time. Rubbing the sleep from his eyes as he gets up yet again, uncomplaining, to tend to Max while I rest.

Then the furrow in his brow as we argue at the top of the stairs.

The way his head falls first, before his body, as if he's a diver on a high board, performing a mistimed backflip. As if he has thrown himself. How his arms don't reach out to break his fall, as if he has given up well before the moment of impact.

Though it feels like I'm reading a book with pages torn out, chapters of the story skipped, I know. Deep down, I know what has happened.

A piece of paper flutters on the breeze of my thoughts. A hand is thrusting it at me. A man's hand with a wedding band on it. Gold and thick. Justin's. I pin the paper down. Unfurl it. Smooth out the creases. The paternity test. A detail written on it that I hadn't processed until now. A letter and a symbol next to Justin's name.

His blood type. O negative. The universal blood type. Capable of donating to anyone. Lifeblood of the emergency services. An unsung guardian angel, right under my nose. Then it's all coming back to me.

The top of the stairs. His admission. My fury.

Just a little pressure.

Just a little push.

44

A small round pill sits in my hand, nestled among the grooves of my palm. One of them is the Lifeline though I've never been sure which. For the rest of my days, however many there are, I will take this medication. Immunosuppressants to defend my husband's heart against me.

The operation was a success. My body didn't reject the interloper in my chest. I was finally discharged five weeks after the accident. I'm making myself think of it as that. An accident. That's how I have to present it to the world. To Dad. To Max when he's older. I have to make myself believe that story too.

Dad has moved in and Steph has moved out, but she's round every other day to help. Steph is one of the reasons I'm still here. She had let herself into the house that day to pick up something she forgot. While I was in meltdown, she called the ambulance. The woman whose life I considered ending helped to save mine.

They've had the bed moved down to the living room for the weeks of my recovery. This time I don't protest. I'd rather not have to climb the stairs every day, relive the things that happened there. What I think I did. At least from down here I can see Max on his playmat, focussed with intense concentration on the projects within the walls of his little kingdom.

Justin's funeral took place yesterday. They waited until I was well enough. A simple affair in the local crematorium, as his will requested. His wishes were concise, with no difficult decisions for me to agonise over. He had the will drafted a few months after Max was born. Just after my diagnosis. How like Justin to be capable of such maturity even amid the emotional turmoil we were weathering.

The room is stuffed with people as we walk in. Every seat full. Nods of respect; people from the local community, the other doctors from the surgery. Amir spends the whole ceremony standing like a bodyguard at my side, blinking uncontrollably. In the row behind me, my best friends are in formation, the rear guard. Dad sits on my other side, holding Max as I stumble blindly to the front to mumble words which can't hope to capture all of who Justin was. But when I look out over this room full of people who don't know the half of it, I dissolve. Billie leaps to her feet and helps me back to my seat.

After the service is finished, as we file out, I pass Louise at the back, red-eyed and blank-looking, Nick ashen-faced at her side. He nods an uncomfortable hello. This poor boy, barely a man, who has lost a father too. I hug Max closer to me and Nick smiles sadly down at the baby's face. As he moves away, Louise steps closer. When she clasps my hand in condolence, she leans forward and mutters something I only just catch.

'Olivia... I wanted to say sorry,' she whispers. 'I'm so sorry. For your loss. And... for what Nick said to you.'

There's something in her eyes that registers even through my haze of grief. It takes me a moment to recognise it. Fear. It's an expression which finally confirms Justin's version of their story. He was telling the truth. Now, as his body is carried into the flames through the curtains behind us, I'm the only person who knows her secret. She looks at me with a rawness that says she knows I could tell her son the truth about his mother.

She needn't worry. I don't even know how to look at Nick after what I've done. I know the lengths a parent will go to in order to protect the one they love, and I've done so much worse than lie.

'Make sure you tell him the good bits too,' I whisper. Nick deserves a better memory of his father, even if it's not real. She nods, biting her lip against the tears.

Post has collected in a pile on the doormat. Cards. Condolences from friends, colleagues. Mostly brief, mostly clichéd. No one knows what to say. No one has the words. A tasteful bunch of flowers arrives from Emily and Dan. I ask Dad to take it away, the one Al sent me from his travels still burned on my memory. A few days later, there's a soft knock on the door. As Dad goes to answer it, I peer through the living room curtains. On the doorstep is a casserole dish wrapped in foil. Disappearing out of the front gate is Irene, with Florrie at her ankles.

Dad and I work through the post slowly over the next few days, so as not to overwhelm me. I'm weak with gratitude that he's here at my side as I go through this. Dealing with the inevitable, unenviable aftermath of life after someone has died. The bureaucracy. We notify the bank, the phone company. Deal with switching bills to my name. I stare in ice-cold dismay at the mortgage statement, wondering how the hell I will cope with the payments. Realising we'll have to sell the house.

In the kitchen, I hear Dad chattering to Max who babbles merrily back. He's growing more communicative every day. I hear Dad repeating 'Mama' to him and I smile. I hope Max inherits his selflessness. Dad brings him in and sets a KeepCup of herbal tea next to me on the coffee table which doubles as my bedside table.

'Here you are, love. Everything okay?'

I nod, stuffing the mortgage statement away. 'Thanks, Dad.'

We sit together on the sofa and watch Max playing with the new toy that Nadia has sent in her unofficial role as 'fun' godmother. A baby drum kit, complete with padded fabric cymbals. Dad grimaces, but it turns out to have both a gentle rhythmic beat and, crucially, volume control. Max has just discovered how to strike the cymbals and keeps looking over at us, face full of joyous self-satisfaction, as we cheer him on.

Dad puts his arm around my shoulders. 'We'll get through this, Olive. We're all here for you. You and Max. This is the hardest part.'

If only he knew.

The days since the operation haven't felt real. I don't know how to move on with my life now. In all these last months of waiting, I'd never thought further than the operation. Further than the white-hot hope for a donor. My desperate scheme to find one. Now I need to face what I've done. Every day that I wake up and swallow a pill, I swallow down the guilt too. I am filling up with it. Overflowing. I move around in a fugue state while those around me celebrate my presence, not knowing the full story. That I am a mother still, but now something else too. A murderer.

Justin's absence is as loud as church bells tolling every hour. It is in every creak of the floorboard that used to bend under his tread. Every turn of the key in the lock. Every time someone switches the kettle on. For these brief instants I think he is in the next room. Just out of sight.

'How's it feeling?' Dad murmurs, nodding at the criss-cross scar down my breastbone that, in jest, he refers to as my zip.

'Still sore,' I say, quietly, knowing that I'm talking about more than just the layers of my skin knitting themselves back together.

'It'll take time, but you won't always feel like this.'

I take Dad's hand, pasting a smile on my lips. I think of his words, what he did to protect me as a child, and wonder what he would say if he knew. Whether his unconditional love could weather even this.

It's not until a few days later, as we're sorting out the study, while Billie entertains Max, with Sinead and Nadia cooking lunch in the kitchen, that we discover the letter. As Dad picks up one of Justin's notebooks, two pieces of paper fall out. Dad stoops down to collect both, glances at them, then passes them to me wordlessly. One is a folded note addressed to 'Liv' in Justin's florid, illegible handwriting. The other is a blank envelope, unsealed. Tucked inside is a second letter in a professional typeface. Dad retreats from the room and closes the door gently.

The handwritten note trembles lightly in my hand. I don't know if I can bring myself to read it. Do I want to know what it says? Can I handle it? Shouldn't I be trying to move on now that what's done is done? Finding a way to put this all behind us somehow.

I unfold it. The date written at the top is a few days before Justin died.

Liv,

Please consider this an explanation of sorts, as much as these things can be committed to paper. I hope this letter, and the enclosed document, will allow you to release yourself.

I've known about what you needed to do for some time. About Junie. About your list. And I wanted to help. I tried with the drink. The first breaking of my oath. Then the night I heard you talking to Al, I followed them home from the pub, Dan in Al's car. Tailed them, the golf club on the seat next to me. I would have done it, but when Al saw me in the rearview, he panicked, swerved. I wasn't chasing him; I wasn't some half-mad cuckold driven to violence. Yes, I wish that you'd left our vows intact, but that is not and will never be who I am. I wasn't there for Al, I was there for Dan. I just wanted you alive. It was all for you.

I stare at Justin's words, blinking away the pooling tears which distort them.

He knew. All this time, he knew everything.

He gave Junie the drink. He broke his Hippocratic Oath, for me. For Max.

In strobe flashes I remember his expression as Irene told us she wants to leave Max money in her will. When he learned Rebecca had Opted Out. Saved from his own excruciating dilemma, I realise; whether he could kill his best friend's wife to save his own. Then his expression at the hospital in his rumpled clothes after Al's accident that I took to mean one thing when it was something else entirely. I got it so wrong.

Justin didn't hit Louise and he didn't mean to cause Al's death.

The tears are tipping down my cheeks now. I wipe at them with my sleeve, heave a shuddering breath, make myself keep reading.

Perhaps this letter is a cowardly act. Perhaps thinking ill of me for always would be easier for you, for you both, but, in the end, I am only human. I need you to know the whole truth. To clear my name.

> *There has been far too much collateral damage now. I am so deeply sorry to have caused it. No one else can come to any harm at my hand. That is why I need to do this.*
>
> *What happens to me isn't your fault; it is my choice. It wasn't just Max's blood I tested; I checked my own too – a full match with yours. I hope you can forgive me for what I am going to do. I have always admired your spirit in the face of the cruel hand you have been dealt. I hope these words will ease the pain when you find me.*
>
> *My track record as a father is not one I am proud of. Since I have robbed Max of a father, I can at least give him his mother. I wish I could be there to see him grow. I wish none of this had happened. But I'll be leaving him the best legacy I can. Remember me to him sometimes*

The letter ends there. Not signed; unfinished. As if Justin had just laid the pen down, still drafting the words of this confession, knowing they would be some of his last.

The paper drops from my hand and I crumple slowly to the floor. My limbs have turned to water at the truth of what he has done. The distance he put between us in those last weeks while he was making the biggest decision of his life. Becoming my last chance.

The blood seems to slow in my veins. The house is quiet, as if it is holding its breath.

Two little words are resounding in my head. Two words I thought I'd imagined that day at the top of the stairs. I hear them again now.

Do it.

My mother egging me on, I thought. But they weren't in my head. They weren't my mother's voice. It was him, Justin, telling me to do it. Telling me to push him, knowing what it would mean.

Shaking, I take out the other document and unfold it. A logo I don't recognise. Words stand out.

Level Term. Decreasing Term. Confirmation. In the event of accidental demise.

It's a statement. An update from an insurance company. As I read the small print it comes together.

A life-insurance policy.

In the event of Justin's death, I receive a lump sum and a monthly pay out to cover the rest of the mortgage and living expenses. I scan the words over and over again. It's a generous amount, enough to remove any financial burden from us. It sinks in slowly; a blossoming pain moving through me.

For this policy to stand, Justin's death had to be an accident. Or to look like an accident. Which it did.

The extent of his sacrifice hits me full force. Justin was planning to die so that I could live. It may not have happened the way he intended, but that was, ultimately, his plan.

The man who vowed to love me in sickness and in health has given up his future and set me free to live mine. Ever in service of others. The man who gave up his good name for the sake of his first-born. The man who loved me, loved Max, despite what I'd done, enough to lay down his life for us. I stare at the illustration he bought me for Christmas, still propped against the wall waiting to be hung, the mother and baby alone together.

As the pieces fall finally into place, my heart breaks all over again.

Dad peers around the door, summoned by my sobs. From his arms, Max reaches out for me. I fold my son close, bury my face into his soft neck. He wriggles an arm free and places his hand on my chest. His little palm rests against the raw pink scar which holds my skin in an embrace around Justin's heart, my flawed, brave, broken, selfless husband's heart, and will do for all my remaining days.

It's the summer before I'm well enough to sit in the cool calm of Dad's house, my pulse thumping as we wait for the knock on the door. Dad gets to his feet first.

'Shall I get it, love?'

He cast no judgement when I told him the truth about Max, only encouraged me to act, like he did when I was a child too afraid to face the music. To reach out to her.

'No,' I say. 'I'll go.'

Hitching Max further up on my hip, I walk in slow motion towards the front door.

When I open it, she flinches like I've hit her. Then her gaze goes straight to Max. His eyes which, now he's almost a year old, are settling into the same shade of green as her own. As her son's.

I look at Al's mum standing there, clutching her bag with the grip of someone who has had to work themselves up to this encounter too. This unconventional family reunion.

'Hi, Annette,' I say. 'I'm so glad you came.'

'Come on in,' Dad adds over my shoulder.

Annette nods. Then Max's grandmother steps inside and I close the door.

EPILOGUE

To my miracle Max,

I've chosen today to write this letter, not because it's a special day; it's not a birthday or an anniversary or a new year. It's just a Sunday like any other, with you sitting at my feet banging together plastic pots, poring over fabric books. I want to tell you about today because it's a day I never thought I'd get. And this is a letter that I never felt able to write before now.

Today, I lifted you up. Today, the scar down my chest didn't tingle as it bore your weight. Today, my eyes didn't swim with the effort. Today, I threw you up in the air, inches from the ceiling, and your face curled into a delight so pure I want to remember the image of it forever. My wild rumpus miracle Max. My creature of divine beauty.

Because, now the future is ours, there will be more days, more ordinary, extraordinary days like these. Now that his heart beats inside me, just like yours once did. You who erupted, volcanic, from me, a body of lava flowing out into the world to become new land.

It's not how I ever would have wished it, but life rarely is. Perhaps, one day, when you're old enough to understand, you can tell me if it was worth it. Perhaps, one day, if you have children of your own to protect, to adore, little lives you would lay down your own for, you will understand why we did what we did. All three of us. Perhaps you won't. That's the risk I've taken. Sometimes you have to do terrible things to protect the ones you love.

I have gone over it in my mind, tried on the other versions of our story for size, other divergent roads. The fact remains that if I had my time over, I would do anything to be here with you now. I would do it all again, whatever it took.

In a heartbeat.

ACKNOWLEDGEMENTS

This book was written shortly after I became a mother, in snatched moments between naps, powered by caffeine plus the faith and help of those around me, so there are a lot of people to thank! Firstly, Hellie Ogden for going beyond the call of duty answering panicked newborn questions (both book and baby related) at all hours. Thank you for your editorial wisdom, patient steering through the process, and for being the reason I'm a published author. Thanks too to Ma'suma Amiri for your enthusiasm and practical support.

Then the brilliant Alison Hennessey at Bloomsbury's Raven Books. The biggest of thank yous for your vision and your exceptional instincts which have made the book so much stronger. There have been few greater thrills than one of your jubilant comments in the margins! Thank you to the whole Bloomsbury team who have performed the sorcery of turning a Word document into a beautiful, tangible thing. Particular thanks to the eagle eyes of Lynn Curtis and Wilhelmina Asaam, to Charlotte Phillips for the gorgeous cover design, to Faye Robinson, Fabrice Wilmann and Craig McKerchar for keeping me on track, to Emily Jones for all you do behind the scenes, and to Ben McCluskey and Holly Minter for getting it out into the world.

I'm extremely lucky to be surrounded by many generous creative minds who gave their time to early drafts of the book. Thanks to Anna Hargreaves, Kacey Carter, Gina Hood, Hannah Price, Keira Duffy Lee, Annelie Simmons, Chloe Wicks and Alya Finch especially for such thoughtful notes and encouragement. Thanks also to the network of other 2026 Debuts who always have time for questions, and to the other B&B Mums who lived the day-to-day of parenting and book news with me. To the wonderful staff at UCLH who looked after us so well, with special thanks to Debra Kroll who held our hands through it all. Thank you to the doctors I spoke to as research for the story: Ginny Caddick, Sam McGrath and Joyee Basu – any inaccuracies are mine alone! And a nod to *Grey's Anatomy*, nine seasons of which kept me awake through the long night feeds, and I can only imagine made an impact on the story which came out.

Thank you to my family for the self-belief and the support that meant I was able to make it through maternity leave with both a book and a baby to show for it. To my mum (who bears no resemblance whatsoever to Liv's) for your gentle encouragement ever since I was young enough to pick up a pencil and imagine a beginning, middle and end. To my dad who, though he's no longer here, I know would be tickled pink to hold a book I'd written in his hands and whose presence is with us always. To the rest of my family for their cheering from the sidelines, and with particular gratitude to my wonderful mother-in-law for keeping us fed, and babysitting so often to give me time to write.

Lastly, to Andrei and to Ivie, my own precious little family, the inspiration for the themes at the heart of this story. You are my greatest joy, without whom I wouldn't have the emotional language or the determination needed to write this book, which I hope will be the first of many.

A NOTE ON THE AUTHOR

Matilda Wilding studied English at the University of Cambridge and now balances writing with working full time as a film and TV executive. *The Waiting List* is her debut novel, which she wrote while on maternity leave. She lives in East London with her partner and son.